BAD NEWS

STACY TRAVIS

BAD NEWS

STACY TRAVIS

Copyright © 2020 by Stacy Kravetz

This is a work of fiction. Names, characters, places and incidents either are products of the author's imagination or are used fictitiously. Any resemblance to actual events or locales or persons, living or dead, is entirely coincidental.

Cover Design: Alyssa Garcia, Uplifting Author Services

Editing: Dragonfly Media Ink

Publicity: Social Butterfly PR

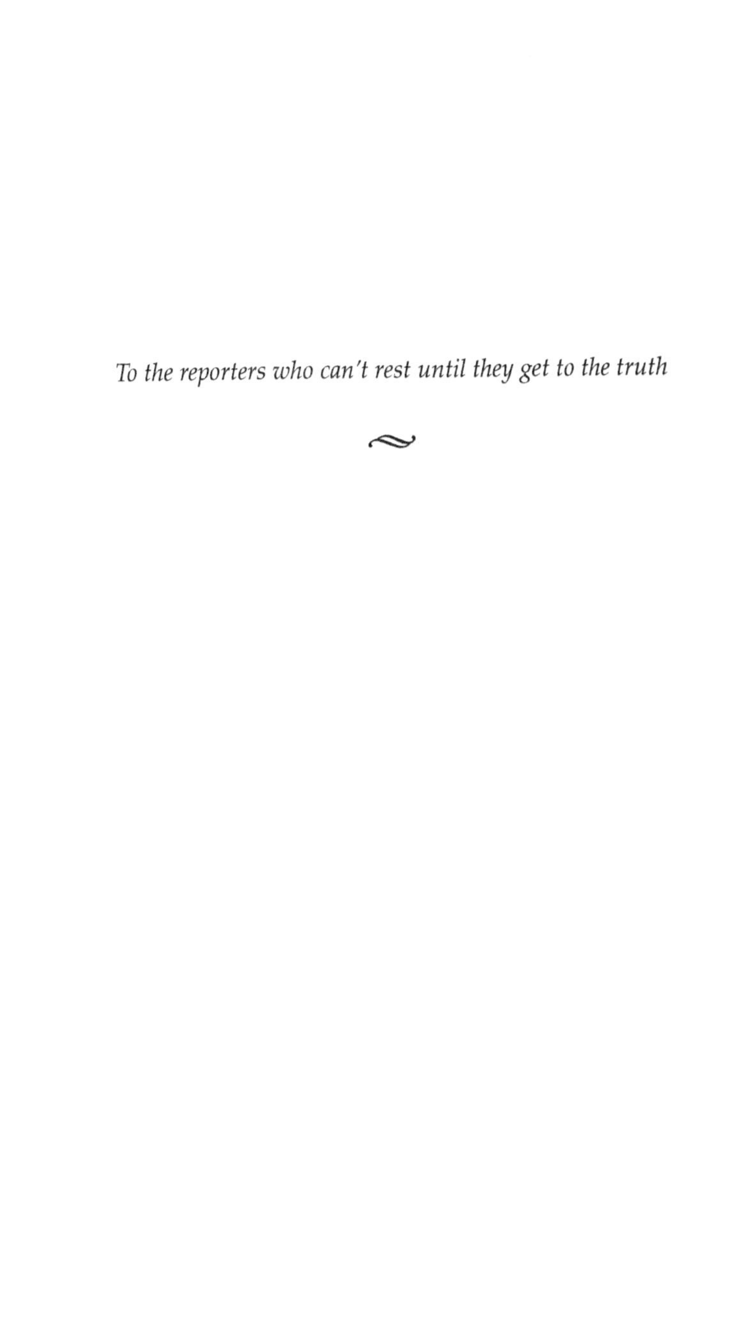

To the reporters who can't rest until they get to the truth

1

LINDEN

I CAN ALREADY TELL today is going to be one for the books.

Specifically, the horror-novel type.

I've been awake for fifteen minutes and I've already stubbed my toe on the corner of my couch and knocked over a potted fern, leaving a trail of dry dirt because I haven't watered it in over a week. I guess wet dirt would be worse, so I have a glass half-full moment of contemplation before telling that sentiment to step off and shove it. Oh, and my hairband breaks and flies across the room like a slingshot.

It's the sort of Monday where I leave my apartment while it's still dark out and I already know it will be dark when I come home. That means I will only see winter's daylight through the windows of the newsroom if I have a moment to look up from my computer at some point during the work day. If news is breaking and I'm scrambling toward a dead-line, I may not even see the daytime sky through the plate glass windows of our eighteenth-floor office.

It's almost just as well. Seeing the sun while not being able to get outside is its own form of torture.

But that's a problem for later.

For now, the soft shag rug feels nice on my feet, especially in the dark when I can't see the fern dirt amid its hideous mottled brown and beige swirls of synthetic fibers. I knew it was ugly when I bought it, but it was on sale and I appreciated that it was super soft and would hide dirt, so I wouldn't have to vacuum as often.

I wish I had the luxury of hiring a cleaning service occasionally to do it for me, but that's a fantasy for a day when I'm not gaming the system by loading up on mushrooms, sprouts, and other lightweight items at the Whole Foods salad bar to keep from spending my entire paycheck on one meal. I would never splurge on a fat cucumber slice or a weighty cube of tofu.

Someday…

For now, there's still a lot of ramen for dinner and protein bars instead of lunch. Reporters don't really make the big bucks, at least not entry-level reporters who still have years to work their way up to plum assignments and decent paychecks. Journalism is one of those jobs people choose for reasons of passion over paycheck, generally because they feel like it's a noble calling or a necessary check on government.

In my case, it's because I love finding a story no one else has and writing about it first. So yeah, I'm just a little bit competitive. I guess it's a labor of love, and I hope that if I hang in long enough I'll work my way up to a salary that allows for a decent robot vacuum and cherry tomatoes on my salads. Goals.

Truth be told, I do have enough money to shop for sensible dinners and modest-priced work clothes. But where's the fun in that? I'd much rather skimp on lunch all week and buy an awesome pair of stiletto boots that are as impractical as they are fabulous. I'd rather socialize with a barista for five minutes at Starbucks over an expensive vanilla latte, extra-shot, extra-hot, than watch my hand-me-down Melita drip machine churn out another depressing cup of coffee. I know I don't always make sound financial decisions. I'm twenty-eight. When I flout wisdom, I go big.

I hear my mother's voice in the back of my head, telling me I could be saving money if I made better choices. Then I actually hear it when I talk to her on the phone. "You have to have a plan. A savings goal. You need to commit to putting twenty percent of every paycheck away," she says.

"I know, Mom. I have a plan," I tell her.

I hate lying to my mother. There's no plan.

"Good girl. I didn't raise a dummy."

The economic term for my situation is cost-burdened. Anyone who spends more than half their income on housing gets to lug around that hyphenate until either they find a cheaper place to live or they get a raise.

And I'm not about to move.

I love my apartment. It's the top floor of a duplex, with blonde hardwood floors, cantilevered windows, and old dark beams across the ceilings. Even with my yard sale decor and bookshelves sitting atop milk crates, it has enough style to look amazing.

I moved in two weeks after I got promoted from news assistant to my reporting job at the Examiner, even though I knew I'd be financially stretched every month. The windows face east and west, and even though there's a tall orange tree outside one window, it's always really bright and perfect for houseplants. There are trailing ivy plants, hanging baskets, and a few fiddle leaf ferns in urns on the floor on opposite sides of my Ikea couch. I may have gone a little overboard with the greenery, but at this point in my life, plants make the best roommates.

Today, I haul myself up before the dawn to hit the gym because I know it's the only time I'll be able to fit in a work-out. The lights are on dimmer switches and only turned on to the lowest light, not because I have a roommate or boyfriend I'm afraid of waking, but because I'm still half asleep and I intend to stay that way for as long as possible, toe stub notwithstanding.

If I keep the lights low and stumble around in a kind of fugue state, I can convince myself that I've actually gotten an extra half hour of sleep. That will come in handy later when I start feeling a little tired and need to fool myself into believing I slept a full eight hours. Well… seven. And really only six and a half. Or whatever.

Really, does it matter?

~

THE REGULARS GREET me at the gym, we adjust our bike seats and handlebars to the heights we like, and I take my usual spot in the back row. I like the vantage point from there. It helps me absorb the energy of everyone else in the class when I can see them all, and at this hour of the morning, I need that extra push.

"Hey Linden." I hear the voice before my eyes can adjust to the dim lighting in the room. But I know who said the words.

"So early," I whine to Cassie, a brunette with narrow hips and the kind of giant boobs that seem uncomfortable to manage in a spandex tank with shelf bra. She always takes the bike on the end and always gets there before me. "If it's still dark out, isn't it technically the middle of the night?" I ask.

Leaning down, I try to balance on one foot while putting the hard-soled spin shoe on the other. I tell myself that it's the early hour that makes me especially clumsy, but I know I could easily fall over at just about any hour of the day.

"I'm a naturally early riser. I did Pilates before this at five-thirty," Cassie says, spinning her legs quickly with light tension, making her bounce up and down on the saddle like she's riding a pony. She's kind of adorable.

"You're a beast," I tell her, repeating verbatim a conversation we've had at least six times this month. I'm not much for new thoughts before seven in the morning.

"I'm just lucky. I only need five hours of sleep," she says, and I mentally curse her and her curvy body. I swing a leg over the saddle and clip in. Then, I give my legs a mental directive to start pedaling.

Come on, you can keep sleeping, just make circles.

Feeling like leaden tree trunks, my legs obey, and I wait for the instructor to turn on the first song so I can lose myself in Lizzo and get my sweat on.

"Did you see *Bachelor Bay* last night?" Cassie asks, unable to keep the squeal out of her voice.

Discussing this reality show is half the reason I'm here. "Yes, and what *was* that thing with Diego?"

"Girl, there aren't enough hours in the day to crawl into his wacky brain."

The show is my guilty pleasure, pure dumb fun watching a bunch of guys get filmed doing stunts as they try to win over unsuspecting women on a yacht docked near a resort town.

Somehow the scenarios that unfold on those ships are beyond scandalous, beyond controversial: champagne-fueled sexcapades, lies, and justifications for infidelity; husbands pretending to be single to compete on the show, all while believing their wives won't find out—and of course they do.

People just seem to combust when they get in front of the cameras. The show has been on for a decade and it's ratings gold. Cassie and I figured out that we were both suckers for it a year ago and we dissect every episode.

"Dean, OMG. Could you believe Jake ended up making out with Sally while that other guy was lying naked next to her in the bed. And she was totally fine with it?"

"It was pretty awesome," I agree. Just thinking about *Bachelor Bay* makes me smile. It's so far-removed from reality that it relaxes me to contemplate it. I'm almost bummed when the instructor gets on the mike and starts coaching us. But not really. I need a good sweat-drenching if I'm going to counteract the day's bad juju so far. We cycle in time with the music, we stand and run on the pedals, and we raise the temperature in the room by at least ten degrees.

Cassie hoots and hollers from the saddle next to me and I sing Pink's "What About Love" out loud. No one can hear me and that's the point. What started out as a slog uphill has turned into a full-throttle, joyous race to the finish. Drenched in sweat and three degrees away from a heart attack, I am transformed.

By seven-fifteen, I am fully awake and feeling almost invincible. I have forty-five minutes to shower, drive to work and pick up my latte from the coffee place in my building before going upstairs.

I love my job, even on the days when I get nasty letters from people who think I've missed the point of a story or even threats of lawsuits from people accusing me of slander. I was taught early on that hate mail is the sign of good reporting. I've wanted to be a journalist since I was a kid, long before I became a reporter for the ThesBEE, a publication for theater news that no one read at my tiny high school.

I worked my way up over the next ten years, through a college major in journalism, internships, terrible beats in tiny towns and semi-successful attempts to freelance in bigger towns. Since I had only ever wanted to be a journalist, landing a job at the Examiner was my dream. The paper has its main headquarters in New York, but there are news bureaus all over the country in all major cities. I was lucky to get hired in the LA bureau, so I didn't have to relocate.

There is, unfortunately, one thing I hate about my job. And it sits in the cubicle next to mine in the fine form of Jack Galloway. He's a star reporter who's treated like he walks on water, which feeds his already-giant ego. Before I'd been at my job for a week, I learned that Jack consistently writes more stories and gets more exclusives—meaning he's beating every other media outlet to report on breaking news—than almost anyone else at the paper.

He also lays claim to the only Pulitzer Prize won by anyone in the Los Angeles bureau for a series of stories he wrote a couple of years ago about a pattern of sexual harassment at several major film studios that led to major reform in the industry. He broke a story each day for weeks and was responsible for billions of dollars paid to compensate victims. When I started my job, Jack's journalistic reputation preceded him. I was ready to kneel at the altar of his skill and experience, grateful to be able to learn what I could from a master.

But he was nowhere to be found.

For the first couple weeks after I was hired, Jack was working at the paper's New York headquarters, so I didn't meet him until I rushed in one day—a half-hour late—and found a broad-shouldered man in a navy sport coat hunched over the news desk. When he heard me and turned around, my first thought was *I'm done for*. As in, there's no chance I can work around this guy every day and not want to have sex with him on the daily, starting right at that very moment.

Yes, please and thank you.

His deep blue eyes did me in at first glance and his perfectly straight, white teeth and dimpled cheeks unleashed a flutter in my belly when he smiled at me. I'm sure he expected me to melt into a puddle when I looked at him.

I almost did.

The only thing saving me was the need to take in the rest of his face: the strong jaw, the cheekbones that could cut glass, and the plush lips that mesmerized me even when he wasn't talking.

He tipped his head up in acknowledgment, "Jack Galloway." Then he looked back at whatever had his attention on the news desk. It was fortunate that he didn't seem interested in conversation because I was having trouble stuttering out my own name. When I did manage to enunciate it, he looked up at me with a smirk, like he was all too familiar with the effect he has on women.

Oh shit, this guy's trouble, I thought.

And I'm a magnet for trouble. Or at least, I used to be. If there was an egotistical, emotionally stunted, magnificent-looking guy within a ten-mile radius, I would find him like a heat-seeking missile. Then I'd let him wreck my capacity to make good decisions until he decided to move on, and I was left like sad roadkill, wondering what just ran me over.

Guys like him were the reason I never got promoted beyond reporting on brush fires and "dog bites man" stories at tiny papers—because I overslept one too many times after making bad decisions. Like going out instead of working late and coming to work unfocused after blindingly good sex.

It's been years since I've made those mistakes because I finally realized that for me, ambition and dating don't mix. So here I am, with no blindingly good sex in my life, no boyfriend, but one hell of an opportunity to do good work for one of the biggest papers in the country.

I'm done with distractions. I'm leaning into the job and ditching all relationships. It's for the best.

But man, if I have to look at Jack every day, it's just going to be painful.

He's the kind of guy who uses his hair for emphasis, running his fingers through it when he's thinking, shaking it forward and back again to settle the loose strands in place whenever he needs to get someone's attention. He comes into work with it wet and slicked back, as if communicating he's just come from the gym. Then he goes ahead and communicates it himself, in case any of us happened to miss the swell of his biceps and the broad span of his shoulders from whatever he does there.

"I caught that on CNN at the gym," he'll say, jumping in

on a conversation about how a company's stock took a turn after a bad earnings report. Or, "On my way to the gym, I saw a three-car pileup. We should do a piece about airbag technology." When he rolls up his sleeves, he has to stop midway up his forearms because his muscles prevent the fabric from going higher.

Some reporters wear jeans and T-shirts unless they have a meeting with an executive or a business lunch. Jack wears a dress shirt and tie most days, even if he's wearing jeans. He keeps a sport coat on the back of his chair for the off chance he has to run out and meet with someone important. He never gets rattled by anything at work. At least nothing that can't be solved by running a hand through his hair.

And while he's nice to look at, that's only when he's not talking. When he opens his mouth, it's usually to tell me something I'm doing wrong. "You shouldn't let a source dictate the terms of an interview" or "never agree to tell a person what quotes you're using in a story. If they say it on the record, you can quote it," he's told me. More than once.

While I appreciate the advice and know I can learn from the more senior reporters, it's the way he says things that annoy me. Like I'm a neophyte idiot who couldn't possibly get it right without his help.

Jack isn't my boss or even a person who has the power to fire me. But that's irrelevant. He's a highly respected reporter and people listen to what he has to say. Most of the time. Fortunately for me, the people who hired me didn't listen to him when he apparently objected, and they hired me anyway.

That didn't stop him from voicing his objection to the deputy bureau chief one morning when he thought I wasn't there. I overheard him say, flat out, "I think it was a mistake, putting her in that job. She's too green. It's going to blow up in her face."

I turned around and walked the other way so they

wouldn't know I'd overheard the conversation. I felt a rolling wave of nausea in my gut and the urge to quit right then. There was no mistaking that the conversation had been about me. I'm the least experienced reporter in the bureau, by a long shot. I'm the only reporter who could be described as green. But instead of giving him the satisfaction of thinking I quit because of him, I went to the bathroom, cried for five minutes, and talked myself off the ledge.

Most of the other reporters treat me like they assume I'm capable unless I show them otherwise. From the attitude Jack gives me daily, I can tell he thinks the exact opposite. Which is why I need him to understand that he can level that blue-eyed stare at me all day long if he wants to, and I'll feel nothing.

2

———

JACK

I don't know why it's so hard for a junior reporter to get to the office before eight in the morning. When I was a junior reporter, I was the first one in and the last to leave. That meant getting here at seven and staying until eight at night, even if no one asked it of me. That was the way you proved you were hungry for the job, the way you let everyone else know you were willing to work harder than them. That way, when you finally got promoted to a prime beat, it felt deserved.

Not the way she did it. Actually, I don't know the way she did it. There was a rumor flying around for a little while that she slept with the assistant bureau chief, but I don't believe it. Not that I know her well enough to assess her willingness to do something like that. I just know that Jeremy would never do it.

If I had to lay odds in favor of one guy on the planet staying faithful to his wife, I'd gamble on Jeremy. He's the epitome of a good guy. Amiable, fifty-seven years old, grey-bearded and stooped-shouldered from so many years spent huddling over a keyboard. He's been happily married for something like twenty-eight years. When I occasionally over-hear him talking to his wife, his voice takes on a sweet kind of reverence that I can't imagine feeling for a person after one year, let alone twenty-eight. It's almost disconcerting that he's still so in love.

No, not disconcerting. It's great, even if I can't see myself ever having something like that. Honestly, I'm not even sure I want it. The kind of relationship he has—marriage, forever love—it feels so… final.

Obviously, that's the point, and it's not my deal. I'm pretty damn happy the way things are, dating—or not dating, as the case may be—and never worrying too much about what will happen, eventually. There doesn't have to be an eventually.

I've ruined every relationship with my career ambition, so I've stopped trying to have a meaningful personal connection. My last breakup left me feeling like an asshole, and that was two years ago. I was chasing a huge story, which required travel, nights and weekends spent reporting, and hard questions that earned me the occasional death threat. I broke a lot of news, sent some bad people to jail, and changed a few industry policies for the better. In other words, exactly what I'd hoped to do when I chose journalism as a profession.

Let's just say my fiancé didn't see it the same way. She gave me an ultimatum—work or her. I chose my job because, truthfully, it seemed like a kinder, gentler option. Guess that should've told me something about the woman I thought I wanted to marry. So we parted ways. Not four months later, she was engaged to someone else. I unfriended her on social media because who needs to see that?

Now I mostly work and occasionally engage in a no-stress hookup. The emphasis is on low mental strain, instant gratification, and little emotional work. It's my safe zone.

Case in point, Linden, who is petite with gorgeous green eyes and a personality as fiery as her auburn hair, and she's made it clear she thinks I'm scum, the reason undecipherable to me. And it's not worth two minutes more of my time to try to figure out why. Who needs that kind of drama? So no, she and I will not be dating.

How did I get sidetracked? Dating her is not the point.

The point is that Linden has gone from being a news assistant to a junior reporter in record time and now she's getting some plum assignments. And she doesn't think enough of this job to get here on time. She needs to show up and do the basics. She needs to learn and get better at reporting, not just reach for big assignments because she's ambitious and no one has the balls to say no to her.

The news desk has to get taken care of first thing in the morning. It's crucial. The whole day depends on getting everything sorted at the beginning. And I seem to be the only one who's in the bureau early enough to get the job done. *Her* job.

She always comes in looking a little defensive, rushed, and apologetic. Then glides right into her chair and picks up where I've left off. She tosses a thank you my way and almost seems annoyed that I picked up the slack, as if I was doing it to make her look bad instead of doing her a favor. Did I mention that she's a junior reporter?

I should just stop doing it. Let her fall on her ass once or twice. It would serve her right. Some people only learn the hard way.

But I guess I'm just a special kind of sucker because I keep coming back for more. By the time she breezes in, I'll have gone through all the breaking news and organized the assignments for the bureau into piles for each reporter to pick up on the way in. *I should be one of those reporters. Linden should be the one organizing the beat work. Why am I such a Type A idiot that I can't stand leaving the incoming wire stories for her to suffer with when she finally rolls in?

I don't want to think about the answer to that.

But I'm here already so there's no harm in having a look at

what's on the wires and the twitter feeds of the companies we cover. It will help me in the long run. Maybe I'll stumble on to a story idea or an angle that I wouldn't have found otherwise.

And right now, I need a good idea.

I work in the entertainment pod at the paper, mainly covering new media. I used to cover the biggest entertainment players like Disney and Comcast, but once Netflix claimed a stake in the content business, all bets were off, and it was a feeding frenzy among the Silicon Valley reporters and the LA reporters to divvy up the reporting territory. I still cover the biggest companies because I've been at it for the longest, but now I also write about everything and everyone, streaming services, old-guard companies, some small tech companies that are creating entertainment. Honestly, it's all kind of a mess.

It used to be that we all knew where the lines were drawn between our various beats. There was tech, there was entertainment. Now it's some combination of all of it and that makes for some infighting over who gets to write the big stories. It also makes for a much more competitive atmosphere among reporters. If I'm not on the ball twenty-four/seven, some reporter in Silicon Valley is liable to scoop me on my own beat, simply because of a better relationship with someone on the inside of some tiny new media company.

It's a total shit show. Which is why I'm here early. My byline count has been a bit... off lately. I've missed a couple of stories because some other reporter at some other paper landed an exclusive story that I should've landed first.

They weren't even great stories, but that's not the point. I'm better than that. I'm almost always first with anything important and my sources know that's my reputation. They tell me what they know so I keep getting noticed, which gets them noticed. As soon as I land another great story, all the misses will be forgotten. Until then, it's all I can think about.

This is the Examiner. The senior editors don't like coming in second place. And they're used to better work from me, as they've been quick to remind me.

I'm not sure why I'm off my game, but I need to get it together, and fast. It's probably just a freak thing, not a real slump. I can get back to it if I can get myself to focus.

The problem is right now I'm so focused on how to get back on top that I'm not doing the work that will get me there. Kind of like stressing that I won't get enough sleep which then keeps me up at night and ensures that I won't get enough sleep. That's been happening too.

It's a phase. I'll snap back into form. I just need one great story idea, instead of the garbage I've proposed over the past couple of weeks. I knew our boss wasn't going to go for any of what I was suggesting but I had to come to him with something.

"Our intrepid reporter Linden has a brilliant take on ripped jeans," I overheard him say to the New York editors, praising some stupid story she brought to him on a Los Angeles-based manufacturer who's using recycled denim. Brilliant? Seriously?

She's obviously ambitious and capable. My desk is close enough to hers to overhear her interviewing people for her stories and she doesn't give up until she gets the quote she wants or the information she needs. God help the person who tries to hold out on her because she doesn't budge an inch.

"I have three people on the record telling me he's being dismissed from his job in the morning. Do you really want to respond with no comment? I don't think that'll look very good for you." I've heard her say things like that without even seeming like she's playing hardball. And they tell her what she wants them to say. But still.

I had a three-column exclusive story on the front page

about a multi-billion-dollar buyout of a media company and she's brilliant for writing about pants. I don't get it. Well, yes, I do. I've set a high bar and now I'm paying the price because the editors expect me to hand them exclusive stories every week. My buyout story was a month ago and I haven't been on page one since. That looks very bad to the senior editors who are paying attention.

And they're always paying attention.

3

———

LINDEN

WITHOUT EVEN LOOKING at my phone, I can already tell I'm late. It's the kind of thing a person knows just from the slight shift in the way the sun looks in the sky.

Okay, I'll cut the bullshit.

I know I'm late because, unfortunately, I'm always late. I always have the best of intentions, but somehow something holds me up. I know it's past eight o'clock, and if I hadn't stopped for coffee, maybe I could've been here on time. But probably not. Something else would've derailed me and I'd be right where I am. It's just how it always seems to work out.

Every damn day.

And that means Jack will already be at his desk, and he'll make sure I'm aware of what time it is and how inconvenient I've made it for him because I forced him to pick up the slack.

It's not like I want him to do my work for me. I actually like the part of my day when I assess all the feeds. If a reporter is working on something big and a smaller story comes through, it will probably get handed off to me to write. Mine is an odds and ends job that still gives me the freedom to dig up my own things to write about. And I'm learning about a lot of companies and getting some good experience.

I don't have a problem doing my job. I don't think it's beneath me. Most people in the bureau had to do it at one time or another and it's kind of a rite of passage.

Unfortunately, I have a tiny issue with punctuality.

I'm somehow reliably late, no matter how hard I try. Jack isn't my boss and my job rarely crosses paths with his, so it shouldn't make a difference to him what I do or how late I am when I do it. Yet he always makes it very clear when I arrive that he's done me a huge favor by going through the feeds for me and sorting everything out. I swear, he just seems like he pitches in out of a need for extra adoration and appreciation. Maybe his teachers didn't give him enough gold stars.

WHEN THE ELEVATOR opens on the eleventh floor, my sole focus is getting to my desk without spilling my hot latte onto my sleeve or down the front of my white shirt. I've already failed so far, thanks to the barista who opted to top off my drink with an extra pour of low-fat milk, which is now leaking from under the plastic lid of my reusable cup.

I can feel a warm dribble running down my arm, even though I'm now holding the cup away from me like a baby with a full diaper. I will my laptop bag not to slide off my shoulder and disrupt the delicate balancing job I've got going with the file folders in my other hand.

In other words, a normal Monday. Hopefully, my revved-up, take-no-prisoners feeling will carry me through midday. Or at least until I'm done dealing with Jack. Baby steps.

I walk toward the newsroom's open double doors, already knowing what will greet me when I go inside. Jeremy, the deputy bureau chief, will have been puttering around since seven, and the box of donut holes he brings each day will already be emptied of its contents. He lives far away and if he leaves past six in the morning, the traffic is awful, so he shows up at the crack of dawn, eats breakfast, and leisurely reads the big national newspapers—in other words, our competition.

"Linden. G'morning," Jeremy says. He's walking from the coffee room back to his desk with a cup of coffee he just brewed. He always takes on coffee duty first thing and he makes it so strong that it has the faint taste of motor oil. I see him glance at my store-bought coffee like it's an affront to his brewing.

"Hey, Jeremy. How's it going?" I'm asking about his day and his life, but he'll answer with something related to news.

"Pauline's got a merger she's tracking but I haven't seen anything else yet. Jack's here, he's probably got something. I dunno. What're you working on?"

"Still chasing sources on my Zumalife story." Zumalife is a small surf wear company that's been giving me the runaround and I'm starting to get worried that I'm missing something important. I'm not about to let Jeremy know that.

"Where are you with it?"

"Still chasing sources."

"What's the timeline? Stuart wants to know."

Stuart is the bureau chief, which means he has a hand in everything that comes out of our bureau and he decides who gets to propose stories to the editors in New York. He's uptight, demanding, and only friendly when a great story is on the line.

Of course he'll want to know the timeline for the Zumalife story. I knew what Jeremy meant the first time, but I don't have an answer.

I also know that I need to come up with something concrete before Stuart asks me himself. Jeremy is kindly letting me know I need to get my shit together and come up with a realistic timetable for delivery. Preferably before Stuart gets to work and I get embarrassed for not having answers to his questions. He's considerate that way.

Stuart is not a person I'd want to invite over to dinner. He's snarky and prickly and rarely interested in what I have to say. I know that sounds like I'm being overly sensitive. When I hear people say their bosses hate them, I always think they're exaggerating or looking for sympathy. I don't think Stuart hates me. He just doesn't deal with me, which feels almost the same.

"Stuart doesn't like people. He likes stories," Jeremy once told me after Stuart berated me in front of the whole news-room for spending three days in a row at my desk instead of going out in the field to drum up new angles on a story.

In addition to only liking stories, Stuart only seems mildly happy when he's editing something one of us has written, deleting whole paragraphs, and rewriting it seemingly just because he needs to feel needed. That's not to say my work doesn't benefit from a strong edit. I just think Stuart enjoys slashing through my words a little too much. As assistant chief, Jeremy does an equal amount of editing but with a lighter touch and I much prefer working with him.

After assuring Jeremy that I'd have a firm timeline for Stuart and a good story for the paper, I walk toward my desk and park my coffee on the rubber Starbucks coaster that came free with a gift card purchase. I hear a soft drone of news from the flat screen monitors which gives the bureau a steady hum of noise that provides a backdrop. And a lot of pressure.

I'm pretty much always stressed, always feeling like I'm behind the eight-ball, one step away from missing a big story. I probably swallow more Tums than the average person, but I justify it because they boost my calcium intake, and you never can be too careful about osteoporosis.

Jack is hunkered over his desk with his back to me, listening to a message on his voicemail, which he always insists on doing over speakerphone. He claims it's so he can be handsfree and type up his call log. But with the Bluetooth option available, it's a thin argument. I am fairly certain he does it so everyone around can hear how many messages he has from important people.

But with him facing away, I take the opportunity to slide into my chair and stash my laptop bag under the desk, so I can look industrious when he turns around. Maybe he'll think I've been there for a while.

He doesn't buy it for a second. Like a bird of prey with an instinct for a nearby kill, he spins around in his chair.

"Nice of you to show, Sandoval," he says, hitting the button on his phone to kill the voicemail playback.

"Morning, Jack." My tone is casual, like he just caught me in the middle of what I've been sitting here doing for ten minutes. But we both know it's a charade.

"Wasn't sure if you were gonna make it. Or whatever. So, I went through the feeds," he says, tossing a stack of printouts at me. "Pauline's already on her merger story and I know about my companies, but there are a few others in there that look important. But you'd know better. Since it's your wheelhouse."

It would be my wheelhouse if he hadn't beaten me to the office. And now I'm in a crappy mood because Jack just rubbed my face in it.

"Thanks. You really didn't have to go through the feeds for me."

"I didn't do it for *you*. I did it for the paper because it needs to get done. You might want to go through everything yourself. In case I missed something." He sneers, daring me to think I could possibly catch something he missed.

"Sure. Of course. I plan to go through everything. It's my job. That's why I'm here."

Early. And I *am* early. The newsroom is empty, and no one else seems upset that I haven't put little FYI notes in their in-boxes, letting them know what companies have been putting out on the feeds all morning. They're not even here to know differently.

"I just thought… never mind."

"What?"

"I just figured since you didn't care enough to get here on time, you might not be in the mood to do your actual job."

"Well, you figured wrong. Why are you such a dick?"

"Excuse me?"

Oops. Was that not in my inside voice?

He stands up and leans on the partition between our cubicles, looking down at me with an amused smirk. His dimples twitch and his eyes sparkle and it annoys me that I notice. I catch a whiff of the aftershave he wears, and I wish I could stop myself from inhaling a little deeper when I do.

"You think I'm a dick?" he asks.

I feel my face flush in what I'm pretty sure is an awkward shade of fuchsia and I immediately start to sweat. Why can't I learn to hold my tongue? My temper is not one of my better qualities and I don't need to give him more reasons to think less of me. He looks like he's enjoying every moment of my misery.

"Actually, yes."

Again, not editing very well.

But I can't help it. It's all I've wanted to say for months now, but I always hold my tongue because the last thing I need is to add the appearance of a temper to the long list of issues he seems to have with me. Until today. Apparently, today's the day I'm working extra hard to get myself fired.

"Well, okay. Thank you for your honesty. I'll try a little harder not to be so dick-like."

"Okay, great. If you don't mind, I'd like to get to it." I swivel my chair away from him and start to look through the pile of pages he handed me. But I can tell without turning around that he's still looking my way.

"Can I just ask you something? I've never quite been able to get clarity here and maybe you can help me understand."

I turn back toward him. "Sure, I guess."

"If you're able to get here twenty minutes late every day, why can't you just leave twenty minutes earlier? Seems like you could fix the whole situation."

I exhale my frustration with the conversation. "I don't know, Jack. Maybe I'll try that. Thanks for the suggestion."

He shrugs and goes back to his phone, dialing up a CEO who loves to give him dirt on other companies and chatting him up like the bros they seem to be.

"Burt, how was the weekend? Yeah, I got my fair share. You never have to worry about me."

He laughs and I can only imagine what the bros are discussing. Probably something sexist and demeaning. "Well, if you're hearing that, I gotta believe there's some truth to it…" More laughing. "When's your next free lunch?" Even a cubicle away I can hear the smile in his voice. He has a way of charming people. "Okay, I'm gonna hold you to that. I want the full story."

He clicks off and dials up his next source, which will be much the same drill. I can tell he's smiling by the tone of his voice and I'm sure his sources feel it too.

"Donna, Jack at the Examiner… yeah, great to hear your voice. So, I'm wondering if Bill has time for me this week… yeah, of course, you and I should meet and go over all the hot takes. You thinking a cocktail…?"

Now I want to gag because as soon as Jack gets on the phone with a woman—any woman—his voice changes and he starts talking in this gravelly, quieter voice, like he wants to melt them into submission. I guess it must work. But it doesn't change my opinion of him as an arrogant guy who's evidently spent too long staring at himself in the mirror because he's clearly in love… with himself.

"Charlie, my man! You so owe me. And I'm gonna collect." He goes on and on like that, sweet-talking everyone in sight and making them think he's their friend. Then he pounds them with a story that makes them look like crooks.

I put on headphones to tune him out.

I'll admit, he's very good at his job. He makes people want to tell him things, even things that are going to make them look very bad when the details are published in a major newspaper. It's kind of a gift. Even over the phone, it's like people can feel his smile and appreciate his good-looking face.

Jack has more bylines than anyone in the bureau. He just has a nose for where to find stories and he's so good at working his sources. The editors love him, and they make room on Page One for whatever he writes, even before they've read it. They simply start every day assuming he'll have at least one story, and generally, he does.

You'd think he might look back and remember what it felt like to be an ambitious junior reporter like me and maybe cut me some slack, but apparently there's not enough room in his head for those memories *and* his fat ego. If he was just slightly less irritating, I might not outright hate him.

I realize that it probably sounds like I'm thinking about him way too much for a guy who irritates the hell out of me. It seems like I've fallen for his charms too and I'm looking for an excuse to daydream about him. I'm not. I legitimately can't stand the guy. Or his body spray or whatever the hell he uses after the gym.

I turn my attention back to the news feeds. I shouldn't let him get to me. This is our morning routine. It's just the way he is. I'm long past reminding him that he didn't need to do my work for me, that he should just leave it. And he's long past failing to remind me of my place on the bureau's ladder —the bottom.

But his point is still well taken. I need to make a bigger effort to get here on time. Tomorrow will be another day.

For now, based on how my morning has gone so far, I get ready for whatever drubbing this one has in store.

4

LINDEN

THE CONFERENCE ROOM hums with idle chitchat, masking the voice of anyone in particular as we get settled in for the meeting. We reconnect with perfunctory stories about our weekends. Pauline drops down in the chair next to mine and I'm grateful. She's about ten years older than me and she's been at the paper since she graduated college, starting as an assistant in the London bureau and moving to a reporting job in the Middle East before landing in LA.

"Hey, you do anything good this weekend?" Pauline asks.

"Eh, went to the farmer's market, took a spin class, went to yoga. Nothing too exceptional. You?"

She drops her voice to a quieter whisper. "Well, it's a little crazy, but I actually did a photoshoot for Essence magazine."

"Seriously?" I don't doubt that Essence would want pictures of Pauline in their magazine. She's one of the most gorgeous women I've ever seen and at almost six feet tall, she looks great in almost anything she wears. I'm just surprised. "Are you modeling on the side?"

She snorts. "Hardly. It was for a piece they're doing on black women writers."

"Still cool. Was it fun?"

"Actually, really tedious. Standing under hot lights and having people fuss over whether my lip gloss was shiny enough is not my idea of a fun Saturday. But it might bring us some new readers."

I'm impressed that Pauline's motive wasn't glamour but readership.

Stuart starts talking without waiting for everyone to quiet down. It's his way of letting us know that whatever conversations we're having aren't as important as what he has to say. "Morning, team. I know some of you have news breaking on your beats, so I won't make this long." I exhale a quiet sigh of relief. Maybe we wouldn't get to the part where he asks me in front of everyone else how my story is progressing.

The truth is, it's not progressing. I've been chasing after the head of the surf wear company for a month, trying to get him to agree to an interview. Something has changed, but I can't discern what's different. But they've gone quiet. Usually, their PR flak is calling me weekly, bugging me to write even a tiny story about the company. If I can, I throw her a bone and write up something on their plans to launch a new board shorts line, but Zumalife just isn't a company that generates a lot of news.

For the first year, I wrote about retail and fashion; I didn't even notice Zumalife. The company is small compared to some of the streetwear companies in Los Angeles and they seem to chug along selling the same board shorts and surf T-shirts year after year. The company has always seemed like a small fish, so I'd take the calls from the publicist and dutifully ask if anything newsworthy was happening, hoping the company would get bought by a bigger retailer so at least I could write about that. But so far, it's just been a quiet small company, desperate for any shred of attention from our paper. Unfortunately, I can't write much more than the occasional story about quarterly profits or a new pair of shorts.

Unless they do something surprising.

In the past four weeks, I haven't heard word one from the company publicist and she hasn't returned my calls. That's unusual enough for me to wonder what's up. It's possible that the company isn't doing anything particularly interesting, but that's the kind of thinking that leads a person to miss a big story.

I need to get a meeting with the head of the company. If he's planning something, I need to know.

"Linden, anything on the promised Zumalife story?" Stuart asks, just as I'm getting comfortable with the idea that I'll get a pass during this meeting.

"Um, I'm working leads on a couple fronts. I should know more a bit later today," I say.

"What are the leads?" Stuart isn't going to let me be vague. I feel everyone's eyes land on my reddening face.

"Well, I have a source at their manufacturing plant downtown, and he tells me they've halted production."

"That's pretty interesting. Do you know why?" Stuart asks.

I shake my head. I wish I knew why. "It could be that they're moving overseas, maybe to cut costs or it could be a downturn in orders. That's what seems likely."

Stuart doesn't look pleased with the amount of information I have. "Anyone else writing about them?" He means our competition. I'd better hope that no one else doesn't get whatever story this is before I do.

"Not so far, no."

"Can you be ready with something today?" he asks.

"Possibly. Depends on whether I can get someone at the company to talk to me today," I say, trying not to let Stuart know how unlikely that seems, based on how they've blown me off so far.

He smiles. "Great. Let's try to get something on the afternoon schedule."

I return his smile, before looking down at my notepad and writing down the words, *Zumalife, afternoon sked,* like I need to remind myself of it for later. Inside, I'm cringing because there's no way I'm going to have this story unless I can get someone at the company to talk to me. And they're stonewalling.

Stuart turns his attention to Pauline's merger story, and she assures him she'll have front page news to report all week long. His smile goes wide, several inches worth of happy that my half-baked attempt on Zumalife could never elicit.

Tyler reports in on a couple things breaking on his beat. More smiles from Stuart. Jeremy is involved in something about processed snack foods that will take months to report and will likely take him to South America in the process.

Then there's Jack. Stuart saves him for last because he's the closer, always guaranteed to have something fabulous Stuart can carry off to his bosses like a ceremonial offering.

"Burt's got a merger cooking. I can tell. I talked to his golfing buddies and he's been a no-show two weeks in a row. That only happens when he's working a deal. I expect him to announce something by the end of the week."

"Which means we'll have it…?" Stuart asks, hoping the answer will be *today.*

"I'm meeting him later. My guess is I'll have it wrapped up after that. No one else's getting this."

"I want you to ping me after the meeting. If we can put something out tonight in the digital edition, even better."

"Yup, I can make that happen." Jack leans back in his chair and casts a look around the room, sizing up the rest of us, daring us to be as good at our jobs as he is. I look away, not wanting to see the judgment in his eyes.

I want to be better, just so I can wipe the satisfied look off his face.

When did doing my job well become about him?

Well, whatever it takes. Maybe a good, healthy dose of competitiveness is a positive thing.

Either that, or it will do me in.

5

LINDEN

I SHOULD HAVE STAYED in bed. I should have feigned illness or made up a family emergency or just quit my job. Any of those things would have been better options than the way the rest of my day unfolds.

First, Jack brings some awful-smelling vegan crap from the food truck downstairs and eats it at his desk for lunch. The smell of broccoli wafting over the cubicle wall actually ruins the taste of my vending machine-bought granola bar, because my brain somehow combines the smell and the taste into one garbage concoction in my mouth. No, I can't leave the office and buy something better for lunch. I'm lucky to have five minutes to hit the machine in the hallway.

The rest of my day is a complete clusterfuck. Despite leaving four messages, I can't get ahold of the publicist at Zumalife. I realize I don't have any actual sources in the surf wear industry who can give me some inside knowledge of what Zumalife is up to, and it's too late to curry favor with people I don't already know well. After leaving yet another voicemail for Zumalife's publicist, I actually feel tempted to drive to the company's headquarters, an hour away in Irvine.

Then I worry that I'll lose valuable time if their doors are locked or the people I need to speak with are locked up in a corporate meeting. I can't risk the two hours on the road for a maybe.

Instead, I take the circuitous route and call analysts to see if they've heard any rumblings of company news. Nothing.

Starting to feel desperate and casting about for ideas, I call several Zumalife retail stores and ask the salespeople some questions, not letting on that I'm a reporter out of fear that they might hang up. I corner one, a nice-sounding guy named Ian, when he has a few free moments between customers. "I'm really looking forward to seeing the new line. When's it expected?" I ask.

"Don't know. Probably next season," Ian says.

"So, do you have a lot of excess stock in the store from this season? Is it all still being manufactured downtown?"

"We have a normal amount of stock. And, I dunno about the other part. I'm not sure where they make the clothes." I start to second guess my strategy when I realize Ian doesn't know anything about the company, other than how to ring in sales on an iPad.

I spend a good part of my day circling the drain, knowing Stuart will be making his way to my desk to find out where I've landed with my reporting. He'll expect a well-reported story. I've got squat.

BY FIVE IN THE AFTERNOON, I'm coming to the realization that I'm not going to be able to deliver anything resembling a newsworthy story. I convince myself it's not the worst thing to have to tell Stuart. In the meantime, I start looking through feeds again, knowing most big announcements get made in the morning, so I'm not expecting to find anything revelatory. Still, it's part of my job to stay on top of whatever's breaking.

That's when I see the headline from the New York Times,

an exclusive story about Zumalife's chief executive buying back all the company's shares and taking it off the stock exchange. He's going private.

It's a big story. It should be my story.

And I don't have it.

It's only a matter of minutes before I hear Stuart's door slam. I don't have to look up to know he's striding to my cubicle to find out why the Times has the story and we don't. I haven't got a good answer for him.

"How did we miss this?" Stuart asks, his voice ten decibels louder than it needs to be for the entire news bureau to hear him.

"I've been trying to get them on the phone for weeks. I—"

"Trying? And then what. Giving up?"

"No, I—"

"This is not good. The Times shouldn't have this before us. Why are they giving an exclusive to the Times?"

"I'm going to get to the bottom of it. I'll make sure they give us their next exclusive—"

Stuart isn't interested in my attempt to turn this around or in any of my excuses, and I'm running out of them. He holds a hand up. "You need to do better. This is a relatively small company that no one particularly cares about. Until another paper beats us, of course. Then, we care."

I nod. It's pointless to try to defend myself anymore. I know he's right. And he's actually being nice, admitting that the company isn't crucial to the order of the universe. But that doesn't take away from my colossal screw-up.

"Get them on the phone. Find a follow-up angle. Something the Times doesn't have. We can still do something good here. We'll run a perfunctory piece tonight, parroting what the Times has, and tomorrow we do better."

"Yes, will do. I'll stay late and set it up. I promise."

Stuart nods, catching something on one of the TV monitors and already moving on to the next item on his agenda.

I'm left at my desk to dig myself out of the hole I created without even trying. I feel like running to the restrooms in the hallway and bawling. But I can't. Stuart said we have to do better. What he means is *I* have to do better.

AFTER ANOTHER TWO hours on the phone, I get a hold of the Zumalife publicist and she agrees to put me on the phone with the CEO in the morning. I will do whatever I can to find a new story angle and write something that will make Stuart dance a jig in his office tomorrow.

But I'm spent. This day started way too early and ended way too poorly for me to have anything left to give.

That's when I hear a voice I wish I could ignore.

Of course he's happily chatting up some slutty woman who, from the sound of it, is probably facetiming him in the nude. "I've seen some good work in my day, but that is one spectacular rack."

I mean, *ew*. Everyone can hear him. Well, to be fair, I'm the only one within earshot, but shouldn't he care about sounding like such a walking hard-on? I stand up and glare at him over the partition between our cubicles.

The second he sees me there, the broad smile on his face fades and he quiets down a tiny bit, asking the chick with the giant rack to hang on a second. He puts the call on hold, his intense eyes locked on me. "Everything okay there?"

"Oh, just fabulous. I'm having a stellar day. The only thing that would be better is if I could hear you objectifying women even louder."

He quickly tells his slutty friend he'll call her back. I'm sure she's grateful for the chance to adjust the angle of the phone camera to give him an even better view. "I'm sorry, objectifying women? What in God's green earth are you talking about?"

"The whole 'spectacular rack' comment. Jesus, you're even more disgusting than I thought if you don't even see how that's objectifying."

His lips bend into a smirk and he stares at me. Then he outright laughs. "For your information, my brother built a fifty-bottle wooden wine rack out of red pine. He's been working on it for months. Figured out how to do it with a couple of YouTube videos. Wanna see a picture? I think even you'll agree it's a spectacular rack."

Oh. Well, I didn't see that coming.

Now I feel like an asshole, and seeing a picture isn't going to make it better, but what else can I possibly do to remove my oversized foot from my even bigger mouth? I grudgingly walk over to his cubicle and look at the picture he has on the screen. It is pretty impressive. I nod. "It's nice."

"Not bad for a dentist who never built anything before, huh?"

I nod again. "I'm sorry. I just… I guess my radar for offensive things is on high alert today."

"*Today?* You always think I'm doing or saying something awful. How is today different?"

I take a deep breath for the first time in what feels like hours. "This has been a truly shitty day. And I jumped to conclusions. So… apologies."

He nods and I skulk back to my desk.

"Hey," Jack says. I don't respond because I assume he's about to say more, but he's quiet until I turn to look at him. He's standing with his forearms on top of the partition that divides our cubicles. The sleeves on his white dress shirt are rolled up to the elbows and he's taken off the tie he had on earlier. He looks sympathetic, but he might just be tired.

I still don't say anything. I'm not sure what he expects, but maybe this is where he tells me that I never should have been hired for this job. So I wait for whatever he's planning to throw in my face.

"It happens."

"What?" I'm not sure if he's talking about my busted story, my mistake about the rack, or something else.

"We all get beaten from time to time. Don't let it get you down." It sounds strange coming from him—compassion. I don't know why he's bothering to try to be nice.

"Thanks. Well, it shouldn't have happened. I know that."

"Do you?" he asks, running his fingers through his hair, pushing it back. I see his blue eyes boring into my face.

And he's done being nice.

"What's that supposed to mean?"

"It means, do you know why it happened?"

My blank look must indicate that, in fact, I don't know.

He grabs an eco-friendly bottle of water off his desk and takes a swig. "It means you didn't have that company on your radar for, like, the first six months you've had this job. You blew off their PR flak. Did you ever meet her for a drink or lunch? Take time to be friendly when there wasn't a story on the line?"

I don't answer. He already knows.

"Then when you figured out there might be some news at the company, it shocked you that they didn't want to hand you an exclusive. It's not your fault. You're still new at this. You didn't know. Times reporter probably worked them for years to be first in line on that story."

I guess he's right. It's a small company and I hadn't paid much attention, initially. I *was* trying very hard to get them on the phone. But only recently.

Yet I feel defensive. First of all, how does he know I blew them off? Is he really paying that much attention to what I'm doing at the desk next to his? Why doesn't he mind his own damn business?

Then I answer my own question. Because he's insanely good at his job and that means he cares about the paper more than almost anyone. Which also means it bothers him when we miss something, even if it's not on his beat. He sat next to me and saw me making a mistake with a company I was supposed to cover, and he let me do it.

Because he wants me to fail.

Now I'm not able to bottle up my frustration—with him, with my job, with myself—any longer. I lash out at the only obvious target.

"You know what Jack, thank you for your fake sympathy, but I'm good."

He looks stunned, then he gets that half-smile, half-smirk on his face that I can't stand. "It's not fake sympathy. We've all been there, is what I'm trying to say. I know it sucks."

"Okay, well, if it's not fake, then thanks," I say. I just need this day to end so I can go home and bury myself under a Sherpa blanket and binge-watch past seasons of *Bachelor Bay* until I pass out. I turn back to my computer. End of discussion.

"Beauty of a newspaper is after one day it ends up in the recycling bin. Tomorrow's another shot."

Goddammit, he's still fucking there, staring at me over the partition. I hate how good looking he is. I hate that his end-of-the-day scruff looks sexy, not sloppy. And I hate that if I didn't dislike him so much, I'd be having fantasies about him.

"I'm meeting someone for a drink. You look like you could use one. I could push it off for a half hour, if you want to go drown it all in a cocktail first."

I'm not sure if I'm hearing him correctly. Is he asking me out for a drink? Is my failure somehow appealing to him or is he just being sympathetic? I'm busy telling myself to get a grip when he holds a hand up because he has to take a phone call.

"Dude, you can't possibly think that... Of course, I'm in... You're on. Let's make it official and I'll put it in my calendar..."

The sound of his voice having his bro conversation with whomever he's talking to snaps me out of my momentary insanity. He's a player. He sweet talks whoever's in his orbit to get what he wants. And his words to Jeremy come back to me, "It's a mistake… she's too green…"

Down deep, I know he doesn't care that I blew it. He's been expecting it since the day I walked in the door. He loves being right, and now I've given him exactly what he's been craving. I tell him he doesn't need to push back his plans with his source. I'm good.

But when he pats me on the shoulder in a reassuring way, I hate that I can feel the heat from his hand long after he's walked out the door.

6

JACK

IT'S possible that her temper is going to do her in, but I think it just might make her a great reporter. It requires a certain kind of tenacity to do the job well, and I'm glad to see she's angry about her missed scoop, even if it means she's misplacing her anger on me.

And hell if she didn't look sexy, all fired up and raging at me, her cheeks pink and her lips turned into an angry snarl. So damned sexy. Too bad I don't date reporters. Actually, scratch that. It's a very good thing I don't date reporters. She would spell trouble for me.

It's not that I categorically dismiss people in the news business as being undatable. I should amend that. I don't date colleagues. Or sources or executives on my beat or anyone else's. Too much conflict of interest.

I tried dating a publicist for one of the smaller media companies on my beat and it blew up in my face. We slept together once and when I tried to leave it at that, she stopped returning my calls. All fine except when one of my bigger companies was trying to buy that little company, I needed information. She stonewalled and I learned a valuable lesson.

There are enough women in the world that I don't need to mix work and dating.

But man, if I did…

I have to stop myself from imagining what someone with her fiery personality might be like in bed.

So. Stop. Imagining. It.

Maybe I've been a little too hard on her, hence the *dick* comment earlier. But she's an accident waiting to happen, as she's just proven today. This is exactly what I warned Jeremy about. He was doing her a disservice by promoting her too fast and handing her a reporting job before she was ready. He was just setting her up to fail. I don't know why he couldn't see that.

Maybe that's why I've tried to make sure she wasn't missing anything in the morning feeds that would make her look bad.

Is that what I've been doing?

Actually no, it's not. I'm just obsessive and I get to work early. I go through the feeds because it keeps me sharp and I might find my way to something good before anyone else gets to it. That's why I've been able to stay on top. It has nothing to do with trying to help her.

Keep pretending you don't like the feisty banter when she gets frustrated after you've done half her job.

Whatever. I need to meet my source and I don't want to be late. I need to convince her to put me in a room with her boss, the CEO of one of the biggest companies I cover. I've been writing a big profile piece about him, but I need access to his private life to round it out, and she's the key to making it happen.

7

LINDEN

I'M WALKING past Jeremy's office when he looks up and signals me to come in. I really don't want to, because there's a fifty percent chance I'll cry if I try to speak and I can't be the reporter who cries.

"Come, sit," Jeremy says, turning around so I can compose myself. He may be one of the most senior people in the bureau, but he has a heart bigger than anyone.

Obediently, I sit in the chair opposite Jeremy's desk. He's looking out the window toward the ocean, but since it's dark out, the only view is city lights.

"You okay?" he asks.

"Yeah. All good."

"Sure, fine. Look, I don't want to belabor it, but you know you can't let stuff like this happen."

"I know. Trust me, I really thought I could get them to talk."

"Right, okay. This will blow over, you'll write your story, and this little company won't be your biggest problem anymore. You just need find something you care about and dig in. That's where the best stories come from."

He looks at his computer, then starts to smile. He turns the screen around so I can see what he's looking at—an image of a large slobbery dog. "That's Zeke. He's part coonhound, part Rhodesian Ridgeback."

"Cool dog."

"Sure is," he says, turning the screen back around and looking at me. "I know you're driven and motivated. I'm not worried about you here. You're gonna do great."

"Thanks, Jeremy. I don't know what I'd do here without you."

"Aw, you'll manage fine."

"That makes it sound like you're going somewhere."

"Not today, not for sure. But I put in to take another book leave. My publisher's ready, but I have to jump through some hoops before New York will let me go."

"Wow, that's amazing. What's the book about?"

He shakes his head. "I can't say anything yet, but the minute the ink's dry on my contract, I'll let you know." He goes back to shuffling papers on his desk. Whatever he's looking for, he doesn't seem to be finding it. "Anyhow, everything worked out on Zumalife?"

I don't want to talk about it anymore, but it's Jeremy, so I tell him. "I'm already set with the CEO for a sit-down tomorrow."

"Exactly, just how I knew you'd be."

Still, I feel like I could use some advice. "What was it, the moment when you knew you were good at your job?" I ask.

He leans back in his chair and runs a hand over his chin in a classic thinking pose. "You know, it was when I found a story I couldn't let go of, something I had to pursue because I knew it was important. When I was reporting that story, I knew I was good." He gestures to a book on his shelf that he wrote. "That story turned into this book."

I know the book. It sits proudly on the top shelf, standing up so the book cover is visible. I also know this book was on the bestseller list for months, but I hadn't ever been aware that its origin was a story Jeremy wrote for the Examiner.

Looking at the cover, I feel almost reverential, like it's something I can't possibly reach out and touch. Jeremy takes it off the shelf and hands it to me. "This is what can happen when you follow a lead, even if you're not sure where it will go. You're welcome to take it home if you want to have a read."

I look at the title, *Hard Choices; One Man's Quest to Find His Mother's Killer*, and nod, thanking Jeremy and taking the book with me. I vow to read it when I get home, even if I need to stay up all night to do it. I need to understand what that kind of passion looks like because I can't seem to find my own, and I can't bear another day like this one.

BEFORE I CAN SKULK out of the building and lick my wounds in peace, my friend Kayla intercepts me and pulls me toward her. "Hey! Did you get my text?"

I look down at my phone and realize I've had it turned off for the past hour. Being unreachable is another cardinal sin in for a reporter. I'm sinking deeper into a hole. "Ah, no, I haven't checked my phone." I power it back on, hoping there's no urgent news-related message I've missed. Other than Kayla's texts, I don't seem to have missed much.

"I wanted to see if you were free. So, perfect timing. Let's go get a drink," Kayla says.

"I can't," I tell her. What I mean is, I don't want to go. I don't want to be around merriment and other humans. I want to take my lumps like a big girl and run home and hide. But that would require a longer explanation than I want to give, and Kayla doesn't give up easily. It's what makes her a great lawyer. She's on the partner track at her firm, and I have no doubt she'll get there. It also means she's not letting me out of her clutches tonight without a fight.

We were roommates until six months ago, when she moved in with her boyfriend, Lucas, and I found housing nirvana in my gorgeous but pricey rental unit. It's been a few weeks since I've seen her, even though her law firm is in the same building as the news bureau. In part, that's because we both work crazy hours, but hers tend to start later and end way later than mine. It's a rare day when she's in the same elevator as me.

"Actually, I had a really crappy day. Maybe I could use one drink."

"Or maybe two. I'm sorry about your day, but I'm secretly happy it works to my advantage." She puts an arm around my shoulder, and we walk through the building lobby.

I realize I miss her, and maybe it would do me good to spend some time with someone who really knows me. I still feel like the new kid at work, and since there's a hiring freeze at the paper, it's unlikely that someone newer will come along anytime soon. For that reason, I mostly come to work, do my job, and leave. Occasionally I'll run out with Pauline to grab a sandwich if neither one of us is working on deadline, but mostly I save the socializing for the friends I have outside of work. They're in the same boat as me—associates at law firms, techies at startups—so we work long hours and have a long way to go to prove ourselves. Those are the people who can commiserate when I need to vent about how much Jack works my last nerve.

"Where should we go?" I'm not in the mood to make a decision.

"Let's make it easy. George's?"

"Perfect," I say, and we walk out the front doors of our office building to the bar a couple blocks away. I pull the hair clip out, feeling relief as my hair falls across my shoulders and the ache from having it up all day starts to subside. I always wear it pulled back when I'm working because it's annoying to have it in my face when I'm typing, but the second I leave the office, I want it down.

"I used to hate when you did that when we lived together, and I have to say, I'm still a little jealous," Kayla says.

"What did I do?"

"The hair thing. You have the most gorgeous hair and when you take it down, it's like a shampoo commercial or something. I expect mermaids to fly down and carry you off to frolic with them."

"I'm pretty sure mermaids don't fly. But thank you for not hating it anymore." I inherited my wavy auburn hair from my mom, and she didn't start to go grey until her early fifties, so I'm hoping I'll get lucky that way too.

It feels good to be outside, even if I've already missed all the daylight. Being in a high-rise all day with recycled air sometimes makes me feel like a rodent in a lab experiment.

The evening commuter traffic is fierce, horns honking and cars clogging the intersections to create gridlock that leads to more horn honking. One more reason to be glad I'm out with Kayla and not boxed in on the road, frustrated and delayed from weeping into my double fudge ice cream at home.

I can hear a flurry of voices as we get closer to George's, which has a patio crammed with people sitting around reclaimed wood high tables and backless barstools. I'm shocked by how many people are out on a Monday night. Then it occurs to me that I don't ever go out, so I'm probably not a good judge of what normal people are doing on a Monday night.

We push inside, where it's a little less chaotic and find a table flanked by low leather club chairs and sink into them gratefully. I look around the room, seeing mostly people our age dressed in everything from suits to jeans and T-shirts. There's no way to discern who might be a lawyer, agent, actor or anything else based on what they're wearing, and the scene feels celebratory but a little desperate, like everyone's trying hard to have a good time but secretly hoping they won't have to go home alone. It gives me comfort to know that I'll be going home alone to the duplex I probably love more than the prospect of hooking up.

A tiny votive burns on the table, and I use its light to help me decipher the tiny black writing on the bar menu.

"It might still be happy hour," Kayla says, checking the time on her phone. "We've got fifteen minutes, so let's order some food too before the prices go up." Even though Kayla makes better money at her law firm than I do, she loves a good happy hour drink deal.

"Ooh, I could go for the tuna tartare and some fries," I say, noticing they're on the list of bar snacks. Even though George's is near the news bureau, I've only been here a couple times and the menu has changed since the last time. "And a tequila and soda. Definitely that."

Kayla flags down a server, who wears her shoulder-length blonde hair in pigtails I doubt I could pull off and blinks her long eyelash extensions at us while Kayla decides between a flatbread pizza and fried chicken. "You girls might want to put in a second drink order if you want the happy hour prices. I can wait and bring the next round 'til whenever you're done."

"That's awesome of you," Kayla says, looking at me for agreement that we should order the second round.

"Why not?"

A few minutes later, I'm squeezing a lime wedge into my tequila and soda and feeling marginally better about my day, mainly because it's over and I'm hoping for something better tomorrow. "So what happened today? Or would you rather not talk about it?" Kayla asks.

I explain the whole miserable episode, including the part about how Jack was almost human about my mistake before telling me it was my fault for ignoring the company. "I mean, for a minute I actually thought he was being empathetic, but then he went back to his judgy self and let me know, once again, that he doesn't think I'm up to the job."

And just as I'm saying this and feeling the heat rise in my cheeks at the embarrassment of the verbal beat down, I glance across the room and see that Jack is standing at the bar, looking directly at me. It's really loud in there, so I'm almost positive he couldn't have heard me complaining about him, but from the smirk on his face, I can't be sure. "Oh crap," I say, looking away from him and pretending to fix my hair so it might seem like I didn't actually see him.

But Kayla ruins that plan, whipping her head around to look over her shoulder where my eyes just were. "What?"

"That's him. Jack, the guy from work who I was just talking about." I'm talking out of the side of my mouth even though I know he's too far away to be able to read my lips. She does her best to casually look him over and swing her gaze back to me like she wasn't just checking him out, but out of the corner of my eye, I can see that his smirk has expanded to a full smile. Of course he expects to be checked out by every woman within range and we've just handed him a victory lap in that department.

I give him a small wave and he tilts his head in acknowl-edgment.

Do I go over there? Invite him to our table?

Both of those thoughts make me nervous and I'm not sure why. He's the same guy I sit next to every day, but somehow in the social, pickup atmosphere of the bar, Jack looks every bit the self-assured, strikingly handsome guy who could easily have the on-air news gig of his choosing. It bothers me that I feel a flutter of attraction in my belly, and I take a sip of my drink, as though the alcohol will kill the butterfly that's taken up residence in there.

"I guess it makes sense he'd be here. It's right by work. Probably where he trolls for rich, divorced women."

"He's hot," she says. "And honey, he wouldn't have to work very hard. He could have any woman in here."

I nod. "I know. It's his personality that's the problem. Immediate turnoff. He's arrogant and his ego is the size of Kansas"

"I kinda think you're full of shit."

"What do you mean?"

"I mean, he's… him. Spectacular. And you have it bad for the guy. I can tell by the way you were making excuses about why you don't like him and now by how you're blushing." She sneaks a look behind her again, which comes off as not at all subtle. "And he's seriously smokin' so I don't blame you."

I hate that I'm blushing. I have fair skin, inherited from relatives who hailed from merry *olde* England, and I turn pink at the merest suggestion of embarrassment. It makes it hard to keep a poker face. I don't care so much with Kayla, but I wish I could keep it under control at work.

"He kind of asked me if I wanted to meet him for a pity drink but I said no."

"He called it a pity drink?"

"No, but that's what it was. He's horrible to me on a daily basis. He thinks I don't deserve to have my job and he never misses a chance to tell me I'm doing it wrong."

"Could it be like the boy who pulls your ponytail in school because he thinks you're cute?

"Only if telling the deputy bureau chief that it was a mistake to hire me is like pulling my hair."

"Okay, he's slightly less good looking because of that."

A tall woman in a perfume cloud blows by us in stiletto heels and a pencil skirt and I follow her scented trail to where she's air-kissing Jack, who looks as happy as a teenager to have the cleavage in her V-neck sweater all to himself. I can't see her face, but her platinum hair and taut body confirm everything I've ever suspected about him and the kind of women he dates.

"He said he was meeting someone, but I somehow thought it would be a guy."

"She's no guy."

"I can see. I don't want to judge her by her heels and foul perfume, but she seems slutty."

"Glad you're not judging."

"Whatever. He can date who he wants."

I look away before Jack catches me staring. I'm happy that his date has arrived because it puts to rest the worry about whether I need to invite him over or even talk to him. I see them move to a table on the other side of the room and exhale a relieved breath. I just want to have my drink in peace and seeing him here is just a reminder of work and the humiliating way I blew my chance at a scoop.

ONE HOUR LATER, Kayla and I have finished our happy hour food and drinks and I'm feeling much better about my life and my prospects for getting through tomorrow without falling on my ass again.

Jack and his slutty date have moved to a low table like ours and he seems completely enraptured by her, not that I'm looking over there. Very often.

Kayla catches one of my surreptitious glances and pokes me with her finger. "Ouch," I say, even though it doesn't hurt that much.

"You need to do something about that," she says.

"About what?"

"Your fixation on him. You either need to fuck him or forget him."

"I'm working on forgetting."

She swirls the remains of her drink in the glass. I notice that hers somehow still has ice, even though mine has melted.

She shakes her head, glancing in his direction again. "Not the option I'd choose if it were me…"

"He's the last thing I need right now. This job has to go well. I might not get another opportunity like the Examiner."

"You might not get another opportunity like him."

"Oh, please. There are tons of guys like him but not a lot of jobs like this one."

"I know, I know. You have the whole theory."

She's making fun of me, but my theory has been borne out by science. Or at least several years of failed experiments in my own life. "I'm not capable of having a great job and a relationship at the same time."

"Who's saying anything about a relationship? Just one night? Get that bad boy out of your system and go back to kicking ass at work."

"You know it doesn't work like that. At least not for me. I get… involved. And distracted. And then I screw up the job."

"Well, I have a different theory."

I take the last swig of my drink, which is very watered down from the melted ice. It tastes like kombucha. "Yeah, what's that?"

"You use the work thing as an excuse *not* to take a chance on guys. I mean, come on. You're a very capable human. I'm sure you could multitask if it came to a guy who looks like that."

I shake my head. "Not true. I'll blow it. Just like I have in the past."

She points a finger at me. "Wrong. Your theory is wrong." There's no point in arguing with Kayla. She's a litigator and she'll badger me until I take her side on any issue. This one is best left languishing.

"Fine. Whatever you say," I tell her.

Our server drops off the bill as Kayla's phone pings with a text from Lucas. She reads it and frowns. "Everything okay?" I ask.

"Yeah, I don't know. It's something with his car."

"We can leave if you need to…"

"No, sit tight just let me call him." She takes her phone out to the sidewalk so she can hear. Out of habit, I check my own phone and scroll through tweets and news feeds to make sure there isn't breaking news I need to know about. Even after hours, if something breaks, we might need to put something in the digital version of the paper. It never ends.

While I'm still scrolling, I hear a voice next to me, "Hey, you guys giving up your table?"

I look up and see a blonde guy in his twenties holding a light-colored beer in a footed glass staring down at me. He smiles. "I'm not trying to rush you. But this is a good table, so…"

"Oh, totally, we're leaving soon. You can have it." I start to get up, looking around to see if Kayla is on her way back. I don't see her. The guy waves a hand.

"No, don't rush," he says. But I'm already on my feet. He stands a good six inches taller than me, which puts him at over six feet. He's nice-looking, and I'm trying to guess whether he's older or younger than me. Wearing jeans and a button-up shirt, he has that startup vibe: casual dress, a few days of beard growth, a few string bracelets on his wrist. "I'm early. I can just lurk around and when you're ready to leave, give me a high sign or something."

"No, really. It's fine. We're heading out."

"I dunno why I always come early. My friends are always late. And then I'm standing here like a fool."

He's standing a little closer to me than necessary for a casual chat while I'm waiting for Kayla to come back, but he seems harmless. It's not until I glance past him, that I see where Jack is sitting at a low table, his eyes on me. I can't tell if he's judging me, maybe thinking I'm planning to hook up with this guy. Not like it's any of his business.

"I can relate. Except that I'm the one who's always late. Unfortunately."

"Oh, well, I guess we're done talking, then... I'm kidding." He laughs, taking another step closer. It's a bit more in my space than I'd like, but he seems harmless.

We chat a little longer, and he tells me he does, in fact, work for a startup that creates an app used by accounting firms. I want to be interested in what he's telling me, but after two drinks, it just sounds like academic information and my brain is telling me it's not taking anything else in.

Kayla comes back and we give up our table to the startup guy, who offers to buy us a drink and let us hang with him until his friends come, but Kayla needs to pick up Lucas, whose car won't start. She looks at the guy, then looks at me.

"I might want to stay," I tell her. It's unlike me and I see the surprise on her face. I've been avoiding dating for the past year after a few too many bad choices led to very bad breakups.

She raises an eyebrow and tries to assess whether I'm too drunk to be making rational decisions. "You sure?" she asks.

I shrug, still considering what I want to do. This guy seems cute and nice enough and I really should take more chances, if for no other reason than for the potential that a good story might lie in the least expected place. Maybe there's a fascinating angle to be found in accounting startups. I don't get out enough. I know that. Stuart has chastened me for not getting out of the office more to look for personal interest stories, and heaven knows my social life could use a little push. This guy is offering me one.

The only problem is I'm self-conscious being in the same bar where Jack is having his date. Each time he stares in my direction, I can tell he's judging me, and I don't want to add to his already-low opinion of me by seeming like I'm looking for a hookup.

Who cares what he thinks? He's not the boss of me.

Kayla looks at me, waiting for my decision, and I can tell she's antsy to get out of here and go help Lucas. She pulls me aside. "You want to stay. This isn't the booze talking?" she asks, quietly.

I shrug. "It's been a shit day. Once I get home, I'll have to face it. I kind of want to avoid reality for a little longer."

She nods. "I get that. I feel bad I can't hang with you."

"Don't. I'm fine. Really."

"You sure?" she asks.

"I'm sure. This guy seems low-stress. One more drink, then I'm calling an Uber."

"Okay, text me when you leave here and again when you get home, okay?"

After she checks to make sure I have pepper spray in my purse, Kayla leaves to rescue Lucas from his car emergency. I turn back to startup guy and smile. "Okay, one drink, then I have to go. Early day tomorrow."

He nods. "On me, since I stole your table."

Glancing to the side, I'm acutely aware of Jack whose eyes are on me again. His date's back is to me, but she must be aware that he's looking past her from time to time. It's kind of rude. I can't decide if it bothers me that he seems to be watching over me like I need a babysitter or if the heat I feel surging through my body is because of something he evokes in me, something I definitely shouldn't be feeling.

I turn back to startup guy whose friends are filtering in through the door and making their way over to us. He gestures to the chairs at what is now his table. I take a seat, my back intentionally toward Jack. It's better if I don't have to look at him.

8

———

JACK

I DOWN THE dregs of my scotch and soda and try to catch the end of what Claudia is telling me but I admit I'm a bit distracted watching Linden with that douche canoe she's talking to. He looks like a million other guys in this city, a few years out of college, living on credit cards, and working at an important-sounding startup that's still deep in debt. I've interviewed a hundred guys just like him.

The bar has filled up in the past hour, obscuring my view of where Linden has been hanging with him and his friends because the woman she came with seems to have disappeared. I know it's none of my business what she does because we're outside of work but after the day she had, the last thing she needs is too many drinks or an ill-conceived hookup that will derail her tomorrow. That's why I'm nursing my own drink. I need to stay sharp. Always.

I want to go over and urge her to make the smart decision and head home. But she had a pretty shitty end to her day, and I seem to be the last person on the planet whose opinion she seems to want.

Plus, it's none of your business what she does or who she does it with.

"...So, if you think that could work, we could try to set it up," Claudia says, and I realize I've missed half of what she's just told me. She's trying to help me get an invitation to spend the weekend with Ken Nichols, who runs Worldvision, the largest entertainment company in the world. I've been writing about Ken and the company for years, but I've yet to do a profile story on Ken. He's notoriously media-shy and reclusive. He spends most of his time at his villa in Montecito, a wealthy beach community near Santa Barbara, and commutes to the corporate offices by helicopter. If he's not in a high-level meeting, he's at the villa.

I've been working on getting Ken to agree to give me access to his non-work life for no less than two years. No one else has beaten me to the story, fortunately, but it's just a matter of time before some other reporter finds a way.

Ken will spout company information all day long, but he's been unwilling to allow a reporter to get an inside look at his life. I've explained to him that it's important for investors and shareholders to see him as more human and relatable because it contributes to the image of the company. "It's a family entertainment company and no one even knows you're a family man," I told him during my most recent round of badgering.

"Oh, I suppose you're right. It just seems frivolous to let people into that side of things. My life at the beach has very little bearing on what makes Worldvision a thriving company."

"That's where you're wrong, Ken. It's just the other side of the coin. People want to have a warm impression of you. Like Walt Disney. And right now, you seem closed off, a company man in a tie who only talks business."

Ken began to see my point and just a week ago, he decided to let me write the profile. To do that, I need access to his private life, and he's still stonewalling. The big prize is spending some time in Montecito.

Claudia knows how much I want the story and she's been great about greasing the wheels to make a Montecito visit happen. Unfortunately, for the past ten minutes, I haven't been paying attention to what Claudia was saying.

Get your head back in the game.

"Sorry, Claudia. I was just thinking about how we do this. Do you have ideas about the Montecito angle?"

"Well, we have to approach it right. You don't come out and ask if you can come to his house. You're a reporter. He's going to be guarded."

"How else are you suggesting I go about it?"

She drains her glass of chardonnay and my drink is long gone, so I flag down our server and order one more round. I need to keep her talking. She's close friends with Ken's wife and she's my best bet at getting an invitation to the villa. We met many years ago, when she came to visit her son Shane, my college roommate, during our freshman year. Every time she'd come to visit, she'd bring a couple loaves of homemade bread, something that sounded good but tasted horrible. Shane and I once made a slingshot and bet on who could launch one of the dense dough rounds farther. I won, but only because Shane misfired and broke our neighbor's window.

Sometime during the past couple years Claudia had some work done on her face. I don't know what she did exactly, but her skin is tighter and pinker than what seems normal. She spends enough time at the gym to have shaved at least ten years off her age, so she looks very good for her sixty-five years. And like I said, she's been very helpful.

"So here's what we do. You know Ken and Judy are having a weekend party at the estate. I have to check my calendar at home, but I know it's soon and I'll suggest to Judy that it might be a nice time to have a reporter come spend some time and get a little background color for a story. She'll be wild about the idea. She loves to entertain."

"You think Ken will let a reporter inside his home because his wife says so?"

"You don't know Judy. She's the way you're gonna get this to happen. But never mind about that. You let me handle it and I'll let you know what's what."

I've spent years trying to get Claudia to utter those exact words. As soon as I figured out the connection between Ken Nichols and Shane's mom, I had to begin building trust. That meant sometimes spending holiday dinners with Shane's family instead of my own, slowly building a camaraderie with Claudia. No source ever wants to feel like she's being worked. It has to be a relationship. She has to want to help me because she genuinely likes me, not because she thinks I need something from her. And I genuinely do like her. Granted, I probably wouldn't spend as much time with her if I didn't need to find a way into the good graces of an entertainment giant on my beat, but I need to get the stories my editors expect. I need to be the best. Claudia can help me do that.

She puts on a pair of reading glasses and starts tapping into her phone. Not a minute later, it dings with a text message, which she reads. "Oh, this is perfect. Judy loves the idea. They're entertaining this weekend and she'll propose it to Ken that you come along." Her phone pings again and she reads. "She just sent me the guest list. It's lots of fun people, besides Jim and me, of course. Ken's golf buddies, Judy's surf instructor, the host from one of the reality shows, *Bachelor Bay*. Oh, this'll be so much fun if Ken agrees to let you come." She looks thrilled.

"Sounds great," I say. I can't muster her level of excitement until I know it's a done deal.

"Are you sure you won't take me up on my offer to drop off a loaf of my sourdough tomorrow? I'll be baking all morning and you know how good it is," she said, sipping her chardonnay.

"You're sweet, but I'm off the carbs."

"Are you doing one of those silly diets?"

"It's not a diet. It's more of a cleanse." I'm not on a cleanse. Or a diet. But her sourdough bread always tastes a little bit like old vinegar and shoe leather. I hate to throw it away, but I can't eat the stuff. Better that she finds someone else who actually likes it.

"Well, any cleanse that still allows you to have a glass of scotch at night is my kinda cleanse," she says, toasting my glass with hers.

I bring the glass to my lips, but I don't really drink it. One is enough for me, but I'm happy to keep Claudia company while she finishes her second. Anything for the job.

By the time she's sipped down half the wine, she's snapping a selfie of the two of us and texting it to Ken's wife. She wants this plan to succeed.

Her phone pings again and she reads.

"How would you feel about bringing a date? Do you have someone special in your life right now?" she asks. She reminds me of my own mother, who always uses the term *someone special* instead of *girlfriend*. Or *fuck buddy*. No, Mom would never say that, even though she knows me well enough to accept that most of my *special someone's* are a lot closer to that than to anyone likely to give her grandchildren.

"I could bring someone if you really think that's necessary."

"I'm just thinking out loud. Sometimes their weekend parties are couples' things. I wouldn't want you to feel uncomfortable being alone."

"I assure you, Claudia, it never bothers me to be solo."

I actually prefer it.

"Okay, well, great. Sounds like we can make this happen, one way or another." She drinks the rest of her glass of wine in a single gulp and dabs the edges of her lips with the cloth napkin, careful not to stain it with her pink lipstick.

I start feeling slightly optimistic about re-upping my

byline count with a Page One profile, which says a lot since I'm always cynical and cautious until I know I have something in the can. A lot of legwork still needs to be done before Ken will agree to let me come to Montecito.

Tomorrow I'll start on a different front, talking to the media relations team at Worldvision and explaining how good it will be for the image of the company to have Ken's face out in public a bit more. People need to see the human side of him; they'll be more likely to go to the company's theme parks and watch Worldvision movies, and the stock price will go up... I'll give them the big sell. They can badger him as well. I need to land this story.

9

———

LINDEN

IN NO WAY do I intend to have three more drinks.

It just sort of happens when a tray of tequila shots appears at our table and everyone hoists one and gestures to me to do the same. One can't hurt, I figure.

Then, there's a second. It hurts even less. A few minutes after that, I'm pretty sure the pain from my day has been thoroughly erased. Thank you, José Cuervo.

Sitting across from startup guy, whose name turned out to be Moss, I sip my tequila and soda and try to focus on what Moss is telling me about accounting best practices, but it's grown increasingly hard with the significant buzz I've got going. He might as well be speaking German for all his words make sense to me right now. I keep nodding like I'm enthralled, and he keeps explaining why the world needs his app, even though it's not much more than a glorified calculator. At least, that's how it sounds to me.

"How about you?" he asks. "How'd you get into journalism?"

I appreciate his taking an interest, but truthfully, I'm not interested in hearing the sound of my own voice enough to lay out my whole life story for him. So I'm vague and he goes back to talking about app design.

Despite my desire to be a go-getter reporter, unearthing fabulous human-interest pieces at every turn, I can't imagine how I can turn his app into a story anyone would read without wanting to gouge their eyes out, unless it involves writing about how too many ill-informed people are developing apps. And I'm pretty sure that story's been done. I smile and nod, and sip my drink. He seems happy to have a barely conscious audience for his story and I zone in and out of focus.

I let my mind drift back to Jack and his date, who I can no longer see because the bar is packed. I assume they're still at their table across the room, probably pushed closer to each other and whispering because it's so loud in here, but I have no way of knowing.

And suddenly, I really want to know.

Images intrude into my thoughts of Jack putting a hand on hers, then maybe lifting it and grazing the back of her hand with his lips. I know he has good lips, even though most of the time they're bent into a snarl at me. I hardly want to prevent him from pressing his lips against his blonde date's cheek, sweeping them across to her mouth and lingering there. Except that maybe I do.

"I'm gonna run to the restroom," I tell Moss.

He bends toward me. "Hurry back," he says in a whisper that might be intriguing if all my thoughts weren't focused on Jack and his date.

My steps are wobbly as I weave through the crowded bar, aiming to walk past Jack's table on the way to the bathroom. I have a nervous knot in my stomach as I get closer, fearful of finding him making out with his date and not entirely sure why it's so important to me that he isn't. As I brush past his table, I look over and see a couple that is most assuredly not Jack and a blonde woman. They already have drinks and look like they've been sitting at the table for a while.

Of course he left. I have to assume they left together, like anyone does once the cocktail warmup is completed and it's time to go back to someone's apartment. I fight the feeling of disappointment that he left without saying goodbye to me, though I'm not sure I could say for sure whether I'd have gone over there to say goodbye if I'd left first. He probably also didn't want to have to introduce me to his date. We do work together after all. Why would he want me involved in his personal life?

Making my way to the restroom, I find that I'm less steady than I'd realized but I plaster a smile on my face and move through the crowd like I'm surer of my footing than I feel. It seems like a very long walk to get to the rear of the bar where the restrooms are even further down a long hallway. I run one hand along the wall as I walk, partly to keep myself on a straight trajectory and partly because the wallpaper has faux velvet flocking and it feels soft on my hand.

I turn toward the first door I find, hoping it's the ladies' room and crash headlong into a man exiting, because of course it's the men's room. He's reaching out to hold me off before I teeter into him and I'm excusing myself for my misstep, but then I look at his face and realize it's Jack.

Shit.

Well, shitfaced is more like it.

"Oh gosh, oops. Hi! And bye. I thought this was the ladies' room," I say, extricating myself from his grasp and making a beeline for the other door. As soon as it closes behind me, I exhale my mortification. When I look in the mirror, I see my beet-red face and glassy eyes. Not the picture of a classy, driven reporter. This is me at my beaten down worst.

As I pee a river, I can only hope that he barely got a look at me. If I'm really lucky, he didn't even realize it was me. If I'm slightly less lucky, he just won't say anything about it tomorrow. If he figures out that I'm plastered and chose the wrong door, I'm screwed.

Looking at myself again while I wash my hands, I blink a couple times, aware that I'm a little unsteady. I think I might actually be swaying. I dig into my purse and pull out a lipliner to rub over my lips, which I can do without even looking in a mirror. The towel dispenser churns out a small paper square, enough to almost dry my hands before I push the door open. I just need to wobble my way back to the table, thank Moss for the drinks, and head for home.

Except that Jack is standing outside the bathroom door. At first, I think he's waiting for me. Then it occurs to me he's waiting for his date, although there wasn't anyone in the bathroom with me. So I'm confused, but undaunted in my determination to get the hell out of the bar. It's just unfortunate because I have to do my drunk weave of shame past him again. "See you in the morning," I say, hoping I'm not slurring.

"Hang on," he says, reaching to put a hand on my arm. I turn to look at him, wondering why he's touching me and how this tiny gesture is enough to unleash a heat storm in my cheeks. His impossibly blue eyes dare me to get lost in them. By now, the scruff on his face is darker with the full day's wear and that much sexier. I want to look away. I need to stop feeling the sweet burn between my thighs that is suddenly making it impossible to look away.

Plus, I know he's probably unhappy I'm here, disappointed that I'm not taking my job seriously enough. Especially today.

"I have to go. Gotta be at work early tomorrow," I say. His hand is still on my arm, so I extricate it.

"Linden."

"What?"

"Are you okay?"

"Sure. All good."

He's looking at me strangely, as if he's trying to figure something out and he can't quite make sense of it.

"Did you… how many drinks did you have?" he asks.

"Um…" I have to count them on my fingers, including the shots. "Five."

"That's a lot. And you're tiny. Plus…" He guides me a few feet down the hall to where a large gilt-framed mirror hangs on a wall under an Edison bulb. He turns me toward the mirror, where I somehow expect to see what a great couple we look like together. Isn't that what he's showing me?

Instead, I see a pink-faced drunk girl with messy hair. And then I notice the source of his concern. My lips are a deep shade of brown, like I dipped them in a chocolate fountain.

Because I grabbed eyeliner, not lipliner.

"Oh, dear God."

Mortified, I immediately try to rub the offending brown off my lips with the back of my hand. It's not working very well. My efforts have the effect of rubbing the brown deeper into my lips rather than taking it off.

I dig in my purse for a pack of wet wipes and rub until all traces are gone. This day needs to end. It can't possibly get any worse, and the last person I want to witness it is standing behind me with the most delectable grin and I know he thinks I'm some special kind of moron. I wait for him to say something mocking. Instead, he brushes the hair off my forehead and turns me to face him.

"You… do you have a way of getting home?"

An image flashes through my mind of me sitting in the backseat of his car while he and his date drive me home. Like a little kid. I wonder if he'll put me in a booster seat.

"I'm gonna take an Uber." It comes out a little slurry. He puts his hand on my shoulder this time.

"No. You're not. I'll drive you. There's no way you're getting into some strange person's car. It's not safe." He's authoritative, just like he is at work when he's telling an executive exactly what he needs for a story. Of course, the next place my mind goes is thinking he's probably authoritative in the bedroom too, commanding and forceful.

Stay on task.

"Why is that safer? Aren't you here too?" I'm trying to ask if he's okay to drive. The words make sense to me, but I know it comes out sounding wrong.

"Yes, I am here." He seems amused and I like the way the corners of his eyes crinkle up when he smiles. And I can't keep my mind out of the gutter, so it's telling me all kinds of things it would like me to do with him right now. Considering my propensity for blurting things out, I know I'm only one brain fart away from telling him I want to ride him all night long like an urban cowgirl breaking a stallion. I make a concerted effort to say only what's necessary.

"Okay, fine. But I don't want you to mistake me being agreeable right now for being agreeable generally."

Again, not sure I'm making sense.

"Noted. I'll try not to see you as ever being agreeable after tonight." He lets out a low, quiet laugh and I realize I don't think I've ever seen him laugh before.

At the same time, I'm not sure he's really getting my point. And I'm too drunk to let anything lie. "I'm just saying, I'm letting you drive me home, but I don't want you to confuse that with me liking you."

Now he's laughing more. "Thank you for clarifying."

I nod and look at him, marveling once again at how great-looking he is. I know symmetry is a thing when it comes to why people are attractive, and he definitely has everything in the right place. The jaw, the hint of stubble, the pale eyes, the cheekbones. I don't know what comes over me, but I find myself reaching up to touch his face. I want to feel the line of his jaw and once I do, I want to feel more.

He's looking at me like it's maybe a problem, but he isn't

moving away. So I bring my other hand up to the side of his face and take a step closer, pulling him in toward me. Just for a minute. I just need to know what it feels like to kiss him. Then I'll stop.

I'm wearing flat shoes and he's tall, so I can't get any closer unless he bends to meet me halfway. We're stuck in limbo, with my hands on either side of his face, lips parted suggestively until he makes a move. The feminist in me knows it's unevolved for me to wait for him, especially when I'm the one with wants and needs right now. But I'm height-challenged, which threatens to derail my entire poorly-conceived idea.

Jack meets my gaze, his eyes questioning. I don't want to explain. He starts to speak but presses his lips together instead. Then he brings them to mine like he's resigned to giving me what I want. The way you'd placate a kid who's pestering for attention. But there's nothing G-rated about Jack's intensity.

He slowly drags his lips over mine, claiming every inch and sinking deeper until I actually feel myself swoon. Then he pulls back, brushing my chin with soft kiss. It's feathery and dreamy and suddenly I'm melting.

For all his daily agita, apparently he's been hiding a softer side. It's a problem. He's gentle when I want to be overwhelmed. This has been the day from hell and now I'm semi-drunk and all I know is that I need to do something that will make me feel better, even if doing it—or him—ends up feeling like a mistake in the morning.

I press my lips harder into his, wanting the lust and sensation to wipe away my ability to think about anything else. But he pulls back. "This is not a good idea," he says.

I nod vigorously. "It's a very good idea."

He tilts his head to look at me and uses both hands to grasp my shoulders and hold me at a distance. "You're not thinking clearly. I don't... I can't... take advantage of that."

"Stop trying to be a nice guy. You're confusing me."

"You want me to be a jerk?" he asks, wary.

"I want you to make me forget about my shitty day."

He looks at me and I see a glimmer of sympathy in his eyes. Or maybe he thinks I'm pathetic. It could be that kind of look. I'm not sure.

Then his lips are on mine with all the fire and heat I've seen him bring to riling up a powerful CEO. It feels so good to lose myself in the sensation of his mouth and the faint taste of alcohol on his tongue. He's being much more agreeable now, curling one hand around the back of my neck and kissing me with the kind of intensity I crave before lightly sucking on my lower lip. It's still way sweeter and gentler than what I'm after, but I'm not about to complain.

He leisurely plants hot kisses across my cheek and curls my hair behind my ear with his finger so he can kiss the side of my neck. I feel breathless and lightheaded. For the first time, I think there's a chance I can forget how mortifying it was to faceplant so royally at work.

"It's helping. I'm starting to forget," I tell him, not sure what I'm even saying or if it matters.

"Good." His tongue flicks across my bottom lip. I shudder and part my lips because I want more. He obliges, his tongue circling mine so slowly that it almost feels like sex. I've never been kissed this way before and it's making me dizzy.

He's also so sweet that I almost have to pinch myself to believe this is the same hot but irritating guy I know from work. His hands are gentle, tangling in my hair. It's not anything like the hurried, angry fuck I have in mind. He's kissing me like we have all the time in the world.

It's nice but right now I don't want nice.

There's a bathroom behind me that's currently empty and I intend to make good use of it. It'll be quick, but it has to make me feel better than I do right now. I take his hand and motion for him to follow me, pulling the door open. "Come."

He gets the drift of what I'm after and he looks downright frightened. "Hold on. Linden, we can't do *that*. At least, not here..." He takes my hand off the doorknob and the door closes with an uncomfortable thud.

And just like that, I start to return to my senses.

Oh my God. What am I doing?

Then the mortification starts creeping in. As if he didn't have a low enough opinion of me already—no-talent, green reporter—I've just added bar slut to the mix. My mind is all over the place, but abject humiliation is the key emotion at the moment. I can't even look at him. "Wow, I didn't think it was possible, but now I actually feel a little bit worse."

He guides my face, so I have to look at him. "Hey. Don't do that to yourself. Like I said earlier, we've all been there. And... we've all been here."

"I can't imagine that's true for you."

"Well, it is. And I've made an enormous ass of myself in a far more public venue than a hallway. In front of a source. And then I yacked on his shoes."

"Okay, that may be worse. I'm sorry I forced myself on you."

He's smiling, which makes me at least not want to cry. "Never apologize for that. It was a nice bonus at the end of my day."

"Ha-ha."

"Let's get you home." He puts his hand on my shoulder like he's steering me, and we walk down the hall toward the bar. I feel like he's guiding me in a straight line, but I have no idea if I'd be able to do it on my own. I'm beyond tired, I'm pretty drunk and I've lost the last bit of fight in me. I'll do whatever anyone tells me at this point.

Back in the melee of the bar, he guides me to the table where Moss is drinking another round of shots with his friends and waits by the door while I say goodnight. Moss asks for my number, which is oddly sweet, considering there's no connection whatsoever. I give him a few fake digits and walk to the door, which Jack holds open for me.

Once outside, the generous cool air hits my face and if I'm lucky, the flush on my cheeks will have a fighting chance of subsiding. "Ah, it's so nice out," I say.

"Actually, it's pretty chilly. You're not cold?" He's wearing his sport coat and he has a scarf wound around his neck.

It's probably the alcohol, but I don't feel cold. "I like it."

"You're gonna freeze," he says, taking his coat off and putting it over my shoulders. It smells like aftershave and even though I know it hangs on the back of his chair like a lonely life raft most days, it feels intimate having it on right now. I can't believe he's being this kind to me. It's a little unnerving because it's so contrary to the tight-ass I'm used to dealing with at work. "I don't get it. I lost a story for the paper, I groped you in the bar and now you've gotta take my drunk ass home. Why are you being so nice?"

He stops walking and tilts his head at me. "Why do you seem so surprised? Oh, that's right. Because you think I'm a dick."

"No, I… I dunno. I'm sorry I said that. I sometimes have a bit of a temper."

He lets out a low chuckle. "That, you do." I immediately feel defensive because he's not supposed to agree so readily, but I decide it's better not to antagonize the man who's offered me a ride. We walk in silence for a few minutes, which feels more awkward than when I was blurting out nonsense earlier. I've never made small talk with him before and I realize that outside of our reporting jobs, I don't know much about him. "Do you live close to the office?"

"I'm in the Hollywood Hills."

"Huh. I wouldn't have pegged you for there."

He casts a sideways glance at me, that amused gleam sparking in his eyes again. "Oh, this oughtta be good. Where did you imagine I'd live? And if you say a troll hut, I'm changing my mind about the ride."

I have to think about it for a minute because, honestly, I'd never given it that much consideration, other than sort of imagining he might live at the gym. "I guess… maybe I envision you living right here. Like, a block from the bureau, so you can race in and cover big breaking news stories whenever they come up. Like a surgeon who sleeps in the on-call room or whatever."

He laughs softly. "You do realize we have the ability to work remotely, yes? The beauty of technology…"

"Yes, but you're a diehard. You have to be there right when the story's breaking and read it on the wires." I'm laughing a little now. It feels good to call him on how obsessive he is. And to take the focus off of me.

It finally dawns on me to wonder what happened to his date. Did he leave her at the bar? Did she bail on him before he saw me? I start to ask him because this seems like a problem—at least for her—but then he puts a hand on my shoulder, and I get distracted again.

We've reached our office building, and if he hadn't steered me in the door, I might have kept walking. I guess I'm more out of it than I realized. I wonder if he's aware.

We take the elevator down to the parking garage, where I see my crummy, beige eight-year-old Honda parked in one of the faraway spots. Jack has a spot close to the elevator and his paint job looks meticulously shiny. In my drunken haze, I'm already distracted by his fancy car and his good parking spot and the reporter's life that might lie in my future if I just work hard enough. It's the dream I want more than anything, marked by a better salary and bylines and a car that doesn't have a window that won't roll down and a crack in the upholstery. "How'd you get the rockstar parking? Lemme guess, because you got here before the roosters?"

"Actually, the parking attendant likes me, so she holds me a space. I butter her up with Peet's coffee."

It doesn't surprise me that a female parking attendant has a soft spot for him. "I don't think that's why," I say.

"What's that supposed to mean?"

"She probably thinks you're hot. Most women think you're hot." I'm still drunk enough not to be in control of my mouth. He smiles and I fight against my instinct to rip his shirt off right here and put my hands on his bare skin. I try to remember my manners. *Colleague offers ride, kindly allow him to stay clothed.*

He looks amused. "Only most? What do I have to do win over the rest?"

"Don't ask me. I think you're a dick, remember?" But I can't help grinning through the words because I think I've already proven that's a lie.

"Come along, little lush."

He leads me to the passenger side of his car, which is a pretty sporty Audi sedan with sleek angles and leather interior. As soon as I slide into the passenger seat, I feel especially tired. And comfortable. "This is nice," I say, settling in.

I don't realize my purse is hanging halfway outside the car until he reaches to move it to my lap. His face is so close to mine when he does it that I catch a whiff of sandalwood and pine, which I can't help inhaling a little deeper. At the sound, he turns to look at me, his face only inches from mine.

He lingers longer than a person would if he was just tucking a colleague into her seat. He looks conflicted.

But instead of leaning in further, he gives me the same tight-lipped smile I saw earlier and backs away.

I mumble my address when he asks, and I take the moment to close my eyes while he plugs it into his GPS. Just for a sec though. Blasted tequila. I can't even remember if I ate the fries I ordered. But I can remember how it felt to kiss him, and damn if I don't want to feel it again.

10

JACK

HOLY HELL, if there was a Pulitzer Prize for keeping my pants zipped and doing the right thing, I would win it. Hands down.

It didn't take any kind of investigative genius to see that Linden wanted me to throw her up against the bathroom wall and have all kinds of fun with her. And like the world's biggest idiot—and a feeble excuse for a stand-up guy—I closed the door on it. Literally.

I could see the look of rejection on her face and I hate being the guy who brought that on. But after a bunch of tequila, on a hundred-pound frame, she's in no position to know what constitutes a good idea. I'm not going to be the guy who takes advantage of that, even if it means rocking a semi hard-on which is not pleasant while I drive. I'll get over it.

It's not a long drive to where Linden lives, and traffic is light at this hour so it shouldn't take us long to get there. I look over at her, resting her head against the seat with her hair loose, framing her face. She's delicate and beautiful with her eyes closed, kind of reminding me of what my sister always says about her kids: angelic while they're sleeping, demonic when they're up.

Not that Linden is possessed by the devil, but she does have a streak. It didn't surprise me that a guy took the opportunity to hit on her the minute her friend walked away. Of course he'd ask her to join them. Of course he'd buy her drinks. I'll admit to being a little surprised she went along with it. Even from where I sat, I could see he was out of his league with her. And she's not one to suffer fools.

So, I'm interested in knowing why she stayed after her friend left. I'm not arrogant enough to assume it was so she could corner me in a hallway. That seemed like a spontaneous decision, though one I enjoyed immensely. Still, I want to know what she saw in the blonde guy because I'm pretty sure she gave him her phone number before she left. It bugs me that I care at all. He looked like a too-tall, boyband wannabe and I want to hear her say she agrees.

"Was that guy your type, the one at the bar?"

She laughs. "I'm not sure I remember what he looks like."

"Made that much of an impression, huh?"

"Something like that." I can't really take my eyes off the road, but I can tell she's looking at me. When I hit a red light, I glance at her, expecting her to look away. But she doesn't. The warm light from the streetlamps and the traffic signal wash over her face with a pinkish glow and she looks pretty in a way I've never noticed before. There's a softness to her face that I don't ever see at work when she's scrambling to meet a deadline.

"Thanks again for the ride," she says. "Definitely better than an uptight Uber driver who's worried I'll puke in his car."

"You say the nicest things. And please don't puke in my car."

She smiles, tilts her head away, and closes her eyes again; a contented smile on her face. The light turns green.

A few minutes later, we're outside her building. It feels like I should walk her to the door, but this isn't a date. I just need to make sure she gets inside safely. I know my place, one step up from an Uber driver. That's all.

"I don't think I have the energy to go upstairs. Can I sleep here?" she says, her voice syrupy and lazy.

"Um, I don't think that's a good idea—"

"I'm kidding. I'm not that drunk," she says.

I come around and open her door. She doesn't make much of a move to hoist herself out of the seat. "Can you stand up?" I ask. She's petite, and five drinks is a lot. Maybe it's hitting her harder now.

"I can, but I'm really happy here. I lied when I said I wasn't that drunk." She smiles. And she's fucking adorable.

"I think you'll feel better if you wake up in your own bed," I say, doing my best to offer her some leverage so she can stand up. But she really doesn't want to move. "Okay, change of plan. Can you get out your keys?"

She digs into her purse and drops them into my hand. Tucking the keys into my back pocket, I lean down and wrap an arm under her knees and another behind her shoulders. Then I carry her up the stairs of her duplex as her purse hangs off one elbow and she leans her head on my arm.

"You have nice arms," she mumbles, and I wonder if she'll remember any part of this in the morning. "It's important for you to know this, even though you're carrying me and I'm not light, so you probably already know."

"You're pretty light. But thanks."

I feel her wrap her arms around my neck, probably just to get secure as I carry her up the stairs, but as her fingers settle lightly across the back of my neck, I fight against how much I like the sensation. It's probably subconscious, but she's running her fingernails through the hair at the nape of my neck and it feels amazing.

I focus on getting the door unlocked and carrying her

inside without bumping her against walls or furniture accidentally. I'm able to flip the light switch on with my shoulder so I'm not moving blindly through a dark space, and it seems like a better idea to settle her on the couch instead of taking her to her bed.

"Thank you," she says softly when I place her on the soft velveteen of the grey couch. I look around for a blanket but the only thing nearby is a scratchy-looking wool throw, so I find her bedroom and return with a softer dark green blanket and a pillow. She settles in when I lift her head and put the pillow underneath. Her eyes flutter closed. "*Mmm*, sleep is the best invention ever. There's room here if you want to try it," she says, patting a three-inch space that most definitely wouldn't accommodate another person. And I need to leave before I cave and snuggle in next to her.

"Thanks, but I'll see you in the morning."

"Early. Before you and the roosters," she says, her voice dreamy and half-asleep. "Don't worry."

"I'm not worried."

I pull the throw blanket from the end of the couch and lay it over her. I can't do much more for her without helping her out of her clothes and I'm not about to step over that line. "Do you have an alarm set on your phone?" I look at her for an answer, but she doesn't respond. She's already asleep. Gorgeous, with a faint smile still on her lips, hair splayed on the pillow.

I have to force myself to look away. And take the damned high road, which feels awfully fucking steep right about now.

11
______

LINDEN

THINGS LOOK SLIGHTLY BETTER in the morning, even though my head smacks with a hangover. The tequila drinking was definitely stupid. Then there's the vaguely horrifying memory of throwing myself at Jack at the bar which lingers in my mind. I'm a little surprised that I don't remember exactly what led to me shoving my tongue in his mouth, but I recall every bit of the kiss. It was perfection. But, for fuck's sake, what was I thinking?

The only thing to do now is hold my head up at work, thank him for the ride and move on without discussing anything about last night. Minimize it, and maybe it will be insignificant.

I'm short on sleep because I set an early alarm in order to read Jeremy's book. I didn't finish, but I think I get the gist of what it's about—the passion I need to do this job right—and I need to work harder to find that story I can't let go. I'm determined.

I skip my spin class, but by the time I get to my desk, I am in possession of large coffee, this time courtesy of the office coffee room. I make sure to arrive by a quarter to eight. Other than Jeremy, who is reading three newspapers at his desk, I think I'm the first one here.

Since I'm not rushing through the office like an escaped felon, I have plenty of time to work through the news feeds and sort out the information for the other reporters. I make little piles for each person and write a few texts about information I've seen on twitter as well. It feels good to be there early, and a tiny voice in the back of my head tells me, *that's why you're supposed to get here at eight, dummy.*

I don't bother going to my cubicle right away and putting myself under Jack's microscope, so I don't even know if he's in the office yet. I assume he is, if for no other reason than hoping to reprimand me for being late. After yesterday, I'm really not in the mood for his lectures about my reporting skills or my punctuality. I don't want to hear him tell me that it was irresponsible to be at a bar last night when I should have been making sure I wasn't neglecting any other stories and letting everyone down at the paper. And I desperately don't want to talk about how I cornered him in the hallway and tried—if I'm remembering correctly—to get him to have bathroom sex with me. OMG, kill me now.

Even though a part of me wants him to see that I've arrived well before eight o'clock, I don't want to give him the impression that I changed my ways because of his annoying nagging. I'm honestly hoping I can avoid seeing him at all.

As I'm pulling wire copy from one of the printers, I hear the staccato buzz of the main phone line. The receptionist doesn't arrive until nine thirty, so it's my job to answer the phone until then. It's my least favorite part of the day, that hour and a half when I pick up the phone to hear things like, "My paper arrived wet this morning" or "I have a real problem with an editorial that ran in your paper, which should really be called the Bleeding Blue Commie Rag" or "I have a great tip for you on a Ponzi scheme that's being run out of the basement of my apartment building."

In other words, calls from certifiable crackpots and people who have nothing better to do than dial up the main phone number of the paper because they know someone will answer and have to listen to whatever they have to say. I have real respect for our receptionist who has to deal with these calls all day long. I always bring her lunch on the days when I get a chance to leave the office. She deserves an appointment to sainthood.

I'm already wearing my Bluetooth headset, so I punch the blinking button on the phone to connect to the caller. "Examiner," I say into the phone, bracing myself for whatever nonsense I'm about to hear.

There's a pause on the other end of the line and I figure I'm being crank called, which also happens a lot. Before I hang up, I hear a noise on the line, so I pause, then a throat clears and the caller starts speaking, shaky and uncertain, "Um hi, is this a reporter?"

"Yes, Linden Sandoval. How can I help?"

"Would you be someone I could report something to?" She still sounds uncertain she wants to be making this call.

"Depends what you want to report. If it's a crime or an emergency, you should call 911."

She cuts me off. "No, it's not an emergency… it might be a crime, though."

"Sounds like it could be something you might want to report to the police," I say, but the haste with which I apparently dismissed Zumalife's importance to my life at the paper hangs over me like a death veil. I can't be quick to push her away when there might be a story someplace. "But why don't you tell me what made you call us."

She's silent again. Again, I think maybe she's reconsidering whether she made a mistake in calling. "I can't tell you too much over the phone, not yet. But I have something I think you'd be interested in. It could be a big story." I'm trying not to be cynical. But in the year and a half since I joined the Examiner, I've heard dozens of people tell me they were certain they had a huge story. Exactly zero of them panned out into anything.

"What's the basic gist?" I ask, knowing I'll be able to tell her within two minutes whether her idea is worth more of my time.

Again, she hesitates. Another phone line is ringing now, and I need to put her on hold while I answer it. I figure there's a fifty-fifty chance she'll be there when I return to the line. But she's there, her voice a little bolder now. "I had a job… somewhere, and I think there's something happening that shouldn't be. I've seen some things and written down some notes, but before I tell you more or show you anything, I need to know if I'm safe."

"You mean, do we protect our sources?"

"Yeah. Like even if you had to testify in court. This can't lead back to me." She sounds legitimately nervous and I decide she's either paranoid and a little nutty, or she really has something here that I shouldn't ignore.

"I would protect you. We don't reveal confidential sources. To anyone," I tell her, remembering an old episode of the Mary Tyler Moore show when she's trotted off to jail for not giving up a source. I'm not above imagining this turning into my Mary moment. "Would you feel more comfortable talking in person?"

I hear her exhale. "Yes, thank you. I'm at work now, and I'm so nervous to be making this call," she says. I can't believe she's calling me from work. That seems foolish and potentially dangerous if anyone is within earshot. "It's a different job than the one I want to talk about, and I'm in the bathroom on my personal cell phone but still, it seems like I shouldn't tell you more over the phone, just to be careful." It's sounding a lot more like *Deep Throat*.

I arrange to meet her later in the afternoon when she says she'll have a break from work. There's a Starbucks near the bureau and it's always loud enough in there that no one would be able to overhear our conversation. She agrees to come. I'm thinking there's still maybe a slim chance this will actually lead to a story, but I tell myself to follow every lead, no matter where it goes.

Before we hang up, I ask her one more question that will give me a sense of whether or not there's likely to be a story somewhere.

"What's the name of the company, the place where you used to work?" I ask.

"Um, it's the show, *Bachelor Bay*?" she says, as though she's asking whether I've heard of it.

"Yes, I know the show," I say, not volunteering that I've seen every episode. Multiple times. For all of its ten seasons. "Okay, well I'm looking forward to meeting you and hearing whatever you want to tell me."

She thanks me and promises to find me at Starbucks. The line has already gone dead but I'm still holding the phone in my hand, dumbstruck.

The idea of a scandal or some wrongdoing at a splashy pop culture mainstay like *Bachelor Bay* intrigues me. It could be the makings of a good investigative piece, and with a popular show at the center, even a small story would get pretty good placement in the paper. That could be great for me, since I need to find the quickest way out of the doghouse. Jack is right, though, and the best way to forget about yesterday's news—especially bad news—is to publish something even better the next day.

There's only one problem. *Bachelor Bay* is a TV show, which means it falls under the purview of the entertainment pod, and Jack is at the top of the food chain among those reporters. But *Bachelor Bay* is, by all accounts, dumb entertainment. Jack writes about billion-dollar mergers and management shakeups at giant companies. It's hard to imagine him writing about a dating show set on a yacht. And he might not want to waste his time on a maybe-story that could turn into nothing.

I consider whether to tell him about the call. There's a part of me that knows it's probably going to be a wild goose chase and Jack will hand me my ass for wasting his time or even indulging the crazy caller with my attention. I don't want to look more like a newbie than I already do.

But what if there's something to her story?

I consider my options and decide I should meet with her first, before saying anything to Jack. That way, if it's a non-story, I can put an end to it, and he'll be none the wiser. And if it turns out that there's something there, I'll hand it off and he'll have to give me credit for doing my job. Either way, it seems like I need to meet with her by myself first. What's the worst that could happen?

12

———

JACK

WELL, holy hell. She managed to get here early.

After the beating she took yesterday, I'm not surprised she figured out she has to take her job seriously. I wasn't so sure how she'd be feeling this morning and I almost called to check in, but now I'm glad I didn't. Driving her home already felt like overstepping the colleague relationship but it seemed like the right thing to do.

I'm pleased to see the neat stack of wire feed items she's left in my in-box, although I'm still going to check everything myself because I can't afford to miss anything.

"You made coffee?" I say, when she comes back to her cubicle after dropping pages off on different people's desks.

"Yeah, how'd you know it was me?" Linden asks, scooting her chair in and swiveling halfway around to look at where I'm standing by the printer, waiting for a few pages to hit the tray.

"It doesn't taste like shit, for one thing."

She laughs. "Yeah, I can't handle Jeremy's concoction, so I made my own."

"Appreciate it."

She turns back toward her computer and scans the news

feeds. I should get to work, but I find myself wanting to linger. "You doing okay?" I ask.

"Yes. Good. Great. Thanks again for the ride. And, you know, from now until the end of days, for never, ever mentioning that I tried to kiss you… just, thanks."

Tried? You were damn successful. But um, okay…

"Sure."

"Anyway, moving on, right? I'm gonna choose not to dwell on the embarrassment that was last night, if you don't mind, and focus on work."

"Okay by me, but you don't need to feel embarrassed."

"I'll feel a lot better if we stop talking about it."

"Fine. Done. What's on the wires?

"You haven't already looked? Come on, Jack, don't pretend you haven't already written the whole paper in your head."

"I may have glanced at the feeds."

"So you know, then."

I don't know why I'm lingering by her desk. I'm clearly making her uncomfortable because she keeps looking away, as though she'd prefer to get back to work. But I don't want to leave it at that. I saw a different side of her last night and I'm curious.

"So… did you have fun? At the bar?"

She turns to look at me with a little scowl, maybe annoyed that I'm not letting her work. I can't help enjoying the way her cheeks are turning pink at my question.

"I thought we weren't going to talk about it," she says, a little edgy.

"I mean generally, earlier. How was your night, with your friend? And those guys?"

"It was alright."

"Yeah?"

"Yup."

"Great."

"Uh huh," she says, eyes narrowing. She looks determined to win this test of wills and tell me nothing. It frustrates me and makes me want to dig deeper. Maybe that's just a bad reporter habit.

Or maybe it's a need I have to satisfy. But why? What do I want from her?

I want her to say she's glad I came along when I did to save her from those overgrown frat boys. Which is ridiculous. She's the last person in the world who needs saving, and I have better things to do.

"Okay, well next time we end up at the same place, you should come say hello," I say, throwing in the towel on the conversation.

She opens her eyes fully and looks confused. And, for some reason, even more annoyed. "What makes you think there will ever be a next time?"

"Statistics. We work in the same place. There are only so many bars and restaurants near here. What, you don't plan on ever going out after work again?"

"Probably not." She's winding her hair into a bun before twisting a rubber band around it. Pieces fall out around her face and it's a little messy and extremely sexy. I have to stop looking at her or I'm going to run this conversation off the road. I want to tell her to take the goddamned rubber band out of her hair because it looks gorgeous when it's loose. And now my mind is off and running to how her hair would look strewn across my pillow in the morning after a long night of sex.

Stop thinking about that.

I return to the conversation we're having, or at least the one I'm trying to have with a woman who doesn't seem to want to engage. "You can never imagine yourself going out after work? Why not?"

"I don't really go out much in general, so it seems like the odds are slim."

That interests me. I want to know why she's so against getting out in the world. Is she getting over a bad breakup? Is she just antisocial? But I also don't want to pry, and she already seems disinterested in me and in having a conversation.

"Huh. Okay. Well, in the event you ever do find yourself in a social setting where I happen to be—ever, even in a case where the slimmest of odds work in my favor—I'm just saying, feel free to come say hello."

She's silent. Then she nods. "Okay."

I can tell the conversation's over as far as she's concerned, but I'm not satisfied. Her cold shoulder drives me crazy and I don't know why. I do know why, but I'm ignoring it. I don't date reporters, especially ones who are as aggravating, sassy and stubborn as her. And yet, I can't let it go.

"That's it? Okay?" Even I don't know what I'm getting at, at this point, so I sure as hell don't expect her to know how to answer.

"What do you want from me, Jack? Are you that desperate to parade your manliness around that you need me to get up close and personal with you at a bar just so I can see you with your hot date?"

Well, I wasn't expecting that.

"I'm sorry. Parade my manliness? My hot date? What the hell are you talking about?"

She shakes her head like I'm the densest idiot to walk the planet. "I already sit next to you. I already have to hear you talking to women you date or screw or whatever the hell you do with them. Do you really need me to come say hi at a bar so I can see them up close?"

"Um, no?"

"Great." She looks at me with no emotion in her eyes. "So, are we done with this conversation?" she asks.

Honestly, not in the least, but I'm so confused by her whole demeanor, accusation and lack of interest in talking to me in general that I just nod and watch as she straightens the notepads and pens on her desk. But I do feel the need to correct her impression of me, as the kind of guy with a preference for blonde, Botoxed, sixty-year-old women.

"By the way, the woman you saw me with, she was a source. It was a meeting for a story I'm working on." I wait to see the information land on her, but she doesn't flinch. "I don't go out that much either, except when it comes to work. I wasn't on a date."

She looks at me, poker-faced. "Oh."

"You jump to conclusions like that on a story and you'll be printing retractions 'til the end of time."

"Sure. Okay. Sorry."

She doesn't say anything else. She stares hard at the computer screen in front of her and doesn't give me the satisfaction of looking back in my direction. But I can see the pink flush on her cheeks and the hint of a smile curl on her lips.

It tells me all I need to know.

13

LINDEN

MEGAN IS ALREADY at Starbucks when I get there. I can tell it's her by the worried expression on her face when she sees me walk in the door. She's the only one in the place that looks like a frightened deer and she's parked herself at the furthest table from the door.

"Megan?" I ask when I get to her table. She nods and I extend my hand. "Linden Sandoval. Can I grab you a coffee or something?"

"Sure. A coconut latte?" She starts to take out her wallet, but I wave it away.

"On me. Please."

A few minutes later, Megan is gripping her paper cup and looking at me like she already regrets her phone call earlier this morning. I try my best to put her at ease, launching right into my reporting disclaimer, which is loosely based on what I've heard other reporters say and also based on the no-nonsense way I attack stories. I get the people on the phone who need to comment, and I make sure they tell me what I need before hanging up.

"We're just talking on background, so nothing you say is

attributable to you. I won't quote you or use your name without your permission."

"Okay…" she says, though the arms she crosses in front of her chest and the frown she wears suggests that she doesn't trust me and isn't going to say a word.

That's when it dawns on me that Megan isn't some CEO or publicist who's used to reporters who are playing hardball. She's not like the other people I've learned to interview using scare tactics and coerciveness. She's terrified of being found out for whatever she's about to tell me and she's probably never talked to a reporter in her life. It might have taken her weeks to work up the courage for the phone call she made this morning. If I approach her like she's a resistant executive, I'm going to lose her.

I wish I had more experience at this. When I worked for the smaller newspapers before the Examiner, I never had to coax stories out of people. I was covering local events. Brush fires. Convenience store robberies. Pageant queens. All of my reporting was done after the events had already taken place and there was no investigating needed. People wanted to share their stories and they were excited to be in the paper. I try to keep Jack's words from making their way into my brain.

She's too green.

I desperately want him to be wrong. I'm equally worried he's right.

I glance around the room and notice tables of other people wrapped up in casual conversation, their body postures much more relaxed than Megan's or mine. Maybe I'm going about this all wrong, launching right in with a stranger and asking her to tell me things she's scared to say out loud. So I take a different approach.

"Where's your office? Is it far from here?"

"Hollywood. Not too far," she says. Okay, that wasn't so hard.

"There's a restaurant I love in Hollywood, the Honey Dragon. Do you know it?"

She leans back against the chair, arms still crossed, but her face relaxes a bit. "Yeah, it's not far from where I work. But I think I told you, it's a new job. I haven't checked out the restaurants yet. It's Thai food, right?"

"Crazy good Thai food. Definitely go if you can. I mean, I'm not a fan of curry and I order their green curry every time. It's amazing. Though you have to be specific about how spicy you like it, because once, I said I was fine with spicy and I bit into what I thought was just a green pepper but it was some kind of ghost pepper, and my tongue was on fire. I was practically crying. Seriously, I thought my tongue was permanently injured, which is a problem for many reasons. But it's fine now. And I still go back. It's that good."

She nods. "I like spicy, but noted on the ghost peppers. Thanks for the rec." My oversharing seems to be working. She uncrosses her arms and picks up her cup, waiting for my next question.

"It's funny," I say, not really knowing what to follow it with, but trying to keep the conversation casual. "There are some great restaurants near here—near my office—but I never go to them. When I'm done with work I just want to get as far away as I can."

She laughs a little. "Yeah, I can relate."

I start to relax a little myself. She needs to trust me. She needs to believe I'll safeguard whatever she tells me.

We talk a little bit more. She tells me about her last vacation, a weekend in Crested Butte, Colorado, and I admit to fangirling over *Bachelor Bay*, as a segue into the real reason we're here. She seems comfortable enough to start talking.

"I have to say, I'm glad you're the one who answered the phone this morning. If it had been some scary-sounding guy, I might've hung up."

"Well, I'm glad you didn't. Although I should warn you that most of the guys I work with are terrified of me."

She smiles. I feel like she's ready to tell me whatever she called to say.

"I'm going to take some notes, but they're just for me," I tell her, taking out a small spiral notebook and pen.

"Okay, so here's the thing. If you've watched the show, you know this season was kind of… different."

I'm not sure I understand and I don't want to put words in her mouth. "Different, how?" I ask.

She looks into her coffee and seems to be searching for the right words. "Well, normally from week to week, one bachelor may have a really romantic moment, and the next week some other guy has everyone's attention. You never really know who's going to end up winning the money and falling in love with the female lead and all that."

"Got it. You mean how Jake is so crazy popular this season."

"Exactly. People just love him. I mean, if he was voted off too early, I think fans would revolt." She looks pained at the idea. I'm still not seeing why she thinks it merits a news story, but I know she called the paper for a reason. I decide to wait and let her tell me what she came to say. She looks into her coffee and lowers her voice. "The thing is, he's not a good guy."

My senses jump to high alert, and not because the Bachelor Bay groupie in me wants to know the salacious details. The way she says it makes me think she has personal knowledge of her claim.

"Define not a good guy," I say, fearing the worst: harassment or assault, which would take her concern to a whole new level.

She takes a deep breath and looks around at the other patrons, none of which are close enough to hear our conversation. She exhales and fixes her gaze on me. "He and I were…

involved, like romantically, at the beginning of the season. Just for a minute."

I don't know much about reality shows. In fact, I'm probably less savvy than the average viewer because I only watch the one show and I consume it like the mindless entertainment it is. Still, I'm pretty sure the contestants aren't supposed to be involved—even just for a minute—with other people while the show is being filmed. "Involved how? Can you be more specific?" I ask.

"It was during week three. I'm so embarrassed now, but he seemed interested and I was flattered because—well, you've seen him—and it just kind of happened. A couple of times. The details of how and where aren't that important, are they?"

"It depends. Did he force you into anything?"

"No, no. It was totally consensual. Are you kidding? Just a couple nights in my room after the camera stopped rolling. But totally inappropriate because I worked for the show. Also because he's a contestant and it's against the rules."

"When did you work there?" I ask. I'm focused on the fact that she's referring to her job in the past tense.

She nods, looking again into her coffee. She blinks heavily. "Up until a month ago. In the camera department. I was downsized. Of course, right?"

I can't jump to conclusions about the reason, even though she seems to think it's obvious. It's fair game to eliminate someone's position. But with the show still in production, it does seem unusual that her job suddenly became redundant.

"Did other people get laid off?" I ask.

"Nope, just me. About a week after Jake and I hooked up. I'm sure he got me fired. He's a slimeball. I know he seems smooth and desirable to the audience, but trust me, it's an act. He's not interested in winning because he wants to fall in love. He wants the money."

I put up a hand to stop her. There are too many accusations coming all at once, and frankly, it wouldn't be the first time a reality show contestant was more interested in money than love. The main issue seems to be that they both violated the rules and she's the one who lost her job over it.

"Did you tell anyone on the show that you two hooked up?"

"A few people know, but they're my friends. I trust them to be discreet, but obviously someone reported it because I was fired," she says, pressing her lips into a line.

I have to be careful here because she's leveling accusations without evidence. "Can you prove you were laid off in retaliation? Did anyone say that to you? I mean, why are you certain you weren't downsized as part of normal cost-cutting?"

She levels me with a stare. "Because I live in the real world. We both know this kind of shit happens all the time. I ended it with him after a week because I knew it was a stupid lapse in judgment and I didn't want to jeopardize my job. Turns out, I did anyway."

"Did anyone reprimand you for the affair before you were laid off?" I ask.

She shakes her head. "Because, think about it. If they reprimanded me, they'd have to reprimand him. Which would mean he'd be kicked off the show, and that's not something they want when he's a ratings magnet," she says.

"So you called me."

She nods her head. "You can investigate. Maybe you can prove they got rid of me and let him slide because they wanted to keep their audience favorite. I can't say anything publicly or I'll be blackballed from the industry. Television is a small world. That's why they paid me a generous severance, so I'd go away. Worldvision makes so much money on that show, they can't risk losing fans over a scandal."

Suddenly, the coffee bean grinder sounds like a power drill in my head.

How do I continually hurl myself into such deep caverns of crap? How did I not notice that Worldvision produces *Bachelor Bay* when I watch it every single week? Worldvision is the biggest company on Jack's beat and of course he's going to care about this. I've just dug myself another deep hole.

"Okay," I say, my brain spinning out scenarios that include my public hanging in the newsroom if I'm lucky and career suicide if I'm not. For now, I try to keep it together. "This is a lot of good information. I'm gonna need to take a beat and figure out where to go from here."

"Of course." Megan looks relieved to have unburdened herself, even though I haven't said what I plan to do with everything she's told me. I wish I felt as good.

After Megan leaves, I use my phone to do a little digging. From what I can see in the annual reports that Worldvision has released over the past few years, the company makes nearly half its money on its television division, but it's not broken down by show. I find a list of all the shows produced by the company, a couple low-rated dramas, and a few other reality shows, but I can already tell that none of them have the earning power of *Bachelor Bay*. It's their cash cow, so it makes some sense that the company would want to maintain its success. But if they're knowingly burying a scandal involving a contestant and a crew member, they're leaving the company exposed if anyone talks. It sounds like a handful of people know about it, and all it takes is one who blabs. Why take that risk?

I've been a reporter long enough to know the answer to that. It's the same reason anyone does anything with questionable moral underpinnings: to make money. Dollars drive everything in business. What I don't know yet is whether what they did—if it's all true—is a crime.

14

———

LINDEN

WHEN I GET BACK to the newsroom, it's relatively quiet. A few reporters are out at meetings and some have already filed their stories for the day and gone home. In the time since I left Megan at Starbucks, the self-doubt has crept in. It seems like a story. It's a story, right? Am I crazy to think this is a story? She was downsized and she thinks it's retaliation for sleeping with Jake.

I consider the possibilities. Maybe the show was just cutting costs. Maybe it's unrelated to Megan sleeping with Jake and telling only a few people. Maybe they all kept quiet. If I go to Jack with my investigative lead and I'm wrong, his contempt will be etched in my brain forever.

Why don't you stick to your own beat and stop pretending you know how to do my job?

I can see his sneering smile, enjoying my failure. Again.

The problem is, my instinct tells me Megan is right. I've seen every episode of *Bachelor Bay*, and I can understand how a scandal involving Jake would tank the show. Megan is more expendable than Jake, but he's equally culpable. It galls me that he can continue on unscathed.

Even though I just drank a latte, I head for the coffee

room, knowing that more caffeine will push me into jittery territory. Maybe I can find something soothing. Like herbal tea. Or valium.

I need a little more time to think before I go back to my desk. The coffee room is a dumping ground for lunch leftovers, which fill up most of the fridge, and assorted sodas, flavored waters, and teas, none of which appeal to me. I forage around in the cupboard for a mug, which I fill with water from the dispenser against the wall.

I can't decide whether to talk to Jack about the potential story or whether I should take it to Stuart and see what he thinks. Stuart will want to know everything Megan told me, which is fine as long as I tell him it's off the record, but then he'll want to know how I plan to investigate the rest. I don't have a good answer to that, not yet.

After a few minutes and two more mugs full of water, I have to admit to myself that I'm scared of Jack. That's why I'm hiding next to the photocopy machine and inhaling the smell of burnt coffee.

Then there's the other thing I don't want to admit: the idea of going to Jack with a story he might actually appreciate has me all kinds of excited in places that definitely should not be active while I'm at work. I mentally tell those parts of my body to quiet down while I steel myself for what I need to do next: find Jack and explain what I've gotten myself into. And possibly get the verbal beat-down of my life.

JACK ISN'T at his desk when I get back to mine. I look at the interoffice memo system where reporters post messages to let each other know if we're out on an interview and when we'll be back. Jack posted one a couple hours ago: *Jack OUT: meeting with source, avail on cell.*

I take a peek over the partition to see if he's left behind

any telltale items that might indicate he'll be returning to pick them up before he goes home. His laptop is gone, but he could be using it to take interview notes. His jacket is no longer on the back of his chair, but that too could be something he put on before he met his source. There's a half-full cup of coffee on his desk and a water bottle, but I have to admit I've never been interested enough in what he does to know if he leaves those kinds of things overnight.

I sit back at my desk and go through the news feeds, looking for any breaking news that someone in the bureau needs to cover for the online Examiner before the end of the day.

Pauline has been working on a follow-up to the merger story from yesterday, so I know she's on top of her companies, but there are a few items that the biotech reporters should know about and a story starting to hit the wires about the energy markets. I do a quick roundup of data and let Davis, Judith, and Tyler know about the info I've dug up for them.

I figure it can't hurt to do a little more digging into the financials of Worldvision to see if I can figure out exactly how much money the company earns from *Bachelor Bay*. I ask Blaire, one of the other entertainment reporters, what the budget is of a typical reality show.

"Depends on the show, but it's pennies compared to scripted television. That's why they're so easy to make."

"Is there a ballpark?"

"I mean, it mainly depends on whether there are celebrity hosts. Those salaries are the biggest part of the production budget. Why do you ask?"

"Just something I'm looking into for a potential story."

"The person you should ask is Jack. He knows the financials backwards and forwards." I figured as much, but he's not here.

"Good idea," I say, as though it hadn't occurred to me. "Any idea if he's coming back today?"

"Nah, no idea. But you can ping him on his cell."

"Right. Good idea."

I have no intention of pinging him. I'll just wait and see if he makes it back to the office today, and if not, I'll corner him first thing in the morning and fill him in on everything Megan told me. I feel like I'm carrying around a secret and the weight of it feels suffocating.

I already filed my follow-up story to yesterday's Zumalife news. Stuart seemed mildly placated by my efforts. I convinced the company publicist that my oversight in the past was a colossal screw-up on my part because I'm new and still learning, and could I please be given a chance to make things right and write a nice profile of the Zumalife CEO? Yes, I groveled. She was mildly sympathetic. The CEO spent an hour on the phone with me and I turned in a nice 1,200-word story that will run on the front of the business section tomorrow.

While I sit waiting for Jack, I try to keep busy. I put in one more call to the Zumalife publicist to thank her for giving me access and to make sure there isn't any other news about the company that I might be missing. I can't afford to let my guard down for a minute.

"No, that's it for news around here. I imagine taking the company private will be the most exciting announcement to come out of this company for a long time," the publicist tells me. Nevertheless, I plan to make it my job to call her weekly just to make sure. I promise her we can meet for a drink soon. Despite what I told Jack, it looks like I'll make it out to a bar near the office again.

～

IT'S past eight at night, and everyone has left the newsroom except for Stuart, who's doing the final edit on Pauline's story and anything else that needs to be sent to the New York editors before the end of the day.

I decide to end my Jack-stalking mission since he's obviously not coming back to the office. I wonder if he's out having a drink with another source. Or with someone who's not a source. Despite what he said about not going out much unless it's work, I know he has women lining up to do whatever he wants. That's been made abundantly clear from the phone calls I've overheard.

"Hey, you're here late," he says, as I'm bent down putting my laptop away. His voice sends a chill down my spine and I force myself to believe it's only due to nerves. I glance up to see Jack in his navy sport coat and tie with his laptop bag slung over his shoulder. Looking hot. Nerves, be damned.

Oh, for the love of God, Linden, please stay focused.

I blink to shake myself out of my trance. "Yeah, I was… hoping we could talk about something. I wasn't sure if you were coming back."

"Oh, you could've called me. But whatever, I'm here. What's up?"

I bite my lower lip, something I do when I'm stalling and already regretting what I'm about to say. He leans against the low wall that separates our row of cubicles from the next one.

"Do you have time right now? If you have to go, we can talk tomorrow…"

"I'm good. What's up? Everything okay?" He looks relaxed, ready to wrap up his day. He's not expecting what I'm about to tell him and now I'm regretting staying here to talk. I haven't figured out what to say.

"Yeah," I begin, but the tremor in my voice is not reassuring. "I took a call on the news desk this morning…"

He pulls a chair up and sits on it backward, leaning on the headrest. "Spill."

I outline the broad strokes of the phone call from Megan

and the meeting at Starbucks. I'm careful to tell him that I didn't want to bother him if her tip turned out to be nothing, but that I thought I should pursue the lead just in case it panned out.

"Of course, the second I realized the show is a cash cow for Worldvision I knew you'd want to be involved—"

"Involved?"

"Well, I mean, I know you cover the company. I just didn't know… initially… if a dumb reality show was too small potatoes for you to bother with."

I tell him how I've spent some time looking at the financials of the television division and compared those with the revenues from the rest of the company and also checked out line items that might be disguising payouts for lawsuits. I'm unable to stop my rambling. I know I'm telling him things he already knows about a company he studies like he's prepping for an exam. I wish I could stop myself from blathering on and on, but since he hasn't said a word in minutes, I keep going, trying to justify the fact that I waited all day to tell him. Wishing I had an off switch on my mouth, so I'd stop filling the air with useless information he already knows.

He's not helping the situation. As I'm talking, his expression is inscrutable.

Finally, I get a grip on the verbal carnage and shut up. I wait for whatever's coming next.

"Goddammit, Linden," he says, voice caustic. Being murdered with a ballpoint pen might be more pleasant than his quiet wrath.

"I know."

Do I? I'm not sure I know anything.

"No, I'm pretty sure you don't. This was a massive fuckup on your part. You never should have taken that meeting."

I've been slowly figuring that out on my own, but hearing him say it only makes me feel like the neophyte reporter he knows I am. And I'm a little pissed that I can never do anything right where he's concerned. I'm also mad at myself for giving him proof.

"I get that. I'm trying to do the right thing now," I say.

"The right thing? I don't think you can possibly know what that looks like, based on today."

"Fine! Tell me. I'd like to learn from this. You can't possibly think I enjoy being constantly beaten down by you."

I see a minuscule softening in his face, just a muscle twitch in his cheek, but it doesn't do enough to disrupt the tight set of his jaw. Finally, he blinks his eyes for a long moment and shakes his head. "I need to talk to Stuart." He gets up and starts walking quickly to Stuart's office.

"Should I stay? Go?" I ask. I have no idea what he's thinking or whether I should be following him.

"Don't go anywhere!" he shouts, still striding away.

I look at the piles that are stacked and spread across every inch of my desk. I need to organize the Zumalife files and check the wires again. This job never ends. News never ends. That used to excite me, the never-ending parade of events and information. I loved being at the center of it, knowing what was happening in the world first, even if I wasn't the one who was writing the big stories.

Now it just feels like I'm racing a bullet train with no chance of keeping up. I'm exhausted from this day that has already stretched past the twelve-hour mark. Is this what he does every single day? Is this what it takes to be at the top of a person's game around here? If so, I'm not sure I want it.

Oh, I'm lying. Of course I want it. Knowing the peak is so far out of my reach makes me want it even more.

Over in Stuart's glass-walled office, I can see Jack pacing around, gesturing with his hands while Stuart swivels in his desk chair to follow the conversation. It's horrible to know they're talking about me in there. I can only imagine the awful things Jack is saying. All the things he's been wanting to get off his chest since I stepped into my reporting job. I've just given him the ammunition he's needed to convince Stuart to demote me back to the news assistant dungeon.

I try to tune them out by organizing my piles and checking my twitter feed, but I'm aware of every ten-second interval that ticks by on the analog clock on the wall.

Finally, I hear a violent twist of Stuart's door handle and his voice calling to me from across the quiet news bureau. "Sandoval, could I have a word?"

I get up and cross through the cubicles to his corner office, hoping he'll let me explain my thinking before ripping my job out from under me. "Stuart, I want to apologize. If I had thought—"

"Yes. It was the wrong call. You always contact the beat reporter as soon as you get a lead on a story."

"I understand that and I'm really sorry."

"It's not just a policy at the paper; it's a matter of respect. Jack has been working his sources and his companies for years and he knows them better than anyone. You should have gone to him immediately."

I can't see Jack because he's still lurking behind me, but I can hear him exhale in frustration. Even his non-verbal's are irritating. "I realize that. And truly, I'm sorry."

He waves a hand, dismissing me. "No time for that. We need a plan of attack. Come, sit." He motions me to one of the chairs opposite his desk. Jack still paces behind me, but Stuart gestures for him to sit as well. "All three of us."

I don't dare look at Jack. I know he doesn't want to be a part of any plan which involves me. When he drops into the chair next to mine, I'm too aware of his scent, the combination of earthy cologne and laundry soap. I wish that sitting this close to him didn't send a thrill of longing through my entire body.

It's just chemistry. Basic biology. Ignore it.

He's hard to ignore.

"It's not just the phone call. I'm working on getting Ken to do the profile and it's a very delicate balancing act. This isn't helping. Does she understand that?" Jack asks Stuart like I'm not even there.

"Okay. You'll meet with this whistleblower and get specifics: who she told, what she told them, who she interacted with at Worldvision. If there's a story there, your profile of the CEO just got a helluva lot more interesting. Now it's not a puff piece on a reclusive billionaire; it's a scandal at the company's most popular show," Stuart says. He looks elated. I'm starting to understand what Jeremy meant about him liking stories better than people.

But there's a problem.

I don't see the story happening with Jack at the helm. Call it instinct, but I can't imagine the magical seduction of womankind that's Jack's stock in trade working on Megan. She's a scared rabbit. His magnetism will work to his disadvantage and she'll crumple into a ball of insecurity. I know women like her. Lots of them. I'm not wrong about this.

On the other hand, I'd like to keep my job and Jack can figure this out for himself. He's the star reporter. It's not my problem.

"I'm completely fine handing everything over, of course," I say, making a hand gesture like I'm dumping my files on Jack's lap. "But the whistleblower... no offense, but she's not going to talk to you."

And there it goes again, my unstoppable mouth.

"I'm sorry?" Jack asks, actually seeming incredulous. So now I have to explain.

"I met her. This woman is a meek camera assistant, and this is her one Norma Rae moment. She wants to talk, but she's terrified of getting in trouble. I could barely get her comfortable enough to talk to me and I'm a non-threatening junior reporter. You're intimidating. She won't talk to someone who isn't an empath."

"I am not intimidating." Jack looks at me like he can't

believe I have the nerve to talk to him like this. I meet his gaze, wanting him to know that unlike Megan, I don't find him intimidating.

"Um, okay." But it's all I can do not to blink before he does. His mouth bends into a small smile and he nods.

"And what do you suggest?" he asks in a calm, slightly amused voice.

"I mean… I could meet with her again and see what else she has to and then I'll go from there…"

"You're saying you want to write the story," Jack says, incredulous again. He looks at Stuart for confirmation of how ludicrous I sound. And I know it's crazy, but I feel like I rose to the occasion today and got Megan to tell me things she wasn't planning to say. So maybe I'm actually a little bit good at my job and maybe I deserve to write this story.

"I—"

Stuart doesn't let me finish. "I think it's a good idea."

"What?!" Jack's eyes are practically bugging out of his head.

"She has a point. And I want to encourage initiative. Linden followed a lead and here we are."

"Yes. Here we are. I'm going to the Nichols's house for the weekend. I'm sure I can find a minute to interview this game show host—"

"Reality show host—" I say.

"—Or whoever the fuck he is when I'm there. I need to control whatever this other story is and weave it into the narrative. I can't have someone else following leads all over the goddamn place without me."

"Fine. Write it together," Stuart says, rubbing his hands together. I'm liking Stuart more and more for his zen-like calm in this situation but I'm not sure I like this suggestion.

"Together." Jack says it like the word makes no sense. I have to say I agree. I'm not sure Stuart understands what he's unleashing, based on the chipper tone in his voice. He's putting two people who currently can't stand each other on one assignment and hoping we don't kill each other. But in the interest of not getting murdered right here in his office, I don't dare say a word.

"Or she writes and you edit, which would be good for you—"

Jack holds up a hand and interrupts him. "Not happening." Only he can get away with talking to Stuart this way.

"Fine. Share a byline, divide it up however you decide. You each have a unique in with the company now. You both take different approaches to sources, which I think can be useful. This is a situation where the parts will add up to more than the whole."

"I'm not sure I agree with your strategy—" Jack starts to say, but Stuart waves a hand.

"I understand, but hear me out. I think this is an opportunity. Come at this company from all sides. You work your angle, Linden works hers. She's good with people." Stuart's excitement almost has me convinced it could work. The look on Jack's face says otherwise.

He's shaking his head, his whole body in danger of convulsing. A vein in his temple is bulging and I'm a little worried it might explode. His face is a shade of pink mine only gets when I'm mortified, and I know that's the reason in his case.

"Stuart, I need to focus on the profile. If I can wrangle an invitation this weekend, I can close it."

"So, take Linden with you."

"I'm sorry?" I can see the vein pulsing from where I sit. I wonder if it will be hard to get his blood out of my clothes when he has an aneurysm and it blows all over me.

"Just an idea. If the reality host is going to be there, you can kill two birds. She can interview him too."

"Stuart, this is feeling complicated."

"Do it or don't do it. Figure out what will get you your story, is all I'm saying."

Stuart sits back and looks from one of us to the other, his way of saying the meeting is over. We each stand silently and walk back to our desks. I don't dare look at Jack or utter a word to him. I can feel the anger emanating from his body like a force field, threatening to knock me over with how much he hates that we have to work on something together. I don't blame him. I'm not happy either.

15

JACK

I CAN'T DECIDE if I'm irritated or impressed. No, I'm defi-nitely irritated. Okay, and a tiny bit impressed.

First, she goes and meets with someone on a potential story that's clearly squarely in the middle of my beat without telling me. Then she tells Stuart her source only feels comfort-able talking to her. It's ballsy, which is why I'm impressed. She needs that attitude and killer instinct if she's going to be successful at the job. But not at my expense.

That's why I need to plow ahead and get my profile done and written. I know it will either run on Page One or it will be the lead story in the Sunday magazine. Either way, I'll blow all the other publications out of the water. I need to nail down my invitation for the weekend a and finish my reporting. No, it's not a done deal yet. That's another issue. Claudia hasn't confirmed and I've got a lot riding on getting it to happen. This reality show garbage is an annoyance I don't need.

I'm also pissed as hell at Stuart for suggesting I edit Linden's work because no one is supposed to know that may end up being my fulltime job. Jeremy told me a few months ago that he's probably leaving the paper to go on an extended book leave. He has a deal with a publisher to put out a massive personal narrative of corruption in the solar industry, rounding up years of reporting on the subject. He'll be on a two-year leave of absence from the paper while he does more extensive reporting and writes the book.

With Jeremy going on book leave, the assistant chief job needs to be filled for at least a year and it's been offered to me by the New York editors and seconded by Stuart.

It's a big deal to move from reporting to running a bureau. It's the right career move, but I haven't committed yet to taking the post. The last thing I need is for everyone in the office to know about it before I've made a decision. Jesus, Stuart almost blurted it out like it was a done deal.

Isn't it? Assistant chief is a huge promotion and most reporters wouldn't think twice.

I don't have time to think about a new job right now. I'm trying to do the one I have.

I call Claudia to see how she's coming along in trying to land me an invitation to Ken's weekend event. I pretty much told Stuart that my going out there this weekend was a lock— it needs to happen.

"Hi love, I was just talking about you. Were your ears burning?"

"Oh, yes, definitely. I wanted to follow up on the weekend event you mentioned."

"Yes, I knew that's why you called. And we're all set. They'd love to have you and your wife or girlfriend. I told them I was pretty sure you're not married… yet. I didn't see a ring the other night, and Shane never said anything."

"No, not married." Jesus, this again?

"So, girlfriend it is. They can't wait to meet her."

Hold up. When did this become a plus-one situation?

"D'you think it would be okay if I just came by myself? I'm not sure my… plus-one is free this weekend."

My mind returns to our conversation from last night when I'd unequivocally told her I'd like to come alone. She'd completely invented the idea of a girlfriend—or a wife?—and I'm not about to complicate things by having some date trailing after me all weekend long. Not any of the women I've dated this decade, that's for sure. And definitely not Linden, despite Stuart's suggestion.

I can hear her pout over the phone. "Oh, that's a shame. Well, I'll have to check and see if there's another weekend that would work. This time it's just a small gathering of some of their couple friends. Okay, let's see… I know they'll be in Europe next month and Ken has a golf tournament, so maybe in the summer…"

Ordinarily, it would be fine to wait. Profiles take months to nail down and write. It's never just about the one-on-one interview. Executives are prepped for those. They keep their responses conservative and toe the company line. It's not until I can get closer, see them outside the office, that the real magic happens. Two hours ago, I might have been okay taking a raincheck on going to Montecito. But with Linden talking to a whistleblower and a potential scandal brewing that could come to light at any time, I have to move now.

I can't wait on this story until summer. I need to make this weekend work. "Claudia, hang on. Lemme try to see if she's available. If you're sure I can't just come alone."

"No, not alone, love. They won't be comfortable with that. It'll feel like you're there to spy on them."

Which I am.

"And having you as a reporter or whatnot fights the tenor of the weekend. It won't feel right unless you're there as a social guest. It's a gathering of friends."

Which I'm not.

I need to make this happen. I'll rent an escort if I have to. "Claudia, can you give me until tomorrow to see if she can clear her schedule? I'll get back to you then."

I can hear the clap of her hands on the other end of the line. "Lovely."

After I hang up, I throw my Bluetooth headset across the room. It skitters on the nubby grey carpet of the newsroom floor and lands someplace where I can't see it. *Fuck.* "Day just keeps getting better and better," I mutter, unaware that anyone is close enough to hear me.

"I really am sorry." I turn to see Linden standing next to my desk, holding my headset in her hand. She puts it on top of a stack of binders that sit on my file cabinet and backs a few feet away. I exhale the frustration about Worldvision, her whistleblower, the hot water I'll be in if I can't produce a great profile. This job works me over sometimes.

"It's not your fault," I tell her. She looks confused.

"It's totally my fault."

"I just mean, you were doing your job. It's fine."

She lingers, frozen, like she's not satisfied with my response. "Okay, well, great." She turns to go and suddenly it irritates the hell out of me that she's not suffering enough for putting me under the gun on a story and making me share a byline with her. I'm angry enough to say something I'll probably regret later. Or, as the words are coming out of my mouth.

"Actually, it's not great. Nothing about this is great. You've put me in a position of having to rush on a profile and now I have to add in a possible scandal that could be a complete waste of time or it could change what I say in my profile. I control the narrative of this job, not you."

"I know I made a mistake. But aren't we in the business of reporting news? Even if I'd passed the call on to you, it would still be a story you'd have to deal with. It would still affect your profile."

Of course she's right, but I'm not about to concede that. "Here's how this is gonna go down. I have to spend this weekend at Ken Nichols's villa in Montecito to get the rest of my profile done. I'm now forced to deal with this game show train wreck because of you."

She doesn't dare respond, but I can see the fire building behind her eyes. She's dying to say something she'll probably regret but for now, she's holding her tongue and waiting for me to finish ranting. "Apparently there will be a lot of couples, and everyone would feel a lot more comfortable if I didn't come alone, so you're coming with me. But to be clear, I don't have any illusions that this is anything but strictly professional. You can use your empathetic ear or whatever the hell you said back there to quietly work the room and help me report the story."

Her mouth has dropped open and she's looking at me like I've grown another head. "You want me to come with you?"

"Not with me. You'll be there too, so I can do my job without anyone thinking I'm some kind of spy. You'll do whatever I need you to do. You'll work harder than you've ever worked at this job. I take this shit seriously."

I don't know what I expect. Maybe I think she's gonna cry or tell me to go to hell because I know I'm acting like an asshole and basically ordering her around. But her face cracks open into the biggest smile I've ever seen on a person. "Okay. Yes. I'm totally in. Great." She looks like she's been told she's getting a new puppy when what I'm telling her is that I'm going to make her suffer and work her tail off all weekend long.

I'm doing my level best to keep my mind on the story and to strategize how we're going to work on it together, but my brain is fighting me tooth and nail because her smile absolutely slays me and it's making me almost look forward to a whole weekend with her. And that's wrong for so many reasons.

"Great," I tell her, leaning back on my chair, grateful that it's there to absorb my full weight. It hits me that she's exhausted from the day and I'm pretty sure it's coming on ten o'clock at night. I expect her to take my cue and go home, but she lingers, her smile still glowing.

"So… I know it's late, and we don't need to talk about it now, but I wanna make sure I don't mess anything up. Can you give me a download on everything I need to know before we go?" she asks.

I nod, running a hand through my hair because it somehow helps me think. I wish I'd done that for more than a millisecond before blurting out what now seems like a horrible plan. She's right. She knows nothing about Worldvision or Ken Nichols or anything else in the media landscape that's been my beat for the past ten years.

This is not a woman who sits quietly and picks up information. She charges in, blurts things out, and speaks before she thinks. The chances are high that she'll turn my reporting mission into a disaster.

"What's wrong?" she asks.

"Nothing? What?"

"You look like you're in agony."

I am in agony. I don't share bylines with junior reporters, and I don't get railroaded into spending the weekend with them. I shake my head, but the headache is creeping in. "I really can't get you up to speed by Friday. I have no idea how I'm gonna do this," I say.

"Why don't you try. I'm a pretty quick study."

I don't know why that annoys me so much, but it does. Her comment speaks to how little she still understands about this job, about what's required to command a beat. It takes years. "This isn't like cramming for a history test."

"Seems exactly like that," she says.

"That's because you don't know any better."

"Oh, here we go. I couldn't possibly know because I'm too new. Too *green*."

"I didn't say that."

"You pretty much did."

My head is pounding, and I don't know what she's talking about, nor do I have the energy to argue with her. I can't think anymore. My head feels like it's about to split open and I need to get home and shower off this day before I say anything else I'm going to have to apologize for later.

"Fine, here you go. Study this" I say, pointing to the binders on top of my filing cabinet. They contain years of annual reports and data I've collected on Worldvision and I know I'm being a jerk by suggesting she read through all of it. It's definitely unnecessary. It would be more helpful for me to coach her on how to get the most out of her source and give her small assignments that will get the information I need. I'm about to backpedal and tell her she doesn't need to look through the binders, but she's already shoving them into her bag without batting an eye. There are three of them and she can't close the zipper on her laptop bag because two of the binders are sticking out, but it doesn't seem to faze her one bit.

"Great. I'll check in with you tomorrow," she says. Then, without a hint of annoyance, she turns on her heel and walks away from me. Her bag, filled with the awkward load of binders, bounces against her hip. I've just sent her down an unneeded rabbit hole to chase irrelevant information.

I'm such an asshole.

I'm also not above checking out the sway of her hips as she goes and noticing her perfect, tight butt. I'll try to convince myself that it's okay to be checking her out like that sometime later when I'm busy lying to myself about how much I dislike her.

And now I've stepped in it. There's no chance I can get away with doing the story without her. If there's something to this whistleblower's claim, we can write the story and share a byline and I can get Linden out of my business. If not, I'm doubly screwed because it'll be one more delay in getting my profile done and she'll have wasted my time.

It's good that I'm still so pissed off about her manhandling a story on my beat. It will keep me from thinking about her as anything except an irritating junior reporter whose presence I have to endure for a weekend.

There will be plenty for me to do if I want to get everything I need for my profile, plus find out what this reality show clown has to say about the allegation of foul play on his show. I just have to make sure to explain to Linden exactly what her boundaries need to be so she doesn't go off and start asking people questions she shouldn't. The last thing I need is for her to jeopardize the access to Ken that I've fought hard to get.

If I could stop thinking about how good it felt to kiss her, how sweet her lips tasted and how much I'd like to kiss them again, maybe I'd have a fighting chance to get on top of my story. I hate the idea of seeing her all weekend long gives me the kind of hard-on I haven't felt in a long time.

I need to keep it one hundred percent professional.

Shouldn't be a problem. She hates you. You've made sure of that.

LINDEN

SOMEHOW, the remainder of the week flies by and I make it to Friday. Maybe the blur of the past few days is due to the fact that I've been consumed with reading the binders Jack gave me on Worldvision and digging through the bureau's archives for material on the company from before he took over the beat. My brain is a caffeinated stew of data, news stories, merger factoids and entertainment journalism. I'm afraid to turn my head too abruptly for fear of some important piece of information being bumped loose.

On Friday morning, I have to get up extra early and turn the bright lights on in my apartment to give my luggage the once-over and make sure I'm not forgetting anything. I'm determined to make it to spinning before work and I need to get to the office by eight. There's no way I'm starting my weekend reporting tour of duty on a sour note by having Jack lecture me about being late.

I really have no idea what to pack. The Nichols family lives in Montecito which is one of the wealthiest cities in California, and I can only assume the weekend will be a dressy affair. But the city is also right near the ocean, so it could be beachy. I'm packing for both, every and all eventualities. I have bathing suits—bikini and tank-style—shorts, jeans, dressy casual pants, blouses, dresses, and even big straw hats. No, I don't own most of these items, but Kayla came over and loaned me half her closet. Between the business casual clothes she wears at her law firm and the cocktail dresses she's accumulated over the years, she had almost everything I think I need to get through the weekend. Lucky for me, we wear the same size.

Shoes are another story. I pull out some strappy stiletto heels I wore as a bridesmaid a few years ago and a pair of beach sandals, along with pumps I bought when I had my interview with Jeremy and Stuart. I haven't had a need to wear them since that day, but now they may be just the thing to add some sass to my dark denim skinny jeans and a few inches to my height.

I almost forget to pack underwear but fortunately, I open the top drawer of my dresser in search of a couple long necklaces and notice the untouched pile. Going commando all weekend would have been the icing on an already awkward cake. I grab a bunch of lingerie and stuff it into my bag, not stopping to match up bras and panties because, let's be honest, no one is going to see them.

By the time I get to my spin class, I'm wide awake, something Cassie notices right away. "This is not the Linden I know well. I'm betting you had a really great night and you're still up. *Amiright*, girl?" she asks.

"No, but I've taken a page from your book and I've been up an hour already."

"Again, I have to believe that's for a man, otherwise, why bother your circadian rhythms?"

"No, no man. I just have a work trip and I needed to pack."

"Aw, well I'm sorry to hear. I always root for you." I glance over at her ring finger, realizing I don't actually know if she's in a relationship. She's wearing a wide opal cocktail ring, next to several gold bands, and a square gold nugget on a third finger.

"How about you? You waking anyone up at four in the morning when you get out of bed?" I ask her.

"No, not in a year or so. I was engaged to a surly Brit for two years before that but then we broke things off."

"Oh, sorry to hear."

"Don't be sorry, girl. He was a pain in my arse, as he liked to say. Trouble from day one. Big drinker, big, bold lover... The whole accent thing just had me though."

The spin instructor cranks up a Pitbull song, which is our cue to shut up and start pedaling. I clip in and get my workout on because I know I'm going to need to sweat out a reserve tank of frustration if I'm going to get through a weekend of Jack nitpicking everything I do. I put everything into the bike. I'm pedaling and soaking up the music like it's my lifeblood.

When the class ends, I waste no time showering and heading to work. When my day begins at eight, I'm going to have to buckle in, because my workday will last until Sunday night. I take a deep breath and dive in.

JACK

TODAY IS NOT GOING AS PLANNED. I want to make as much headway on the Ken Nichols profile as possible, plugging in the background information I already have so it won't take me as long to lay out the story after the weekend.

Instead, I'm staring at a blank computer screen, uncertain how to begin. I've been here since six, trying to take advantage of the quiet newsroom to make some progress, but after two hours, I barely have the outline of an idea and I'm beyond frustrated.

That's when Linden breezes in the door, the faint scent of lavender shampoo wrapped up in her hair, which she has spiraled and stacked on top of her head like a donut. She's wearing tight jeans and a pink T-shirt with a navy-blue blazer and I'm pretty sure my jaw hits the floor because I've never seen her in something like this. Usually, she shows up in baggy boyfriend jeans and some kind of bohemian shirt which looks comfortable to work in, but doesn't do much to highlight what I now see is a knockout figure. Maybe that's why she wears the big flowy shirts—to keep lechers like me from checking her out.

"Morning," she says, not looking in my direction. Clearly,

she knows I'm here, since she just spoke to me. But considering we're about to spend the next two days together, it's odd that's she's so brief.

"Hey. How's it going?" I ask. Maybe I need a little human interaction after two hours of battling with the inanimate computer that's sucking every last bit of humanity from me. She looks surprised when she turns to look at me.

"Um, fine. How about you?"

"Eh. You know. Writer's block can be a bitch…"

For the second time in two days, her face breaks into a smile the likes of which I've never seen in the year and half she's worked here. I wonder what I've done to bring it out, because I'd sure like to be able to do it again sometime. "*You* have writer's block?"

"Why the word emphasis? We all get stuck sometimes."

But she's shaking her head in disbelief as if I've just told her I ate baby sea lions instead of toast. "I didn't think *you* did." Again, emphasis.

"Well, I do. It's a normal thing for a writer."

Now she's nodding. "Right, and if I was a better or more experienced or a more devoted writer, I'd know all about it."

"I didn't say that. I wasn't even about to say that." I feel defensive but I'm not sure why I need to defend myself against something I didn't do.

"Oh." She looks contrite but still suspicious of me. "Sorry. I… tend to assume stuff, occasionally."

I can't help but smile at her partial self-awareness. "Occasionally… often. I kind of get the feeling you think I'm a much worse guy than I actually am."

"*P-ha!*" It's almost like she doesn't mean for a sound to come out, but her laugh is so spontaneous and genuine that it escapes in her utter disbelief.

"Wow. I guess you think I'm an even worse guy than that."

She shrugs. "You're okay."

I can't help but roll my eyes. "Way to salvage a guy's ego. So... okay like a guy you appreciate because he carries you up the stairs when you're shit-faced or like a guy you can only look at from a vast distance without wanting to throw up?"

"I thought we weren't going to talk about my night of ignominy."

"I'm game, but only if you admit I'm actually a good guy. Or—" I hold up a hand, "Let's not even go that far. Let's just say I'm better than you thought."

She smiles, not as brightly, but I'll take it. "I can admit that." She wheels her desk chair over to my cubicle and sits a few feet away, examining me like a therapist. "So, spill it. Why are you so blocked? Are you stressed? Overthinking?"

We're the only ones in the newsroom and her gesture feels intimate, even though I'm certain from our previous conversation that she doesn't mean it to be.

"Probably both. I need to get the profile right, but I can't seem to get it flowing."

She narrows her eyes in confusion. "Is this a different profile than Ken Nichols? How many things do you work on simultaneously?"

"Probably a dozen. But, no, it's not a different one. It's Nichols."

"But you haven't done the interview yet."

"I've sat with him dozens of times. I should be able to get a framework to fill in after the weekend and I'm just stuck."

She wheels her chair a little closer and looks at my legitimately blank screen. "Yeah, looks like writer's block. But I don't understand. How can you even outline the story before you've spent the weekend with the guy? And what about the *Bachelor Bay* stuff? That could change your whole direction if he talks to you about it. Whatever you write now will probably go in the garbage."

"I'm flattered at your high opinion of my prose."

"It has nothing to do with your writing. You haven't gotten Ken to open up. You don't have the story yet. No wonder you're blocked. I mean, I know I'm inexperienced and all, but it seems obvious. Is there something I'm missing?"

She's not wrong. Of course I'm going to have a lot more material after the weekend, or at least I hope that will be the case. But the way she's saying it, it seems obvious in a way I hadn't thought of until now. Because what I don't want to admit is that I don't have this story at all. I'm depending on what comes out of this weekend to make or break my profile and if I come up with nothing, I'm sunk. It's a new experience for me to second-guess myself and I don't know why I'm struggling with the story.

Maybe it's a sign I should take Jeremy's job when he leaves and start editing other people's stories instead of writing my own. But I don't want to think about it now.

I don't say any of this to her, though, because the last thing I need is to have her second guess my authority when I ask her to get bits of the story for me from other guests. I need her to believe I have a plan. "No, you're right on some level. But I should be able to do better. I probably just need more coffee," I say, standing up and starting to push past her. She swivels around in her chair and stops me with her hand.

"Hey."

I look at her because it's definitely the first time she's touched me since the night at the bar, and I'm surprised at how much I like it. "What?"

"Just tell me what you need from me this weekend and I'll make sure I get it—whatever you need so you can write this."

She removes her hand and scoots her chair back to her own desk, immediately busy with whatever she sees on her computer terminal. But my brain is still spinning, thinking about her words, "tell me what you need from me this weekend," and thinking about all the ways I could interpret them the way I wish she meant them.

I can't spend a whole weekend with this woman and hope to keep my mind on work. I can already see I'm fucked and I still have more than two days ahead with her.

Forty-six hours to be exact.

18

LINDEN

THE DAY FLIES by thanks to multiple cups of coffee and the slew of small news items I have to write up for the Saturday paper, which I'm not sure anyone actually reads. With the "welcome cocktails" at the Nichols's villa taking place at six, I need to leave the office by four if I want to be on time.

I want to be on time.

Jack has kept busy this week. I think he's had a front-page piece and three business page stories in the past two days. He's either been on the phone or off writing in one of the private offices, which means we've barely spoken until this morning. But reading through the hundreds of articles he's written on Worldvision over a decade has made me feel like I know him slightly better. He's thorough and doesn't pull punches in his reporting, which is why he's so good at it.

As I'm stuffing my laptop and one of Jack's binders of company data into my bag, I see him standing next to my desk, watching me. Without a word, he takes the binder out of my bag and puts it back on the file cabinet where it sat until he gave it to me for homework. "You don't need that," he says.

"I figured I might have some free time and I can read through it again."

He looks surprised. "Again? You read through it once already?"

"You told me to," I remind him, wary. Is this a trick? "I have all the sector growth numbers from the past ten years in my head, but I want to look at last year's expenses again for any irregularities that could be hiding write-offs for severance cases like Megan's."

"You have all the sector growth numbers in your head? From the past ten years?"

"Yes." I worry that I should have memorized more.

He shakes his head. "I shouldn't have made you read all those documents. They're not gonna help you this weekend. I'll let you know what you need to know."

"So why did you tell me to read them?"

He hesitates, then closes his eyes for a second before answering. "I was pissed off that I was going to have to work with you on the story, and I wanted to make you suffer. I know that makes me..."

"A dick." I can't help it. I have to call it like I see it.

"Exactly. So... sorry."

I look at him, trying to decide if he's really sorry. Finally, I shrug. "It was interesting to read through everything. I feel more prepared now."

"Okay..." he says, in a tone that says he's planning on saying more. He opens his mouth, then closes it in a hard line. His blue eyes bore into mine and I feel a flutter in my stomach under his gaze.

"Is this going to be a problem, us working on this? Having to deal with each other?" I ask. It's hard to talk when he's looking at me like he wants to rip into my brain.

"No. It's going to be great." He sounds like he's trying hard to convince himself. "So..." He looks at the clock on the wall. Now it's five after four. "We should get going. I can drive."

"You mean, drive us both?" I can feel my face heating up, the way it does. I wish it would behave itself and stop outing my embarrassment. I can't handle two hours in the car with this man.

"Wow, sound less enthusiastic?"

"I just mean, don't you have to, like, listen to annual reports on audiobook or something?"

He smirks. "I can still do that with you in the car. C'mon, let's get out of here."

I follow him out of the office and down the elevator to where his car is parked in its usual spot. "Hang on, lemme grab my bag out of my trunk," I say, heading toward my Honda.

He backs the car out and drives to where mine is parked— so I don't have to lug my bag across the parking garage—and hops out to make room in his trunk next to his own bag. I heave my large duffel out of the car and catch his dumb-founded look. "You planning on moving in up there?" I notice that everything he has is packed into a carryon-sized leather weekender which is stashed in a corner of the trunk.

"I like to have options." My duffel weighs close to fifty pounds thanks to all the shoe choices, and it barely fits in the trunk while still allowing it to close. Hefting it into the trunk causes Jack's shirt to come a little untucked and it forces a lock of hair to fall into his eyes. He straightens up and pulls himself together before going over to open the passenger door for me.

"I might've pulled a muscle there," he said. "I wasn't expecting to have to do weight training this afternoon."

"Guess you need to get in better shape."

The last thing I see before he closes my door is a grin that tells me he's not done giving me a hard time. I can't say I mind.

~

AN HOUR LATER, we're driving on Pacific Coast Highway alongside one of the most stunning ocean views I've ever seen. In the past year and a half, I've never left work early enough to get down to the ocean in time for sunset. On most weekends, the drive seems far and I feel lazy. But right now, the sun is high enough in the sky that its shiny yellow rays paint the ocean with streaks of light which I can't help but stare at through sunglasses I almost never get to wear on weekdays.

It would be easy to mistake this for a weekend getaway with a phenomenally hot guy who seems to enjoy pushing the speed limit and God knows what else. I have to reel myself in every few minutes and remind myself I'm here for work.

"I never get down to the ocean. It's gorgeous," I say, unable to take my gaze away from the view.

"Yeah, hazards of the job. I'm not much of a beach-goer myself."

I decide this is my opportunity to learn a little more about this high-strung, successful man who can do no wrong at the paper. "Has reporting always come easy to you?"

"What do you mean? It's not easy."

"I mean, you're always on the ball; you always have sources and CEOs wrapped around your finger."

"Yeah, that's a ton of work. I'm on it twenty-four/seven."

"That's what it seems like. You're very devoted." I notice his shoulders tense and his face pull into a frown. I'm not sure if I've offended him by agreeing with what he just said. "Sorry, was that the wrong thing to say?"

He shakes his head. "No, it's not you. That's just been a bit of a… sore spot in the past."

"How so?" I'm not getting it and he brought it up, so I'm gonna keep digging.

He looks at me and I can see from his pained expression and the way he's white-knuckling the steering wheel that he regrets opening the door to the conversation. I hold up my hands. "No, it's cool. We don't have to talk about this."

He sighs, eyes focused on the road. "It's okay. I guess... so here's the deal. A few years ago, I was engaged. And now I'm not."

I absorb this information while I wait to see if he's planning to elaborate. He's looking straight ahead at the road and still holding the wheel in a death grip. While I wait, I think about the idea of Jack with a fiancé. "Was she a reporter?" I imagine the two of them breaking important news together and celebrating by framing their bylines side-by-side.

"Realtor."

"What?"

"She was a real estate agent. She sold houses."

"Okay," I say. "Did she die?" The way he's talking about her in the past tense makes me wonder. I can feel my forehead crinkling at the sad idea.

Then I hear him chuckle. "No, she didn't die. She's married to someone else and is probably very happy." He lets out a sigh, but before I can ask any more dumb questions, he continues. "We had a year to plan the wedding and I didn't think that much about it. But apparently, I was too absorbed in my job."

I'm not sure I'm getting the issue. "Too absorbed to plan the wedding?"

"That was the fight initially. But that's not what it was about. She thought I put my job first, before her."

"What did you think?" I ask.

"I thought I was doing important work and doing it well. I thought she'd be proud of that."

"She wasn't?"

He shakes his head without looking away from the road. "That was the year I won the Pulitzer. She didn't come to the ceremony. She was at a cake tasting. I guess that was proof we had different priorities."

"That's about the best example of different priorities I can imagine."

He smiles at that.

"It's complicated, isn't it? That's why I don't date. I ruin relationships with my work obsession. It's better this way, though. I need to focus on doing good reporting and not get distracted. The job we do is important," he says.

"I hear that. Except I'm the opposite. I've ruined work opportunities with kissing."

"Kissing?"

"And other stuff." I wave my hand around as though to indicate what some of that other stuff might be, swirling around us in the car, which makes no sense. I settle my hands back in my lap. "Anyway, that's why I don't date." He looks at me for a second and I see a brief smile of understanding cross his face.

With that one area of common ground, I start to think maybe I'll be able to get along with Jack for an entire weekend. The alternative is too painful to consider.

~

AFTER AN HOUR ON THE ROAD, we shift to basic get-to-know you questions because even though I've forced my tongue into his mouth, we don't know each other that well.

"Favorite movie?" he asks.

"Tie between *Dead Poet's Society* and *Moonstruck*."

"Ah, you're a romantic."

"I just like old movies. You?" I ask. I'm betting dead to rights he's going to say *The Pentagon Papers* or something with journalistic heroes.

"*Rainman.*"

"Seriously. That's depressing."

"No, it's such an uplifting story. Watch it again. Trust me," he says.

"Okay, deal. How about favorite snack?"

"Grain bowl from the place downstairs."

"*Ew*, the one that smells like rotting garbage?"

"I hadn't been aware of that. But I guess, yeah. And now I'm too self-conscious to ever eat it again. So thank you." He looks at the road but every so often he glances in my direction. "How about your favorite?"

"Nutella and celery."

"Is that a thing?"

"It's like peanut butter and celery, but better. It's like *Rainman*. You need to try it and contemplate it before you disparage it."

"Fair enough."

I wind my hair into a bun to keep it out of my face and catch what looks like a grimace pass over Jack's face.

"Everything okay?"

He raises his eyebrows and stretches his neck, as though trying for a reset. "Yeah. Fine." I decide not to pursue it, lest he find some fault with something I didn't know I was doing wrong. As I'm wrapping the band around my bun, I hear his voice, barely above a whisper, "You should leave it down." He's still looking at the road and I'm not sure I heard him right.

"What?" I ask.

"Nothing."

I pause for a second, then I let my hair fall, still not entirely sure what he said. When I cast a side-eye in his direction, I see one side of his mouth tick up into a smile.

We drive in silence for a while, not because we've run out of things to talk about but because we're both aware of how much is riding on our reporting this weekend. He's already filled me in on Worldvision dos and don'ts of the weekend. "Engage people in casual conversation. Try to get the *Bachelor*

Bay host talking about himself, his hobbies, whatever he does outside of the show. If he's a drinker, let him drink. Don't ask him anything important until after he's had a few..."

I've taken notes on my phone and I'm committing them to memory. I'm more than a little nervous. This is a potentially big story and it's not my beat. There's a chance I'll come away with a great story but there's probably a bigger chance I'll screw something up. Jack has made it clear that's not an option.

"So, what's the point of this whole weekend thing? Is it just something Ken Nichols likes to do for fun?" I ask.

"Pretty much. He hosts people in his orbit, his wife gets to busy herself during the week putting the whole thing together, which she apparently loves, and he invites just enough work-related people that he can write the whole thing off."

"And he's really fine with you writing about his house and his non-work life?"

"Yes. He seems suddenly really excited about it, which is a little odd because he's very protective of his personal life." Even though he's looking straight ahead at the road, I can his eyes narrow. He doesn't look as certain as he sounds.

"Yeah?"

"Yeah. It's the first time he's invited me up here. The stars aligned."

"So, anything you find out this weekend is fair game for the profile?"

"Unless it's explicitly off the record. I guarantee Ken's not expecting me to ask him anything about your reality show other than numbers."

"Will he be annoyed?"

He shrugs. "I can handle him. And if there is something to your story, I'll take great pleasure in holding Ken's feet to the fire." He can't hide his smile. I get the feeling that nothing thrills him more than printing something no one else has.

And pissing off powerful people. He probably likes it more than sex.

"Ah. I see. Well, I'll take this opportunity to learn from the master," I say.

He steals a sideways glance at me, his smile still wide. "Oh, I might be able to teach you a thing or two. But I'd expect you to return the favor." At that point, I'm no longer sure he's talking about reporting.

No, of course he is.

He doesn't date. I don't either. We're on the same page. It's such a relief.

I'm such a liar.

19

JACK

THIS PLACE IS MASSIVE.

It's quite a testament to how much money can be made running a giant media company. Even knowing how much Ken Nichols earned last year in sheer dollars, it didn't fully translate until now. The property is bigger than most hotels.

I won't begin to debate CEO salaries and whether they're justified. Worldvision itself is valued in the hundreds of billions of dollars, and it has the power to influence the entire industry. It's why I work so hard to stay on top of everything Worldvision does. This weekend is important, and I need to make sure Linden doesn't go rogue and stir up trouble.

"Oh, Jack, ever a bright light. So good to see you," Judy Nichols says, smiling with toothpaste commercial teeth, as a white-gloved staff member opens my car door. She winks at me.

Linden has been welcomed on her side by another staff member who helps her out of the bucket seat and leads her out of the car to where I'm standing with Judy, who wears a dress with flowing pale-yellow layers that match her hair. She stands next to a small high-top table covered with a white cloth and a silver tray of champagne flutes. She holds one out to me and a second one to Linden, extending a hand to her.

"I'm Judy Nichols. So pleased you both could make it up for our weekend party."

I introduce Linden, who is gracious, confident, and charming in a way most reporters lack. We're generally so dogged about asking questions that we sometimes come off like we're conducting an interrogation, not a conversation. Linden sweeps in like the daughter Judy never had and with her smile, she puts Judy at ease and makes her want to be her friend. It's a gift.

"It's just lovely here. Thank you for the invitation," Linden says, for which I'm mildly relieved because she has a tendency to blurt things out and I'm not sure what she is making of the rolling lawns and manicured grounds in front of us. To say the Nichols's Montecito home looks like a five-star hotel would be an insult to this six-star palatial villa.

"Oh, you're sweet. We love it here," Judy says. "Okay, so, not to sound like a drill sergeant or anything, but you two should take a minute to freshen up and then join us when you're ready in the west garden. I don't want to rush you, but the sunset is at seven, so you'll want to make sure not to miss it. Cocktails first, then dinner. Hugo will show you where the *casitas* are. We've set up our property to mirror a hotel we visited once in Mexico, even hired the same architect."

"I'd love to hear more about it. Do you have pictures of what it looked like before the renovation?" I ask.

"Oh, ever the eager reporter. Yes, I'll show you everything. But not until you've had time to unwind. You need to get a feel for the place before I fill your head with facts."

"Good plan."

We're told there are a few required "recreational activities," Judy says, explaining that we all need to come to the lower lawn overlooking the ocean for cocktails and dinner tonight, and there's an afternoon sailing outing tomorrow.

And of course, more cocktails and an optional dinner. Other than that, we're on our own. We're told to think of ourselves as guests at a luxury hotel.

"Hugo, can you run these two lovelies down *Casita* Lane?"

It's the second time she's said the word—*casita*. I didn't take Spanish, but I know enough to understand it means a small house. It doesn't surprise me at all that this property has space for multiple residences. From the sweeping circular driveway, I can't even see the main residence, let alone any other buildings or the ocean, which I know is close by. I'd done a little research on Montecito and learned that Ken and his wife bought the property for eleven million dollars five years ago. At the time, there was only a low-slung mission-style house on the property and several acres of orange groves. I'm eager to see every square foot of the property, but I know I can't rush our hosts. I'll get a better story when they're ready.

Hugo has us hop in the back of a golf cart and drives us and our luggage to a corner of the property and pulls up in front of, sure enough, a small house. While we drive, Linden goes into full reporter mode, asking Hugo everything about himself, his family, his childhood. She's not doing it for a story. She's taking a genuine interest in him because that's what she's like, fascinated by people and their stories.

By the time we get to the *casitas*—which are not far away —Hugo has told us he's the youngest of six children born on a horse farm in Brazil. His parents and four brothers still live there, but he and his sister have been living in the US for fifteen years. "I was a cowboy who studied dentistry and now I work here. I have to say, this is the most fun."

He parks the golf cart and picks up our bags, motioning us along with him. "Follow me," Hugo says, leading us down a winding path to the front door of the house, past potted cacti and low hedges of lavender. At least I think it's lavender. It's purple and I'm not really a plant guy.

Linden looks at me, a little unsure. "Are we both staying here? Together?" she asks. I shrug.

"Yes, this is for both of you," Hugo tells us. I avoid Linden's gaze in case she's shooting daggers out of her eyes.

I hadn't thought to ask about the accommodations. I assumed the villa would have lots of rooms and we'd each have one. But Ken Nichols is a billionaire and it doesn't surprise me that his property has individual houses instead of guest rooms.

"This place looks big enough that a small family could get lost in it, so I'm sure we'll barely cross paths," I tell her, trying to be reassuring.

Hugo opens the French doors that lead out to a patio with a sweeping view of the ocean. Linden heads straight for the open doors while I thank Hugo. He has to make one more trip to the golf cart for Linden's other bag. I leave the door open for him and we look around. "This is the most beautiful place I've ever been. It's nicer than my apartment and I love my apartment. I want to move in," she says.

I breathe a sigh of relief that she seems enamored of the place, since it's a little awkward that we're shacking up, as it were. I'm so glad she doesn't seem to mind. I also make a concerted effort to look at the view of the ocean and not the gorgeous way the afternoon sun lights up her face, but it's hard.

"You probably could. This property looks big enough that Ken and Judy wouldn't even know you were here."

Then she turns to me, and her expression is hard. "Okay, What the hell is this? We're sharing a *housita* or whatever this is? You thought this was okay?"

Oh, shit. Guess she's not so enamored.

"It's a *casita*. A small house." If I steer the focus to nomenclature, perhaps I can distract her.

"Whatever. I didn't take Spanish. You thought it was okay to make me stay in a small house with you? And you didn't say anything? We had a two-hour drive with nothing to talk about."

"I thought we talked about lots of stuff."

"That's not the point. What were you thinking?

"I wasn't. I had no idea what the accommodations would be."

"You didn't think to ask?"

"No."

"Oh my god, you're such a guy."

"That, I am. Guilty." I throw up my hands. "I mean, look. It's a really nice small house. I'm sure it has five bedrooms or something. There's a hallway this way and that way. You don't even have to see me if you don't want to." I walk down one of the hallways and she follows.

At the end of the lane of hardwood is a spacious master bedroom with quilted pillow shams, a king-sized bed with a thick white cover, and a little couch in a corner. Same French doors to the patio, same view. "You can have this room," I say, unable to avoid the image in my mind of her naked on the bed. With me.

"Hell right, I'm having this room. You can stay in the kiddie bunk beds or whatever."

"Nice. Care to complete the tour with me and check out my dungeon?"

She looks gleeful. "Oh, I wouldn't miss it."

We retrace our steps down the hallway and spend a few minutes in the communal area, which boasts a full, well-appointed kitchen, with dark stone countertops and four barstools pulled up to an island. "Can you believe this is just a guesthouse? It's crazy. Look at this gorgeous granite," she says, running a hand over the countertop. "And how this toile sets off the cedar. I love it." I look at where she's gesturing to the blue and white fabric on the chairs, which sit opposite a fluffy white couch. The table is low and made of wood. I'm not much for home decor.

"Yeah. It's nice," I say, eager to see where I'll be laying my head for the night.

"Okay, impatient, are we?" she asks, tearing herself away from furniture ogling to go down the other hallway, which has three closed doors in different directions. One turns out to be a bathroom. The next is a laundry room combined with gym equipment. We go to the door at the end. Linden pushes it open, then turns on me and glares. "Well, enjoy sleeping on a desk." She turns and walks past me into the living room.

I take a look into the room, already knowing what I'll find —a large partner desk with an Aeron chair for ergonomic posture and a small beige couch. Of course there's no second bedroom. That would make my life too easy.

When I go back to the living room, she's standing there with her hands on her hips, furious. "Do I seem like a stupid person? Like someone who's just easy, who will shack up with you just because the opportunity presents itself?"

I kind of wish she'd settle down because the more irate she gets, the sexier I find her.

Behind us, I hear the doorbell of the *casita* ring and turn to find Hugo standing in the doorway, looking a little awkward. I don't know how much of her tirade he heard. From his expression, I'm guessing all of it.

"I'm sorry, I think there was a mistake. I think Mrs. Nichols assumed you were staying together…" His face is the shade of a beet. "Miss Linden, we have an empty casita if you'd like it. I'm really so sorry."

"Oh, it's not your fault. We just drove together but it would be *great* if we could stay separately," Linden says, walking over and giving Hugo a hug. I wish she didn't seem so joyful about our separate accommodations. On the plus side, I have to admit she has a way with people. She'll be an asset this weekend if some of the guests tell her things they might not feel as comfortable telling me.

Hugo picks up Linden's giant duffel and leads her out the

door while I take my much smaller suitcase into the master bedroom. The light scent of Linden's shampoo lingers in the room and I'm annoyed at the small part of myself that wishes it was her lingering instead.

Get your head in the game.

I'm here to do a job and I should be immensely grateful that we're not, in fact, sharing a *casita*. If the five minutes of Linden's ire was a sample of what lay ahead if we'd been stuck in the same space, I'd dodged a bullet when Hugo corrected the mistake. Looking at my phone, I see that I have a good half hour before the mandatory cocktail and mingle hour and I intend to use that to prepare. There's no chance I'm risking the opportunity to get close to Ken Nichols's life and take down every detail. To start with, I take out my laptop and start writing a couple of paragraphs of background color, just based on first impressions of the villa.

But not ten minutes later, there's a knock at my door. It's Linden, looking apologetic and a little sheepish. "I... I owe you an apology. I'm sorry I was being a jerk. After you were nice enough to drive all the way here and deal with the traffic, and agree to even have me along, which I know you didn't want to do, and I want you to know that I get that, and I really am grateful to be working on this story," she says, getting a little out of breath at the endlessness of her sentence.

I hold up a hand to stop her. "It's okay. It was a misunderstanding."

"It's not that I think you'd be a terrible roommate or anything. I just thought I was being tricked."

"I am an excellent roommate, actually, though it's been a while since I've had anyone around who could attest to that," I say.

She leans against the doorframe. "Okay, well, that's all I came to say." But she's lingering. And fidgeting. I also get a better look at what she's wearing now: a short skirt and some silky-looking top with a lightweight wrap and stiletto heels that make her nearly as tall as I am. Thankfully, she's left her hair down and it's now rolling over her shoulders. The woman standing in front of me is a near-total transformation from the jeans-wearing junior reporter I'm used to seeing every day. I could be done in by her hair alone.

"Do you want to come in for a minute? We don't have to be in the garden for a bit," I say.

"That's true. We've got a good hour."

I don't have to look at a clock to know we have way less than an hour. I'm not starting this weekend off giving Linden the chance to be late to anything. I know Ken well enough to understand that punctuality is important to him. "No. Not an hour. Twenty minutes tops."

A hint of a devilish smile creeps over her lips. "I'm kidding. I know you hate that I tend to be late."

"I don't hate it," I say. "I just don't get it."

"Yeah, time-conscious people don't. I don't know. I guess I'm just overly-ambitious about how much I expect to accomplish in the time given. So when I'm late, not only am I not punctual, I also feel unaccomplished."

"Sounds like an awful way to live."

"It's how I'm wired. I'm just telling you so you'll cut me some slack when I'm late," she says. She's still standing in the doorway, not making any moves to come in or leave.

"So… are you coming in? Or not?"

"I'm coming in. And you're raiding the little bar in the kitchen there and fixing me a drink." I'm amused by her boldness, but a little worried that if she starts drinking now, I might have to carry her back to her room a few hours later. I must look terrified. "Relax. I'm only having this one drink. I'll have seltzer water at the cocktail thing and at dinner. I'm not going to embarrass you or myself. I'm here to work." With that reassurance, she sweeps into my *casita*, swings the French doors open, and plops herself on the couch facing the ocean.

I'm then left to hustle her up a drink, and as I poke through the contents of the bar in the kitchen, I'm a little dumbstruck by her.

"How did you even know there was a bar in the kitchen?" I ask, finding some highball glasses in one of the cupboards and opening the freezer to see if there's ice. Of course, there's ice. There's everything a person could dream up or presume to want. I start mixing up some gin and tonics.

"I was just in here, remember? I notice kitchens. I'm hoping to own a place with a Pinterest-perfect kitchen someday, so I keep an eye out."

I hand her the cocktail and take a seat on the opposite couch, which means I don't have the ocean view. She immediately shakes her head. "No, you have to look at this view. Come join me in the expensive seats." She's so genuinely happy to be here, and it strikes me for the first time that despite her tendency to be late, she works long hours at the paper. She probably hasn't taken a vacation day since she came on board.

I move next to her, and immediately I'm aware of the precise distance between us, like a chasm I'm desperate to close, even though there's absolutely no precedent for that. And there's that damned lavender shampoo which I can smell as soon as I sit down. This weekend is going to be my own personal hell, spending two entire days and nights around Linden with no reason to be any closer to each other than we are now.

"Sure beats the office. I already feel relaxed," I say.

Linden stifles a laugh by taking another big swig of her drink, which she has trouble swallowing because of whatever she thinks is so funny.

"What?"

"No, I mean, it's just you. You're so not relaxed."

"What do you mean? I'm very relaxed."

Now she can't hold back and she's outright laughing at

me. Maybe it's the alcohol. It was a mistake to make the drinks this strong. I just felt like we needed an ice breaker to get us over the hump of awkwardness. We've never socialized outside of work, unless I count the bar the other night, so I want to make sure we don't annoy the crap out of each other.

"Now I'm getting paranoid. Why are you laughing?" I ask.

She tries to rein it in, but she's got a bad case of the giggles. "It's just funny to me that you think you're mellow, but you may be right. Maybe this is as relaxed as you get. I just assumed that when you left the office, maybe you'd cut loose a little bit."

I'm not sure what she's getting at. "Are you saying I'm uptight?" I ask.

"Not uptight. Just focused," she says.

"Whatever you want to call it, it sounds like you're calling me uptight."

"It's not a bad thing. It's clearly gotten you to where you are which is a pretty impressive place. If I end up being half as good a reporter as you are, I'll consider myself a success." The second she says it, she looks like she wants to take it back.

"That's a really nice thing to say. Thank you. Are you okay? You look like you just made yourself sick by saying something nice about me."

She waves it off. "I'm fine. But you already know Stuart thinks you walk on water. Your ego doesn't need my encouragement."

"My ego isn't the issue. We all need encouragement. Would you like me to say something nice about you?"

"You'd be able to pull that off? She looks genuinely surprised and starts to laugh. "I mean, sure. Have at it."

I take a moment because I want to come up with something good. Not a flippant compliment but something that shows I see what she brings to the table, even if I've given her a hard time until now.

"Oh, tell me it isn't that hard to think of one nice thing," she says, looking horrified.

"No, no, I'm just trying to come up with something really good."

Her face softens. "It doesn't have to be really good. Anything will do." I see the vulnerability there and realize she really doesn't know how good she is. I remember being new at the job and filled with self-doubt, but Linden always comes across as sassy and confident. Now I feel like the compliment has to be even better and I'm psyching myself out of saying anything because whatever I come up with will either sound overblown and insincere or insignificant and worthless.

Get a hold of yourself. You write words for a living. Come up with some.

"You have an ability to see tiny details that no one else does and make your reader experience them. It makes for good reporting."

I can't tell what she thinks for a minute because she looks down. I'm wondering if somehow according to the way her mind works, I've just insulted her. Then she smiles. "Thank you. Why'd I think you were such a bad guy?"

"I've been asking myself that very question for months," I say. She glances at me, then looks away, swirling her drink and taking in the ocean view.

"So, what's the plan? Do we divide and conquer? Go good cop/bad cop?" she asks.

It amuses me that she's so focused on our reporting mission. Not that I'm being blasé about it, but I'm not used to having a sidekick, so most of my planning goes on in my head and I'm not sure how to articulate the Bonnie and Clyde caper she seems to have in mind. "First of all, let's start slow. Get to know the reality show guy.

Then we can figure out if you or I have a better rapport with him."

"Okay, I'm fine with that. So just treat the cocktail thing like a cocktail thing? Mix and mingle?"

"Pretty much. We can't come off the ropes swinging and expect to get anywhere," I tell her. No one wants to feel like they're being interviewed when they're at a social event, but everyone likes to talk about themselves, so it's a fine line between being an attentive, inquisitive audience and being intrusive or probing. Linden is great with people, and she'll have no problem getting them talking. The only thing I worry about is her tendency to make assumptions—and jump to wild conclusions—but maybe she only does that with me.

"Okay." She's nodding and sipping her drink, which I see she's almost finished. I haven't looked at my phone again, but I have a pretty good idea that we need to head out in ten minutes or so.

"Be gracious and pleasant and do more listening than talking. We can reconvene back here later and see where we are. Sound good?" I ask.

"Yup," she says, taking another longing look at the ocean before turning to head back inside. She seems captivated. "D'you think we're going out on a boat like that one when we sail tomorrow?" she asks, pointing at a white-sailed vessel that's working its way along the coast.

"I have to imagine so, if it can fit more than a dozen people comfortably, but I don't know much about boats."

"Could be a multi-hull, like a cruising catamaran. Or maybe a cruiser yacht if he has enough crew."

"I take it you sail."

"No, but I've read a lot about boats and how to sail them. Living vicariously, I guess. In case you didn't figure it out, I grew up in a pretty landlocked place. The ocean is an endless fascination to me."

"Yeah, where'd you grow up?"

"Fresno. Central California."

I'm not sure why that surprises me, but it does. It occurs to me that in the year and a half we've worked together, I've barely asked anything about her. It's a matter of triage. I allocate my time to the stories I need to write, and I don't spend valuable minutes quizzing the people who sit next to me when I could be picking up one more interesting detail about a person or place. It can only be about the reporting.

Except for right now, when it all seems to be about her.

20
———————

LINDEN

CALLING where we're standing a *garden* is like calling Central Park a putting green. Yes, there are flowers and even a stretch of land that's home to an orange grove, a lemon grove and raised beds of strawberry plants, but the majority of the space is a stretch of lawn so large it could probably accommodate a regulation football field.

I have to remind myself not to act as starry-eyed as I feel in this place. The bottom line is that I've never experienced this level of opulence and although I can appreciate its grandeur and luxury, it makes me very uncomfortable. This isn't a life I aspire to have—the helipad and the lap pool and the sunning pool and the outdoor kitchen and cabanas. It's one thing when all these amenities are available at a hotel, but as a way of life? It feels like way too much to handle and way more than anyone needs.

On the other hand, I would be a terrible guest if I didn't do my best to enjoy myself while I'm here. So I head to the bar, staffed by two young bartenders, even though the expected crowd of two dozen could easily get by with one. Dressed in white dress shirts, black ties, and aprons, they look like every bartender I've ever seen at a party.

"What can I get you, miss?" one of them asks.

"Sparkling water with a lime, please?" He uncaps a tiny glass bottle and fills a cut crystal highball glass with ice before tipping the soda water bottle and adding a circular slice of lime on top. "Thanks," I say.

Before I step away from the bar and decide where to begin my mingling, I pause and take in the scene in front of me. Judy is standing with three other women, all of them closer to my age than hers and all dressed in short cocktail dresses and heels. I'm glad I opted for the skirt and heels tonight. I chose a silk camisole under my wrap, so there's a hint of implied sexiness, and right now I can feel the light breeze on the bare skin over my collarbone.

The garden is ringed by flower beds that are crowded with blooming plants, all of which look native to this area of Southern California. They fit seamlessly with the Spanish mission style of the villa. I notice low creeping jasmine mixed with rosemary, taller lavender, and purple salvia plants and hundreds and hundreds of tiny white roses.

Several people are grouped around high tables on the grass, chatting, and drinking. The sun is sinking lower over the water, but there's still ample time before sunset.

A couple of waiters weave throughout the crowd of twenty people who are already here, passing tiny *canapés* on silver trays. I can't see what they are from where I'm standing, and I doubt I'll eat any. The last thing I want is to have an hors d'oeuvre half-shoved in my mouth when someone tries to start up a conversation. Just like drinking sparkling water instead of alcohol, not eating seems like a safe choice.

I know Ken Nichols without having ever met him. He's impossible to miss, the full head of white hair, cream linen pants, and a navy sport coat like he stepped off a yacht. He's holding court among several men, one of whom is Jack. Almost as if he feels my eyes on him, he glances my way and waves me over.

I do my best to walk on my toes so my stiletto heels don't sink into the grass, and as I draw closer, Jack's eyes don't leave me. I'm pretty sure he's checking out my legs. And then my cleavage.

"Eyes up here," I whisper when I get close enough, which elicits a smirk from him, and only a momentary glance away from my chest.

"Ken, I'd like to introduce you to Linden, my date." His eyes bore into mine and he squeezes my hand hard, urging me to go along with his lie, even though I have no idea whether he's just messing with me or not. I grit my teeth in a fake smile in his direction and turn my attention to Ken. I'm determined not to screw up the opportunity for one of us to get a good story. I can't help but think Jack has pulled a fast one to try to throw me off my game, but I refuse to let him win.

I extend my hand to Ken, who shakes it. "I like a lady with a firm handshake," he says, laughing an old boys laugh to the other men in his circle. Then he introduces me. One of them is a golfing buddy he's known for years and the other one is the family doctor who's taken care of Ken and Judy since they moved to the Santa Barbara area. I don't know why I'm surprised that he's friends with his doctor. Of all the influential people he could entertain at his villa, he chooses his doctor. It's kind of sweet.

"So nice to meet you. I really appreciate you having us." I refuse to say anything else that will give him the impression one way or another about Jack being my boyfriend—or my date or whatever—not until I can get him alone and find out what his angle is. Why couldn't he introduce me as his colleague? "I was admiring your garden. So beautiful and all native plants, I see," I tell Ken.

"Something like that. Our landscaper said it was sustainable, which I like because we're in a drought zone. We can always turn off the sprinklers and kill the lawn, but the plants will survive."

"Jack, did you have a look?" I ask, suggesting with my gaze that he follow me to see the sustainable plants. And let me wring his neck.

"Ken, excuse me for a moment," Jack says.

I wait until we're a good distance away before I unleash my wrath through gritted teeth. "Why did you introduce me as your date instead of your colleague?"

"He assumed, so I went with it. That's why they put us in the same *casita*."

"But we fixed that situation. So why didn't you correct him?" I'm still not sure I believe that he didn't plan the mix-up to punish me for trampling on his beat.

"I was about to but then I started thinking… maybe this could work to our advantage."

"Oh, I'll bet you did. Just like sharing a *casita* would."

"That's not what I mean. I just figured you need to chat up Chad Whatever, the game show host—"

"It's not a game show."

"Whatever. I'm saying, if it seems like you're here as my date, you become less threatening because people won't assume you're here to dig up dirt for the paper. That will make Chad feel comfortable—he's used to people dating and arguing and feeling awkward."

"You got that part right."

Jack holds up a finger to stop me. "Most importantly, this saves you from the potentially awkward interaction when he tries to get you to sleep with him at some point this weekend."

"Wow, you've really thought this through. I didn't realize that before your magnanimous decision to aid my reporting by posing as your date, I was going to have to trade sex for a story."

"You weren't and you're not. But now you can talk to him

all you want and get as many juicy details as you can, and he won't push the issue. As I'm told he's known to do."

I'd heard that too. Maybe he has a point. It's just hard to believe he's really being nice to protect my honor and doesn't have some self-serving angle.

"And this has nothing to do with trying to sabotage my story by distracting me with… dating stuff?"

He smiles and it's so damned hot I want to grab him and throw him against a wall. "What kind of dating stuff?"

"Just… stuff that would distract me."

"I'm not saying that's off limits—"

"It's off limits."

He holds up his hands in mock surrender but he's still smiling that cocky smile that makes me wobbly in the knees. And everywhere else. "Whatever you say."

"Okay… I guess I could pretend to be your date. For the sake of my story." I couldn't muster enthusiasm yet for his plan. "But won't he think it's strange that we're staying in two separate houses?"

"I don't think he has any idea about that. But if you really want to play the part, you're welcome to share mine." That wicked smile is back.

"You'll take any opportunity, won't you?"

He laughs. "I'm human. And you're not playing fair with that short skirt and those heels."

I'm momentarily speechless, unsure whether he's flirting or just doing some kind of fake boyfriend impression. Or maybe it's the gin and tonic talking.

"I was taught that good journalists never play fair," I say.

His voice is a gravelly whisper when he leans in. "I certainly don't."

A shiver runs through my body at the timbre in his voice and the suggestion I'm not sure he intends. It's a struggle to turn the tone back to business, though I'm not sure he's implying I should. I take a better look at him and notice he must have changed his tie at the last minute before leaving the *casita*. This one has tiny starfish all over it.

"You changed your tie," I say, looking him over and letting the idea of pretending to be his date take root in my mind. For the weekend. Because we're both here anyway.

But what does that look like?

He runs a hand over it, but his eyes are still on me. "It seemed festive. And ocean-appropriate."

"It is. Quite." It takes an effort to pull my gaze from his face. It's like forcing myself to look away from the sunset right before the last bit melts into the ocean. Why would I ever want to look away? "So. I'm your date, huh? This oughtta be interesting."

"What makes you say that? Because I'm interesting?"

"You are."

"Why do I feel like you have a whole lot more to say? Come on, let's have it. If we're stuck here all weekend, we should at least be honest."

"Okay, I find you a little tightly-wound, a little scary and yes, a little interesting."

"Scary? Why am I scary?"

"Because you have the ability to crush my career in a single blow if I don't do well this weekend."

"I'm flattered you think I have that kind of power, but I'm afraid it's only Stuart who has the say on that." Of course he does. Which is why Jack wasn't able to remove me from my reporting position even though he believed I was too green and hiring me was a big mistake. Thinking about his words blunts the small glimmer of attraction I feel for a small glimmer of a moment. It's better this way. I can do the fake dating the same way I do my reporting, with focus and professionalism.

I'm tempted to ask how he thinks it's going so far, but I fear hearing something worse than what I already know, so I leave it at light flirtation that will go nowhere and the awkwardness of having to pretend to be his lady friend.

"Okay, let's mingle, sir." If I thought this weekend would be awkward it's just reached a whole new level of strangeness, and the only thing I can do is go along with it, unless I want to take a very expensive Uber ride home and throw in the towel on what could be a big story. Not a chance.

Jack starts walking me back toward the rest of the group but before we get very far, he abruptly turns and leads me to the bar. I look at him quizzically, holding up my still-full sparkling water. "I don't need a drink."

"Yes, you do. If we have to pretend to be a couple all weekend, we're gonna need some reinforcements."

"What about your whole stay sober, stay professional diatribe?"

"That was before I roped you into being my better half this weekend."

"Sure you don't have that backwards, given that you're the star reporter?"

"Would you stop calling me that? I'm just a regular reporter."

"With a Pulitzer."

"That's in the past. Today I have the same need as you to find the next big story."

The bartender is looking at us like we're not the first couple he's seen bickering at his bar. I realize that acting like a couple will be easier than I thought. Maybe now I'll be freer to tell Jack what I really think of him, all under the guise of romance. "I'll have a gin and tonic, please," I tell him.

"Make it two," says Jack.

"Sure thing," the bartender says, pouring gin into two glasses and reaching for a couple of tiny glass bottles containing tonic water.

I down the rest of my seltzer water and leave the glass on the bar, taking my new drink and walking back to where Ken is talking with a new group of men. He introduces them to both of us. "Neve here teaches Pilates to Judy five days a week. She's addicted and if I was a better man, I'd do it too. But I stick to golf and my core is the worse for it."

Neve is maybe twenty-five years old, but he's not the picture of the young, hunky trainer that sweeps silver fox ladies off their feet. He looks more like a jockey, just over five feet tall and wiry with a mustache. I can imagine him twisting himself into a pretzel like a performer in *Cirque du Soleil*.

We make our introductions and I see Jack exchanging waves with an older man who's coming down the stairs. He's dressed in similar wealthy man's casual as Ken—khakis, button-down shirt, and a white sweater tied around his neck. Ken explains their connection while Jack excuses himself to greet the man. "Jim Culligan and I go way back. Business school days, actually. He runs a restaurant supply company that pretty much has the rest of the industry playing catch-up. Good man. Jack will introduce you." He steps a few feet away to where another small group of men and women are gathered. "The Foxton crew! So glad to see you all." Ever the charming host, making his rounds.

I walk over to Jack, who is embracing Jim in a bro hug that appears to come with some history. Jack turns to me and introduces us. "Jim's like a second father to me. His son, Shane, was my college roommate," he says. I shake Jim's hand and listen while they reminisce. "How's Shane doing? Last I talked to him, he was thinking about moving back to California," Jack says.

"He's great, still finishing his hours. One more year 'til his Ph.D., I think."

"Shane's studying psychology," Jack tells me.

"Yeah, it's great. One of these days, I may actually be done paying tuition," Jim says, laughing. "But then I'll probably be paying for a wedding. Always something."

"You should only hope to be paying for a wedding. Shane is a confirmed bachelor, last I checked."

"You're one to talk," Jim says, winking at Jack.

Leaving us to chat, Jack goes back to the bar to fetch Jim a drink. I want to ask what Jack was like in college, but I decide to stick to less personal conversation. "I hear you're in the restaurant supply business. How'd you get into that?" I ask, immediately realizing he probably doesn't want to talk about work. I take a swig of my drink. Maybe I'll find conversational creativity at the bottom of the glass.

"Oh, well, my father owned a restaurant and he had so many different vendors for pots, pans, and sauciers; I always thought that was strange considering they were all made of metal. I started working on a vertically integrated solution while I was in business school and turned it into a real business once I graduated."

"You make it sound easy, but I'm sure there were challenging days." I'm genuinely interested in hearing his story, and he seems content to have an audience. He tells me about grades of metals and conductivity and curvature. I'm fascinated.

"Ah, there's my wife and daughter," Jim says, gesturing to a tall blonde woman who I immediately recognize as the platinum skank I saw Jack with at the bar. Now, knowing she's Jack's source who also happens to be married to a middle-aged guy who sells restaurant supplies, I feel seriously stupid for assuming it was a date. It was an honest mistake. From the back, she looks very young. And also, very Scandinavian. Like maybe she sailed in on a Viking ship. Her daughter is probably my age, also blonde but not as willowy. "Claudia's my wife. She was a model back in Iceland before we met. I was on a business trip there, if you can believe, looking for a vendor for stainless steel."

"Oh? I didn't know there was a big stainless-steel industry there."

"It's sizable if you know where to look." He waves them over, but they seem busy talking with Judy, who's talking a mile a minute and grasping Claudia's arm like she's never letting her get away.

"Well, they seem occupied, but you'll have to meet them later."

"I'd love to," I say, with a little too much enthusiasm, still trying to find the balance between grateful guest and fascinated dinner companion who takes an outsized interest in everything the other guests have to say, hoping some grain of information will leak out and confirm my story. At this point, I'm still figuring out the who's who of the guest list and trying to ascertain whether anyone else here is involved with *Bachelor Bay*.

Then I see Chad across the lawn, and with him, an opportunity to do some reporting. I look in the direction of Jack, knowing he'll have a minor coronary if I go after this guy myself. After a minute of staring—for legitimate journalistic purposes, I remind myself—I catch his eye and gesture to where Chad is standing alone, off to the side of the garden. Chad is looking around, getting a lay of the land. Then he heads for the bar. I make my way over there carefully, avoiding dips in the grass with my heels. Before I'm halfway there, Jack is by my side, ever the dogged reporter.

"What'd you say his name is?" he asks, gesturing with his head.

"Chad. He hosts the show."

"Bet you a hundred bucks that's a spray tan," he says.

"Well, you would know."

Jack gives me a look, like he might be offended by the insinuation. I wish I had better edit switch between my brain and my mouth.

At this point, the bartender must either think I have a drinking problem or that I have a thing for him, because it's the third time I've shown up in twenty minutes' time. He greets me with a smile that says he's thrilled either way, so I pretend to be very interested in a tree far beyond his head to avoid meeting his gaze. I've ditched the gin and tonic from five minutes ago and now I'm standing behind Chad, figuring I can just order drinks and spill them out all night if I have to. He senses my presence behind him and turns around.

"Oh, after you. What are you drinking?" he asks, smiling the reality show host smile I've seen on my TV a hundred times. Then he notices Jack and I see the wheels turning in his head, sizing up whether we're a couple or not.

"Gin and tonic," I say, still not making eye contact with the bartender, just in case he has some dumb idea about mentioning that I was just here a few minutes before. I'm pretty sure they're paid to keep quiet on such matters, but I can't risk it.

"A gin and tonic for the lady. And I'll have a bourbon. Neat." He ignores Jack, who asks for a bottle of water. I hear the bartender tell him to hang on a sec while he opens a new case. Chad leans on the bar, smiling.

"I had a roommate who drank bourbon," I say. It's not true, but it's a way in.

"But not anymore? No roommate? Or your roommate no longer drinks bourbon?"

"No roommate."

"Ah, was this a boyfriend roommate or the regular kind?" He doesn't waste time getting to the facts. I look him over, not that I haven't stared at his face on *Bachelor Bay*. But he looks different now and I realize how much makeup he must be wearing on the show because his face is a mess of freckles and there's no evidence of that on TV. Plus, I'm pretty sure he's wearing contact lenses because his eyes are an unreal shade of dark blue that comes from putting blue contact lenses over brown. His dark hair falls over his forehead in a lazy flop and all I can think is that he's got nothing on Jack.

"It was the regular kind."

"Ah, good to know. I'm Chad."

"Linden."

By now, Jack has been hovering silently long enough, so I introduce them. "Nice to meet you, Chad," Jack says.

"Are you two…?" Chad asks, pointing back and forth between us to imply we're a couple.

"She's my date. I'm a reporter with the Examiner." I see Chad flinch, but his camera-ready smile is too wide to betray anything. "I'm working on a profile of Ken this weekend, and Linden is extra fun, so I dragged her with me." He looks at Chad, testing out the lie on him and gauging his reaction. So far, so good. Chad seems intrigued.

"Extra fun, huh? I'd like to see what that means." He gives me his *Bachelor Bay* smile, which exposes his entire top row of straight, white teeth. They're almost too perfect to be real.

Jack puts a hand on my shoulder and whispers in my ear, "I think you'll have a better rapport with him if I'm not here. I'll catch up with you in a bit. Good luck." I'm already feeling a shiver from his breath so close to my ear, but then he kisses me on the cheek before walking away. I blink a few times, reeling a bit from the kiss and feeling a flush creep over my face. I try to refocus my attention on Chad, who doesn't seem at all unhappy to continue chatting with me solo.

He smiles. "Do you need to go, or can I monopolize a little more of your time?"

"Oh, no, I'm good. Tell me, what's your connection to the Nichols family?"

He looks momentarily taken aback that I didn't recognize him from the show, which was my intention. Make him work a little harder and tell me everything. "Oh, I um, work on one of the shows Ken's company produces."

"Maybe I've seen it. Which show?"

"It's called *Bachelor Bay*," he says, waiting for a reaction. I squint at him like I'm trying to place that information in context. "I'm the host of the show." I can tell it annoys the hell out of him that I'm not fawning all over him, but I can also see that he's going to go to great lengths to explain just how important he is to the show.

"Wow, that's so cool. So, you *are* the show, sounds like."

He feigns modesty. "I don't know if I'd say that, but I do have to keep everything on track, so the audience has some context for what the contestants are doing and feeling."

"*Bachelor Bay*. Sounds like a dating show. Am I right?"

"More or less. It's twelve bachelors on a yacht docked in a resort town and they're given tasks to see if they can impress women who they meet in bars or on beaches. And eventually, a bunch of them live on the yacht and the couples are winnowed down until only two couples remain."

"Two couples? Is it a foursome?"

He raises his eyebrows and winks. "Oh, I can see you'd be helpful in creating the spinoff."

I feel like it's working. He's getting comfortable, wanting to tell me more. I still have a long way to go to close the gap and get him to slip out information about the show being staged. But the night is young, and I have tomorrow as well. Baby steps.

Chad has me cornered in a small space with a cocktail table at my back and I wonder if it's intentional that he isn't giving me an easy escape route. Every so often, he reaches out a hand and touches my arm or brushes it against my shoulder. He's on his second drink now and he's leaning in close, breathing his bourbon breath against my face when he talks.

"I'm lucky to be able to do a job I love in such a beautiful location."

"Do you ever want in on the action? What would happen if you wanted to date one of the women from the show? Is it forbidden?"

"Oh, strictly forbidden. It's rule one. All the action takes place on camera." He takes the opportunity, as he's already done several times, to lean close enough that he can look down my shirt. I don't have breasts like spin class Cassie, but they're a full handful and I know he's helping himself to a nice show. I feel like I need a shower.

"Sounds strict." It's not like I expect him to reveal a scandal to a complete stranger, but at this rate, I'm going to have to spend half my weekend with this guy's glassy eyes roaming all over my body if I want him to tell me anything.

From behind him, I catch the eye of Jack and try to give him a signal that I'm making good inroads. But he doesn't look at all happy. Is he just being his usual self and figuring out something I'm doing wrong?

The scowl on his face doesn't disappear when he walks over to the bar and orders himself another drink. I can't be sure if it's because Chad is monopolizing my time or if he isn't the one doing the reporting. But it was his decision to walk away. Until I know for sure, I'm not going to trust him completely.

THE SUN MELTS AWAY into the ocean and there's a momentary silence as we all admire the view. "I'm starting to understand your obsession with the ocean. It's pretty hard to look away," Jack says, stepping next to me for the first time in a while.

"I'm not sure I'd use the word obsession," I say.

"Are you always this argumentative?"

"Pretty much. Argumentative, opinionated, quick to make assumptions. "

He laughs. "At least you're honest."

"What was with your abrupt exit when we were talking to Chad?"

He runs a hand through his hair and shakes his head. "I didn't mean to be abrupt. But I got a quick read on him and saw I was only going to be dead weight if I stood there any longer. He was much more comfortable talking to you."

"You figured that out in all of thirty seconds of talking to him?"

"Pretty much. Some people—and I hate to play the gender card, but I'm gonna—some guys clam up when another guy they don't know starts asking questions. I could tell he was uncomfortable the second he heard the word reporter."

"Ah. I picked up on that too."

"So I hightailed it away, figuring he'd relax and you'd have better luck broaching the subject of your whistleblower's allegation."

"He hasn't told me anything so far. But I have all weekend."

Judy rings a tinkling dinner bell and asks everyone to make their way up the path to the dining area, which I can see above us surrounded by twinkle lights and pillar candles. The other guests turn away from the water and obey Judy's instructions, but Jack doesn't move.

"Is everything okay?" I ask, wondering why he's suddenly frozen.

He's staring at the water, maybe catching a final glimpse before dinner. But we'll have the same view from the upper level where we're headed, so I'm not sure that's the reason.

Then he turns on me. "Are you hoping to spend the whole weekend with him?" His tone is accusatory and I'm not sure if I'm about to get a lecture on getting a source to open up.

I shrug. "If I need to. He's talkative, and he seems pretty easy with the drinking. I'm sure I can get him to tell me more, eventually. On the downside, he's kind of a creeper and I'm going to have to spend a lot more time with him this weekend and he's a little handsy."

"That's nauseating."

"It's fine. I'm a big girl. I can take care of myself."

He takes a long slow gaze over my entire body, and even

though Chad eyed me much the same way, when Jack does it, it feel anything but sleazy. It feels hot and sexy. "There may be something I can do to help."

"Really. I'm fine. I don't need your help."

But he's already wrapped a hand around my waist and pulled me toward him. The suddenness and intimacy causes my breath to hitch. "You sure? Because I can be very helpful."

I feel my heart start to pound and I'm self-conscious that he can feel it too, now that he has his hand on me. "What, exactly, do you mean by that?"

"Chad has no idea what your relationship is to me. Maybe he's the kind of guy who wants what he can't have. Maybe it would pique his interest if he saw us do this." He reaches his other hand up and tilts my chin up toward his face, then lets his fingers trail along my jawbone to where they wrap around the nape of my neck.

I meet his eyes, questioning his intention but his icy stare betrays nothing. He lowers his lips to mine, lightly brushing them with his before sinking in deeper and claiming more of my mouth against his. My insides twist and my brain turns to jelly. I feel myself responding to the soft touch of his hand in my hair and the firm insistence of his lips.

For a moment I forget where I am, what my name is, why we're here. I can only think about kissing him and wanting to follow him down this delicious, slippery slide.

After a moment, he pulls away, but his eyes betray nothing. The tiniest smile forms on his lips and he leans in again, feathering his breath over my cheek, running his tongue lightly over my bottom lip. Once, then again. Coaxing my lips apart until his tongue slips inside. He's in no hurry, lazily letting his tongue roam and tangle with mine. Without thinking about what I'm doing or why I'm doing it, I reach my hand to feel the hard line of his jaw, such a contrast with the gentleness of his lips. His stubble feels rough against my fingers and so damn sexy.

Then he slowly pulls away, keeping his eyes glued on mine.

I can't read the expression on his face. It looks like part relief, part satisfaction, part raw, unrestrained heat. "That might persuade him to keep his paws off you," he says, looking past me. I follow his gaze and see Chad in the distance, but I can't see him well enough to discern whether he looks disappointed.

But now, at least, I understand what just happened.

"So that was for Chad," I say, just making sure we're both clear on the meaning of his kiss. Because my brain is fuzzy and my body is still tingling from the effects of him, and now I'm adding the building anger that makes me want to punch him in the face. "Seriously? You're as bad as he is. I'm not a pawn you can play when it suits you, and I didn't ask you to intervene and make all the other potentially interested men run away. I'm not yours to save from some other guy."

"I never said you were any of those things. And I don't think you need saving."

"So why the little performance for Chad?"

"Sometimes it helps to stir the pot." The glimmer of a smile forms, like he's playing a game of chess and just made a bold opening.

"Oh." I'm not sure what to say, which is unusual for me.

"That's all you got?"

"Um, well, I have questions."

"Of course you do; you're a reporter."

I take a step back and stare at him, backlit by twinkle lights that cast a flattering glow on his already-beautiful face. "Are you going to answer them?"

He shrugs. "You haven't asked anything yet. Is that how you usually go about your reporting? You just wait for the other person to answer questions you haven't even posed?"

"Just when I thought I might like you a tiny bit, you have to ruin it, don't you?"

His smile is a smirk now and he reaches for my hand, pulling me a little closer. "You like me?" he asks, his voice a quiet rumble.

"I'm still deciding."

Then he whispers, "Let me help you decide." He leans his face an inch closer to mine but doesn't close the gap between us. A chill runs through me as my body responds to him, betraying the logical part of my brain that says I need to focus on my job and only my job. The only clear thought I have right now is how much I want to feel his lips on mine again. But he's still inches away, holding out, not willing to give me what I want until I meet him partway.

"I think… Chad seems like the kind of guy who needs a lot of convincing before he decides he has no chance."

"So, for the sake of a good story…" I say, moving an inch closer but stopping before my lips meet his so he knows I'm in control of my emotions. Even though I'm not.

"…I know how important good journalism is to you," he says. I can feel his breath like a breeze across my face. It's hypnotizing and I struggle to keep from closing my eyes and giving in to what I want.

"I'm one hundred percent devoted to the craft." It's a struggle to get the words out when I can barely breathe.

"I'm happy to help however I can." Our faces are mere inches apart and I feel pulled closer, unable to resist the magnetic force of his lips. I tip my head up and feel his lips melt into mine, pressing gently but intentionally. It's sweet but urgent. Tongues that can't get nearly enough, lips that want to consume. This isn't a sweet fake-date kiss. This is a year and a half of working together and wanting to hate him but hating how much I wanted him, all tangled up in a kiss that can't last long enough. Especially at a party. In public. At the home of the most influential CEO on Jack's beat.

It's almost as if we both realize it at the same time and draw back, a little bit shocked at the intensity that caught us off guard and drew us in that far. But he's still holding me against him, and I can feel his heart beating in his chest. His voice is a low growl. "Um, okay. Maybe I got a little carried away there," he says, running a hand through his hair. When normally I might find it amusing to pick up on his tell, which says Jack is just slightly uncomfortable. Right now, it's the last thing I want to see.

"Yeah. I know. Sorry."

He looks taken aback. "Why sorry?"

"Just, this is work. We shouldn't get… distracted." That's what he's implying, right? We need to stay focused on the story and what it takes to get it.

He closes his eyes for a long beat, and when he opens them, his gaze is hard. "Right. I think I got swept up in the whole Chad thing."

"Well if he was watching that, I think it's safe to say he got the message."

"I think he did."

Jack takes a step back from me and for a moment, I think he's going to turn and walk away. Instead, he reaches for my hand and gestures with a tip of his head toward the terrace and we start to walk. He glances to the side again to where Chad stood earlier and looks satisfied with his performance. Like maybe Chad will stay just interested enough to talk to me but not so unclear on the boundaries that I'll feel uncomfortable.

But when I turn around, I don't see anyone there.

21

LINDEN

EVER THE MEDDLING HOST, Judy has arranged the seating so the men sit in every other chair, with women between them. From what I can tell, no one is sitting next to the person each of us came with.

Seated on opposite sides, Jack and I are at one end of a long table that stretches down the middle of a terrace above the garden where the cocktail hour was held. This is no ordinary table. Covered in a series of white cloths, it stretches twenty-four feet in length. I know because my shoe is just under a foot and if I take a short stride, it covers about one foot. And I walked the length of it because I was in sheer awe that a dining table like that even existed. At three feet wide, the square footage of that table alone is bigger than my bedroom.

Along the center of the table, a tangle of perfectly placed tiny twinkle lights wind around bleached pieces of driftwood intertwined with flower vines that look like they've fallen from a fairy tree, but which I know must have taken a florist hours to assemble. Small votives dot the length of the table, which is set with silver charger plates and napkins with seashell rings tying them into a fan shape. The silver-backed

Chiavari chairs are made extra comfortable with silver padded seat pillows. It's a level of wealth and attention to detail I am only familiar with through my reporting, not my own life.

Everyone around seems to have had way more drinks than I had, and people are talking loudly, cackling at inappropriate humor, and having a good time. At the head of the table, Ken beams at his guests and talks with the two men seated closest to him: his doctor and his golf buddy. I can see that Jack isn't going to have a chance for any one-on-one conversation with Ken over dinner, but I can tell his reporting antenna is up, because every so often he subtly makes a note or two on his phone in his lap. At least, that's what I think he's doing.

I'm sitting next to Jim Culligan on one side and Judy Nichols's surf instructor on the other. I can't decide what fascinates me more, the multi-million-dollar restaurant supply business Jim Culligan built from scratch or the fact that Judy has a surf instructor. His name turns out to be Buzz and he's more than just a surf instructor. When Judy introduces us, she sings his praises and lets me know he's won more than one world championship. As someone who's more comfortable on dry land, surfing is pretty fascinating to me—at a distance.

Jim goes to the bar—which has been moved up to the terrace—for a stronger drink than the table wine I'm currently drinking, so I take a little time to chat with Buzz. He tells me he learned to surf in his front yard, which happened to be on the big island of Hawaii.

"I guess if you grow up there, surfing is like playing little league?" I ask.

"Yea, most of my friends grew up on those beaches and learned to take big waves before they could drive."

"How big is big?"

"Fifty footers. Eventually, we started competing, which

meant we had to go over to some of the other islands. My dad had a military scholarship that paid for grad school. He ended up on a base on Oahu at first, then he started working on the big island and we moved."

"What kind of work does he do?"

"He's a psychologist. My mom too. They met in grad school."

This is why I love being a reporter. I'm not even writing a story about Buzz—not today, at least—but I love the excuse to sit and ask people questions. Everyone has a story and most of them are far more fascinating than they believe they are.

"Do they still live in Hawaii?"

"Yup. Never left. They love it."

He takes a bite of the endive salad on his plate and stretches his arms in the air like it's helping him digest his food. I try to catch Jack's eye, but he's wrapped up in a conversation with a gorgeous blonde woman who's seated next to him. I haven't met her yet and I have no idea which couple she's a part of, but from her body language and flirtatious smile, I have a feeling she may have come solo. I remind myself that Jack is just doing the same thing I'm doing, being a good listener, and asking questions to engage the people around him. That's why we're here, to gather tidbits of background information and get what we need for a story.

It shouldn't bother me that she's gorgeous or that Jack looks like he's enjoying her attention so much. But the fact that I'm feeling anything is reason enough that kissing him was a mistake. It's already distracting me and throwing me off my game, which is the last thing I need.

When Jim comes back with his drink, I turn in my chair to face him, intentionally looking away from Jack and the blonde woman. There's a lot I can learn about the restaurant supply business and there's no time like the present.

"Well, my father started a small business which, believe it or not, produced the little paper ruffles that restaurants used to put on the ends of legs of lamb. You're probably too young to even remember those, but I grew up in a house full of little experiments like that one. And it's not an exaggeration to say the whole business grew from there..."

I take a sip of my wine and listen to him talk, his words starting to blend together after a while. I can tell he's an all-business guy who can talk about his company all day long but once I try to pivot the conversation away from it, he'll clam up. I've already tried a couple of times with innocuous questions about his family or his hobbies and he looked at me like I was speaking another language. It's fine. I don't need to glean information from Jim. I can sit and discover more about pots and pans.

In the time I've been a reporter, I've learned to read people and I know when to take my toys and go home. As much as Buzz is an open book about his life, his parents, his love for surfing, Jim is equally closed.

Instead, I look again over at Jack, trying to catch his eye, looking for some sign that his kiss wasn't solely motivated by the story we're chasing.

THE DINNER PARTY setup doesn't allow for much mixing and mingling while we're all seated. The meal itself isn't formal. There are buffet stations set up along the perimeter of the terrace serving prime rib, cracked crab, seared rare tuna, and vegetarian pasta. Assorted salads and side dishes are further down. But once everyone's seated, Ken and Judy engage in a series of toasts and introductory games designed to help us get to know one another. It's nice because it helps me put names to the faces at the table, but it also means we're sitting down for a good hour with no chance to talk to get up and mingle.

Finally, there's a break before the desserts and coffee and

I'm able to get up and stretch my legs. I want to check in with Jack, but before I can even look in his direction, Chad corners me by an oversized piece of Italian pottery that's been turned into a fountain.

"How's it going?" He's standing about a foot closer to me than he needs to be, and I realize that in no way is he deterred by Jack or anything he might have seen us do in the garden. Or maybe he's invigorated by it, because he reaches for my hand and leads me to the bar.

I've kept pretty good track of what I've had to drink: one strong gin and tonic with Jack hours ago, two aborted gin and tonics in the garden, and a glass of white wine during dinner. It's not the greatest combination and likely to leave me with a headache in the morning, but the result is that I'm seeing and thinking clearly now and if Chad insists on pulling me along with him, I plan to work him for my story.

"What are you drinking? Let's see if I remember, vodka soda?"

I shake my head. The bartender has a better memory than Chad and mouths "gin and tonic" to me while already pouring the drink.

"No? Not vodka soda? Don't all women drink vodka soda? It's like a thing."

"If it is, it's not my thing," I say, thanking the bartender for my drink. I don't plan to have more than a couple sips.

Chad has another bourbon and he takes a long sip. I can tell he's pretty drunk already, which means it's probably a pretty good time to chat him up. "Can we sit?" I gesture to a bench at the edge of the terrace and he walks over with me.

"I'm dying to hear more about your job. It sounds so fun and interesting. Do you get to travel?"

He leans back and smiles. "Yes, quite a bit. Every season we film at a different oceanside location, so I've been all over the world at the most exquisite beaches."

I decide this is the time to use whatever charm and feminine wiles I can muster to my advantage. I turn my face up to Chad and smile. "I have a confession to make. I wasn't entirely truthful with you earlier."

Chad breaks out his TV smile, dimples dancing on his cheeks, while he waits for whatever I'm going to tell him like it's Christmas. "Yeah?"

"I knew you were the host of *Bachelor Bay*. You'll have to forgive me for being such a fangirl, but... I am. I've seen every episode. I just love it."

I can see from the way his breath quickens that I've just given him the biggest hard-on of his life. "Oh yeah? Why didn't you say so?"

"I didn't want you to think I was only talking to you because I'm a fan of the show."

He immediately takes me up on the suggestive implication. "Huh. Was there another reason?"

I smile and tilt my head like he and I both know there's a much better reason. From his wolfish expression, I can tell he's willing to find out exactly how good my reason is.

I inwardly hate myself a little bit for using the implication of sex or even just basic flirtation to get what I want. I worry that being a work whore doesn't make me much different than any other kind of whore and I'm not sure I want that to enter the equation.

Then I harken back to what one of my favorite journalism teachers once told me. Sandy Tanner was a pale, freckled redhead who could never be bothered with working out, which meant she had a lanky soft body that was as non-threatening as her sweet face. She'd taken on a story about a cult in her early reporting days and gotten access to the cult leader.

"He kept telling me I looked too sweet to be an investigative reporter. What does that even mean?" she asked me, dimples engaging when she smiled.

"I'd have been insulted," I told her.

"Who has time for that? I used it to my advantage and kept asking innocent questions, playing the part of the halfwit he thought I was and telling him I didn't understand until he'd broken everything down for me in detail. He didn't think I had the guts to write anything bad about anyone. He underestimated me," she told me. She'd gone on to write a scathing ten-part expose on the cult and its inner workings which led to the arrest of the cult leader and a dozen of his disciples who were planning a murder spree that rivaled Helter Skelter.

At the time, I sat like a child at the knee of a wise grandmother, soaking up every morsel of advice she was willing to give. I wanted to be a great reporter and I knew I could learn a lot from her.

"I told him I was going to write horrible things about him, and he didn't believe me. He'd sit and tell me exactly what he dreamed of doing, to the letter, and I wrote it up like a bible for the cops to trace his steps."

If she could use her innocent appearance to break down the reserves of a cult leader for a story, I could use a little flirtation to get Chad to give me some behind the scenes dirt on *Bachelor Bay*. It was a far cry from taking him back to my *casita* for a midnight romp in my *en suite* hot tub. Flirting was innocent.

"Let's just say I wanted to meet you," I say. Chad takes a step closer to me and I can smell the bourbon on his breath. Unlike the way I felt when Jack pulled me close, this proximity to Chad is a little revolting. His eyes leisurely run over my body and his thoughts don't need translation into words to be crystal clear.

"I'm glad to meet you too," he says, picking up my hand and kissing the inside of my wrist. It's so revolting I almost cringe, but instead, I hold his gaze and use this moment to get more information.

"So, this is my chance. I'm here with one of the biggest TV

stars, ever. And I'm so excited. Can I ask you about the show?"

"Sure," he says. "I'll tell you whatever you want to know." I'm counting on that.

"I want to know all about the contestants. I mean, what a bunch of personalities! It's hard to believe you had such good luck finding all of them," I say.

"I know. Our casting folks do an amazing job."

"How many people apply to be on the show?"

"Hundreds of thousands. There's a crazy intense screening process." He's still holding my hand in one of his, grasping his drink in the other.

"Do you have a big part in picking the contestants? You must have a lot of influence because you know what works and what doesn't."

"Yeah, I'm an exec producer, you know, so I play a big part in casting the show."

I bat my eyes like I'm enthralled by his account and the attention he's paying to me. He moves even closer, and I wonder if he thinks this is some sort of foreplay. The way his gaze searches my face like he's fighting how badly he wants to kiss me. I can see that talking about his large influence on the show is an enormous turn-on for him.

"Tell me about Jake. I mean, he's a piece of work, but everyone loves him."

"Totally. He makes my job easy," he says.

"Could you tell he was going to be a fan favorite when he walked in the door?"

"I knew he had charisma and he wasn't gonna say no to anything. That makes for great television."

"What do you mean? What kinds of things was he open to doing that other people would say no to?"

He winks. "If I told you, I'd have to kill you. Can't let you see how the sausage gets made. No pun intended." I ignore the image of anyone's sausage. I'm not expecting to get the down and dirty details yet. But I have only two days to break him down and I need to start now while he's liquored up.

I lean in a little closer, doing my best to meet his gaze. Then I bite my lower lip. "It's funny. I almost feel like Jake is the kind of guy who'd want to break the rules. Push the boundaries of what's allowed."

His eyes go glassy as I release my lower lip and tilt my head up to his, lips parted in the most suggestive way I can manage. He's looking at me with feral wanting, like he can't decide what he wants more: to keep talking about himself or to fuck me in front of twenty people.

Then his face falls because he's not drunk enough to tell me what I want to know. A small part of his brain must be intruding and telling him to keep his dick in his pants and his mouth shut. Because he takes a step back. I can see the focus return to his eyes, just a bit.

"Well, he can't. He may be open to anything, but we give everyone rules and constraints. Within that, they can have fun, but it's not a bacchanal."

I deflate a little bit, realizing I'm not going to get what I want, at least not tonight. I'm also aware that the flirting and suggesting I've already done didn't get me there and I'm a little horrified at the idea of what it might take. I'm not willing to fuck this guy for a story. That's a firm line in the sand I will not cross. But maybe there are more creative ways to get what I want.

I smile at him sweetly, lest he think I'm not still interested in talking to him this weekend. "Of course it is. That's not at all what I was thinking. I just figured with your expertise that you have a great feel for when someone might be a rule-breaker in a good-for-television way."

"Oh, well, for sure I know that. With some people, you can see the fuses lit from a mile away."

I decide it's enough for night one. I've laid some good groundwork for spending more time with him this weekend.

I will flatter him and work his ego until he tells me what I want to know, just like Sandy Tanner did with her cult leader.

From across the terrace, Judy rings a dinner bell, signaling that we should sit back down for more toasts and forced conversation. I wonder if the whole weekend will be orchestrated according to a schedule she controls with a bell. I know myself well enough to realize that I will flat-out rebel if that's the case, so I hope, for my sake and hers, that there's far less structure coming in the next two days.

I also know types like Chad well enough to know that their egos are stroked when women leave them wanting just a little bit. I lean in and put a hand on his chest. "Chad, this has been so much fun. But I guess we're wanted back at the table. Can we pick up this conversation tomorrow? I'm dying to hear more about your work. So fascinating."

On cue, the lust returns to his expression and he nods. "Of course. Tomorrow. I look forward to it."

I turn to go, my hand on him until I step away, hoping the seed of what I need to get is planted. After a few paces, I sneak a look behind me, and sure enough, Chad is still watching me walk away.

Mission accomplished.

"LET'S FACE IT, this guy is probably a non-event," Jack says when I report to him what I've learned so far.

We're standing in a far corner of the terrace, tucked behind a four-foot-tall planter with an equally large agave plant flourishing from within. I've decided to treat myself to a full gin and tonic, not one that I will pretend to sip and abort after twenty minutes in favor of three glasses of sparkling water. Being a responsible reporter is wreaking havoc on my bladder and after all the water, I've needed two trips to the bathroom already.

I can't understand why Jack has such a low opinion of my reporting. "Why do you say that?"

"I just think you're on a fishing expedition and it's gonna be hard to reel this one in unless you do more than ask him to spill his guts."

"Jesus, are you seriously suggesting I chase him down and fuck his brains out?"

Jack looks aghast. "Hardly. Jesus, no. Are you kidding?"

I'm so surprised by his vehement response that I'm momentarily devoid of words. "Oh. Okay. Well, good."

He shakes his head. "I'd never suggest that." But something in his expression seems wary.

"What then?"

"I'm not sure. Two days isn't a lot of time to get someone to trust you enough to tell you their star contestant had a fling and got someone fired over it for the sake of ratings. I'm not sure two years is enough."

Now I'm annoyed. The whole reason I agreed to come on this faux lost weekend with a guy I don't even like was the promise of landing a great story. The last thing I need is Jack second guessing it now that I'm here.

"You're infuriating. Why did we even come here?" I'm tempted to punch him, though I know that won't exactly make me look like a professional journalist in his eyes. Maybe I don't care. Maybe that would make me look more professional.

He holds his hands up in mock surrender. "Easy there. I'm not saying there isn't reason to be here. I just don't want you to shoehorn in a story where there isn't one."

"And I don't need you to assume I can't get him to talk when he still might."

Then I storm back to my seat at the long dinner table,

resigning myself to more conversation with the men sitting next to me until Judy decides I'm free to roam.

I look over at Jack, who has planted himself back between the full-breasted women at the table, but instead of ogling them, he's staring straight at me, possibly trying to figure out what the hell bug flew up my ass to make me so difficult.

If I could answer that question, I'd probably be in a relationship right now.

22

———

JACK

JESUS, is she ever infuriating.

It's not enough I had to watch her practically allow that Chad moron to lick her face while he was talking to her, but now she's stomped away, and I have no idea why she's so pissed.

And I wish I could stop looking at her.

Ever since she walked into my room in those fuck-me heels and that wisp of a skirt, all I've been able to think about is what's underneath.

"So, am I right in thinking you're a reporter," the woman to my right says. Maybe she thinks it because I told her I was a reporter when I introduced myself an hour ago and she asked me how I knew Ken. Or maybe this is just her way of sparking conversation. Either way, it forces me to look away from Linden, which I do reluctantly. Even though I can't hear anything she's saying to that guy who looks like a surfer dude, I can't take my eyes off her. When she's talking, there's such a sparkle of joy in her eyes and genuine gratitude in her smile that I don't doubt she could get anyone to tell her their darkest secrets. Including Chad. Which is why I feel like an

174

asshole for implying she's not going to be able to get him to talk.

What I don't want—what I can't stand the thought of—is her somehow liking the guy. The way she was standing near him earlier and touching his chest, it made it seem like maybe there's a spark there. She could be working him for a story, or she could be falling under the spell of a guy who's so made-for-TV fake-gorgeous that she'll forget all about why she's here. That was the point of my comment. I wanted to light a fire under her and make her stay focused on the story.

I know I need to engage with Hillary, who's just asked me a question and who I'm pretty sure is married to the surfer dude—but I take one last lingering glance at Linden, hoping the vision of her will stay seared in my brain when I'm forced to converse with Hillary. Now Linden is smiling, listening to the surfer dude like what he's telling her is the most fascinating thing in the world. She has the makings of a great reporter because of her genuine interest in people.

And now I turn back to Hillary, who's waiting expectantly for my response. "You're correct. I am a reporter."

"Oh, that must be so fascinating."

"It is." Except for right now when I don't have any interest in her or whatever story our conversation may spark in my brain. But I force myself to focus.

There's a half-full bottle of wine within reach, so I offer to pour some into Hillary's glass and fill my own. That will make the next spate of toasts and roasts halfway bearable.

Even though this is by far the nicest home I'll probably ever visit, there's a reason I dislike events like this one: the forced merriment and socializing. But I'll do anything it takes to get the scoop on Ken, and I'm intrigued by the assortment of people he lets into his inner circle. It interests me that about half are trusted allies like Tim and the rest are paid trainers who attend to Ken and Judy's recreational needs. I have a feeling Ken values their discretion about his non-working life and pays for it with these lavish invitations. I'll dig into that angle later, because right now I feel too distracted.

If I'm honest, the only person I'm thinking about right now is Linden. I know she's pissed over my comment about Chad, but how pissed? Is she going to freeze me out for the rest of the weekend or is she already over it?

Maybe Hillary can help me decide. "Can I ask you something about women?"

"Ooh, this oughtta be juicy. Sure."

"Okay, so when someone says something that annoys me, I stay there in the fight until it's resolved. With some of the women I know—and I know I'm generalizing, so apologies— sometimes they have a tendency to walk away. What's that all about? Why not just resolve the thing?"

Hillary's nodding like she knows exactly what I'm talking about. She picks up her wineglass and swirls the contents like she's thinking about how to respond. "I can only speak for myself, but if I walk away it's to avoid saying something I may regret later."

"Okay, I see your point. But then when do you come back you'll resolve whatever the issue is?"

She shrugs. "Sometimes never. It depends. Some stuff doesn't need to be resolved. Walking away, that ends it."

"That makes no sense to me. I always need a resolution."

"Yeah?" she says, sipping her wine and looking at me over the rim of her glass. "You need a resolution, or you need to be right?" She's looking at me like she's caught me in a lie, as though she's determined to make me admit I'm cheating on her with the truth.

"I don't always have to be right, but I need someone to tell me why I'm not."

She laughs. "I'm not sure I even understand what that means. But my advice to you is to say you're sorry for whatever stupid thing you did to make her mad and move on. It will be the best thing you ever did for your sanity."

She drinks some more of her wine and puts her glass down like the discussion is closed with the gesture. I've evidently become a lot less interesting—reporter or not—because she turns toward the man on the other side of her and boxes me out with her back.

It's fine by me. Now I can look back over at Linden and try to gauge whether Hillary is right. I'm not sure I should apologize for my suggestion that her story is going nowhere because I'm pretty sure I've given her exactly what it takes to motivate her. Then again, I'm making that assumption on the basis that she's exactly like me. And in watching her—at ease talking to anyone she's with—it occurs to me that maybe she's nothing like me. Which scares the shit out of me, because I can't predict what she's likely to do next.

23

LINDEN

A COUPLE HOURS LATER, dinner is wrapped up and about half the guests have made their way back to their rooms or their *casitas* or wherever they're staying on the property. It still amazes me that one family owns a home large enough for two dozen guests, but it tells me a thing or two about how big a company Worldvision is and what a big deal it will be if I can pull off an investigative reporting coup by exposing *Bachelor Bay* to be hiding improprieties. And, not to get too far ahead of myself, but if *Bachelor Bay* turns out to be a scandal, there's no telling what else Worldvision might be hiding. But that's Jack's beat to investigate.

The chair next to Jack is empty now, so I sit down. I'm still annoyed at his earlier dismissive comments, but I try to let it go. I'm here to report a story, and I'll do that regardless of what he thinks.

"Are you getting some good color for the profile?" I ask him, trying to keep our conversation on non-controversial territory. Work is always a good bet.

He shrugs. "Enough. I know I'll have time with Ken tomorrow, so I'm just gonna enjoy tonight and not work."

I can't help but smirk at that. He looks at me quizzically. "Why is that funny?" he asks.

"I'm just interested to see what that looks like."

"What *what* looks like?" He doesn't have any idea what I mean, which makes me laugh even more.

"You. Enjoying and not working."

"We're back on that? The relaxing thing?"

"I just find it funny that you think you're doing it when you're all wound up."

He puts his phone in his pocket and scoots his chair back a little bit so he can lean back on it, trying his best to seem relaxed, but looking very awkward doing it. "I can relax. I'm doing both right now, enjoying and relaxing."

"Well, yeah, you're working hard at trying to seem relaxed. But I'm not sure that's anywhere close to the same thing as actually relaxing." He's very amusing. I knew he was intense at work, but now I'm starting to see that he's intense all the time, in a frustrating but endearing way.

He throws up his hands. "Well, maybe you're just not good at reading me. I feel very relaxed right now. I'm not at work. This is… fun. And we're around great people."

"Oh, you're such a liar! You barely got the word fun out of your mouth without choking." I lean in and whisper to him, "Because this is *not* fun. It sucks."

He smiles. "I'm glad we're on the same page."

He looks down and I know he's thinking about taking his phone out of his pocket to write down some detail he can use later in his story, but I reach and grab his hand before he can do it. He looks at me, surprised at the contact. I put both of our hands on the table, but I don't take mine away. "Is that your safe place, reporting?"

"I'm not sure what you mean by that."

I'm not sure I believe him, but I explain anyway. "Like a default personality you take on so you're in control of a room full of people. If you have your reporter hat on, you direct the conversation, you ask the questions and you avoid talking about yourself."

"That just sounds like being a reporter, which is what I'm here to do."

"I know that, but not at this very moment. You said it yourself. There's very little reporting to be done at this dinner, so why not hang it up for a couple hours and have a conversation that has nothing to do with reporting?"

"Isn't that what we're doing?"

"Ugh, you are frustrating. Let's talk about something that has nothing to do with work."

"Fine." He looks down at my hand which still has his pinned to the table. It's more to prevent him from reaching for his phone, but now that he's agreed to have a conversation, I relent enough that he can take his hand away if he wants to. He doesn't move but I can see the internal struggle.

It makes me laugh. "This is really hard for you, isn't it?"

"What?"

"Not looking at your phone, not being in charge of the interview, having a conversation where you might have to say something spontaneous."

"Hardly. I can talk about anything you want. That's what makes me a good reporter."

I shake my head, needing him to pull himself further from his comfort zone. "Not good enough."

"I don't know what you're getting on about. I told you about my favorite snack in the car earlier."

"True, that was a big glimpse into your soul. Can we talk about something that has nothing to do with food or the field of journalism?"

He inhales deeply, like he's forcing a meditative condition that doesn't come easily to him. His face softens. "Sure. What do you want to talk about?"

"Lots of things."

"Super specific. Can you do better? Ask me whatever you want, and I'll do my best to answer."

"Anything?"

"I'm not saying I'll answer, but sure. Shoot." He turns his chair to face me more squarely and I can see more of his face. Those blue eyes which lock on mine and don't let me go. The playful smile that dares me to ask him whatever I really want to know. The tousled hair that I just want to touch.

I could ask him why he thinks I'm unqualified to do my job or what I need to do to prove myself. It's important to me that I earn the respect of my colleagues and since he's the most accomplished in the bureau, his approval means more than it should. I think about how to ask what I want to know without sounding insecure about my abilities.

Here's my golden opportunity to get beneath the surface and find out who he is outside of work, but all I can think about is how plush his lips look and how much I want to feel them again. So I ask him the question that's been on my mind for the past half hour, and it has nothing to do with his childhood or his hobbies. When I do open my mouth, as if controlled by forces beyond my control, I ask him something else entirely. "Did you really kiss me for Chad's benefit?"

"I thought you didn't want to talk about reporting?"

"It's only very loosely related to reporting. And you evaded my question."

He smiles in a way that exerts a near-magnetic pull on me. The warmth and playfulness of his eyes make it impossible to look anywhere else. "Well you have to admit, it worked. The guy's so hot for you, you just might get him to sell out his career and tell you what you want."

"Still haven't answered the question."

"Okay, sure. Yes, it was for him, for the story," he says. Then he adds, "Partly."

I'm careful to control my expression, not wanting to give him the slightest indication what I think about his answer. Then he leans closer and indicates that I should do the same. I tilt my head toward him and he comes in a little closer, so now his lips are just grazing my ear, which sends a shiver through my insides that doesn't stop until it dead-ends right in between my thighs. His voice is a gruff whisper. "But no, it was mostly for me."

I feel a rush of heat in my cheeks and a growing pang of wanting.

It may be the first time in my life I haven't had a ready retort. He draws back, his lips barely grazing my cheek along the way. Now he's watching me, waiting for a response. And I've got nothing. I'm so dumbstruck by what he just said that I'm unable to speak.

"Wait. What?" I finally manage, trying to keep my breathing steady. I'm still trying to put his words into some sort of context that makes sense.

If it was for him, it means that... Hang on, is he saying that...?"

And now I don't have time to think anymore because his lips are on mine, gentle but insistent, letting me know that is what it feels like to kiss him when I'm not drunk and he's not doing it for show. He slides one hand along my cheek and into my hair. His lips linger, barely brushing against my chin and wrapping around to kiss me softly on the cheek before he whispers in my ear, "Okay, I was lying. I don't give a shit about Chad. It was entirely for me." He kisses me behind my ear and down my neck, his breath warm as he whispers, "And I hope, for you too."

I feel my heart beating in my throat and a muddle of thoughts competing in my head. This can't happen. I can't get into a relationship with anyone, let alone someone I work with. Boyfriends derail me. But then... who said anything about a relationship? "I… okay," I finally manage to articulate. Which makes him laugh.

"Yeah? Can I assume, then, that you're good with me going off-script, darling date?" Now he's smirking like he knows the answer to his question. And despite the fact I'm absolutely good with how his lips felt against mine and I can barely think of anything besides how to get them back there, I can't help giving him a hard time.

"Because you've yet to meet a woman who didn't swoon after you kissed her?"

"No, because you're all breathless and confused and that's usually a pretty good sign that a person enjoyed being kissed."

He's right. I'm just not used to being this swept away. "It is a good sign," I say, but really, it's a terrible sign. Because here's where I blow it. I fall for all the breathless parts and forget about how the late nights don't mesh well with early mornings at work and how falling headlong for another person doesn't work when my whole focus should be on making my dream career happen, now that I've finally been given the opportunity. And I can't help thinking that maybe he knows this. Maybe it's just one more way for him to prove he's right, that I'm not really fit for my job.

"So why do you look so distraught?" He leans closer, his lips inches from mine and I so want to close the gap and think about nothing else except how good his lips taste and how they'd feel running over every part of me. He tilts my face up so I'm looking into his eyes, which are warm and considerate in their desire to have me tell him what I'm thinking. I just don't know if he has my best interests at heart.

"I can't kiss you. I can't do anything with you."

"Because…? Are we actually siblings, separated at birth? That's the only issue that immediately comes to mind that could be a problem. I mean, it's not illegal, just icky."

He's so sure of himself, I almost want to go with his bold

attitude that seems to say everything will be okay if I just follow what my body is telling me to do. But I'm wary. He gets people to trust him and open up to him for a living. I can't afford to be one of those people, especially when I know he has a low opinion of my reporting skills.

I look past him, trying to see past the glare of the twinkle lights on the terrace to where the ocean is churning in the distance, as though it will give me some perspective. But all I see is those annoying garden lights. Jack reaches a hand to my chin and turns my face. I have no choice but to look at him.

"Hey. If it makes you uncomfortable, say the word and I'll back right off. I just thought… when I kissed you, what it felt like… it's hard to believe that wasn't mutual."

"Well, maybe I'm a really convincing actor."

"Are you?"

Here's my opportunity. I need to do the right thing and extricate myself from this potential minefield that will only lead to me lying naked on a bed screaming Jack's name in about ten minutes. I need to put my career first and remember how hard I've worked to get the opportunity to write for the Examiner. I can't blow this. Or even think about what he could do to me and how it would make me moan in ecstasy, no question about it. No, here is where I need to stand firm in my conviction that having sex with anyone—let alone this man who is so damn magnificent I can't actually look at him right now—will spell nothing but trouble. I take a deep breath and ready myself with the long list of excuses and reasons I've been preparing for just this sort of occasion.

Then my mouth takes over, irrespective of my brain.

"No. I'm a terrible actor. I couldn't even get a non-speaking role in our high school play. And it was a relatively big cast at a relatively small school. Nope. But that's not the point."

He smiles and tilts his head toward mine, so our fore-heads are touching. It's such a sweet gesture of intimacy that runs in direct contrast to the frustration I'm feeling, in more ways than one. "What is the point?" he asks, his voice soft.

When I don't answer, he cups my chin in his hand and angles my face so my lips are perfectly lined up with his. He brushes his lips against mine, barely touching but sending little tremors through my chest. He changes the angle and kisses me more deeply, moving his hand behind my neck and moving it through my hair.

I reach my arms around his neck and sink into his lips, which taste faintly of gin and lime. He sucks on my lower lip and I feel my breath catch in my chest.

When we break the kiss, I can't remember why I thought this was a problem. I'm also seriously lost in the magnetism of him.

Then he runs one finger along my cheek and under my chin, which he tilts up again, so my lips are too close to his luscious mouth for me to resist their intrinsic pull. I give my brain a time out and let sensation take over until all I feel is his soft lips and the sweep of his tongue along my bottom lip. He coaxes my lips apart and I'm swept away by the sexy way his tongue roams over mine, slowly and luxuriously like we have all the time in the world. Like we're not sitting at the dinner table of one of the biggest media magnates in the world.

Holy shit. I draw back instantly, remembering where we are and what I'm supposed to be doing here: reporting a story. Not macking on my colleague, no matter how good it feels or how convincing we look to anyone wondering if we're actually a couple.

But when I glance around, most of the crowd has scattered. The three or four people who remain are talking amongst themselves, sitting in a circle of chairs on the far end of the terrace, where a fire pit sends up an orange glow. No one seems at all interested in what we're doing.

"You okay?" he asks, looking more amused than concerned at my sudden panic.

"No!"

"Then please explain the problem because I'm not seeing it."

I could tell him I'm tired and need a good night's sleep. I could tell him it's not a good idea to mix work with… this. Instead, I say what I've been thinking for months. "I don't trust you."

Jack throws his hands up. "Seriously, woman. What did I ever do that made you hate me so much?" He stands up, looks at the sky and paces in a circle.

I don't think before I blurt out my reason. "You told Jeremy it was a mistake to hire me!"

He stops pacing and looks incredulous. "I did what?"

Now it's my turn to look incredulous. I stand up from the table and close the space between us so I don't have to yell, even though I want to. "How can you not remember? Right after he hired me, you said he was making a mistake. You said I was too green for the job."

He runs a hand through his hair. Twice. He must be really thinking hard and trying to come up with something to say. Then he closes his eyes, like the memories are beginning to edge their way back into his mind. "Oh. That."

"It was more than a *that* to me. You tried to undercut me from the beginning."

He shakes his head. "No. You misunderstood."

"How could I misunderstand when your words were perfectly clear? Do you think I'm that stupid?"

"I don't think you're stupid at all. But I think you're new at this and the Examiner is unrelenting. Working there is constant pressure and demand for near-perfection."

"And you don't think I can handle it. I get it. You don't have to spell it out."

"No," he says, shaking his head. He's just making it

worse. Now he's going to tell me that I can't hack it all over again because I can't handle the pressure. And I've just added fuel to the fire by going off the reservation and letting him know I'm worried I can't. "That's not at all what I meant. I could see how ambitious you were, and I knew you wanted to take on a beat and start reporting bigger stories but that can be career suicide if you're not really experienced. I was asking Jeremy to let you warm into the job so you'd be protected from scrutiny. I was looking out for you because even then, before I even knew you at all, I already liked you."

I start to walk back toward the long dinner table, which still hasn't been cleared. Despite my frustration with Jack, I still have the wherewithal to think it's unlike Judy to have a mess like this go untended for even a moment. "And now you're just gonna walk away?" he says from behind me.

I turn to look at him, at his gorgeous face which looks even more beautiful with its legitimate concern that I'm leaving. It's not for show. He's hurt and that makes my heart relent.

"I wasn't leaving. I just wanted some water." I grab the water glass from my place at the table and carry it back to where he's standing. "So, it seemed like you were starting to say something nice."

His expression softens. He almost relents to a smile. "If you believe a dick is capable of being nice."

"I'll be the judge. Let's hear it."

He exhales, hand rumpling the already-messy head of hair once more. "I was worried. You had big dreams and a lot of talent but not enough experience. Learning on the job at a place like the Examiner can be brutal. I've seen reporters full of promise get chewed up and spit out before they knew they'd done anything wrong. I didn't want to see that happen to you."

It's a pretty sweet thing to say, but he barely knew me at

all back then. It's hard to believe he had so much invested in my success at the job. Unless… "For the sake of the paper?"

"Well, sure… It wouldn't be great for the paper if you were given an assignment you couldn't handle, but no, my primary concern was you. You have way too much talent and drive to risk it on a high-profile job at a top paper when you're not prepared. If you fail, you fail big. You fail publicly. And more times than not, you're never given a second chance."

"But you barely gave me a first chance. You assumed I'd fail."

"I never assumed that. But if I'd waited to see what would happen, it might've been too late. If I assumed anything, it was that I could do something to help. I can see now, all I ended up doing was making you think I doubted your ability."

I have to admit that makes a certain amount of sense. And it would take a master salesman to dream all that up on the spot to talk me down from my irate stance on not wanting to kiss him. So maybe I choose to believe him?

Then it dawns on me. "All those times you were all over my ass for being late, all those times you ripped wire copy before I got there to make sure I didn't miss anything…"

"I was trying to have your back. Now, looking at it from your perspective, I can see how it maybe conveyed a certain lack of confidence in your abilities. So, I'm sorry for that."

But I'm not hearing him. "You had my back?"

"Yeah."

"That's… so unbelievably sweet. No one's ever had my back before."

"That's a shame."

"On behalf of my back, thank you." I turn around so he can see the appreciation my back is giving him.

"Truth be told, it's not really your back I'm interested in having right now."

"No?"

He shakes his head slowly and looks me over, appreciation in his eyes. "There are many other parts of you that interest me, and I'd like to have all of them. Starting with those gorgeous legs. And your lips, which taste like a dessert I could eat for the rest of my life. And lest you worry I'm objectifying you, I think your brain is gorgeous too."

That pretty much does me in. There's no way in hell I'm about to resist him right now. "That's the sexiest thing anyone's ever said to me."

He laughs. "I'm doing pretty well so far, then."

Then the doubt starts creeping in. "But we work together. You don't think it'll be awkward when we get back?"

"Look, we're in a beautiful place, with ocean views and drinks flowing all weekend long. You have your own *casita* if, at any point, I start to annoy you. But if not…"

"Like colleagues with benefits in Montecito?"

"Kind of like that."

"In that case, I only have one thought: Whose room is closer?" I look at him and I size up what he's wearing: khaki pants and a nice shirt, good flat shoes. "I don't mind running in a skirt, but hell, I can't wear these," I say, pulling off my shoes and looping the straps around my hand. I yank his hand and take off at a sprint, the patio stones rough beneath my feet as I head toward the set of stairs that leads to the main expanse of the property. Jack is right behind me until we reach the top of the stairs.

Then we're both running across the wide lawn of the villa that separates the main home from the guest *casitas*, racing like two little kids caught in a rainstorm and trying to stay dry. We reach the fork in the path, where one direction leads to my room and the other to his, unsure which way we're headed. Jack takes over, pulling my hand to lead me down the path to his door, which he wrenches open with a hand that's behind him because his mouth is already on mine and we're stumble-walking to the big plush couch in the living room where he lands on his back, pulling me on top of him.

It's a frenzy of hands in hair and lips on skin and hands roaming and tongues intertwining. I want to feel him pressed against me. I want to experience all the things I've been thinking about all night as I've observed him from afar and from much closer. It all stays behind when we leave Montecito, so I'm not holding back.

He pulls me to the couch and I can feel how hard he is. Our bodies rock into each other and my hands roam to his face, where a day's worth of stubble feels rough and so sexy against my hand.

My brain has finally run out of reasons to protest because every other part of me feels too good and I'm not sure anymore why kissing this man could ever possibly be a bad idea. His hands are in my hair and his tongue makes a sweep across my bottom lip, which unleashes the tiniest moan that I've been holding in since I first tasted his lips hours earlier. And then a bigger one when he grabs my face with both hands and kisses me harder.

He backs away for a second and tips his forehead to mine, like he did earlier, one hand wrapped around the back of my neck. "Hi there."

"Hello." I like this side of him, the non-critical, non-reporter side.

The race that got us here from the terrace in mere seconds slows to a less hurried pace as I roll sideways, still pressed up against him but now able to wrap my hands more fully around his back, which is strong and toned. Our tongues tangle and I let my hands run from his broad shoulders down his toned biceps. I've never been so grateful for every moment he's spent lifting heavy objects. "You. Are. So. Hot," I pant out, coming up for air from the kiss.

"Back atcha," he says.

He lowers his lips back to mine but this time he just

brushes lightly against them, teasing me with the gentle touch and making me want more. He angles his head the other way and sweeps against my lips again. I feel myself responding to every move, pressing my body into his. He takes a nibble at my lower lip, then licks along the seam. It makes me want to meet his tongue with mine. We're moving slower now, taking our time with the melding of mouths and the languid grinding of our hips.

Jack runs his hand over my skirt, which somehow hasn't ridden up entirely, and continues down my thigh. "Your legs are spectacular." He rubs a hand over the skin, continuing down past my knee and up again slowly while I swear to myself that I will owe Cassie and every one of my spinning people forever for motivating me to get my legs into shape for this moment.

Jack is clearly a leg man. He makes his way down and up my leg again, this time continuing under the hem of my skirt and all the way to my hip, rubbing a hand over the fabric of my panties before bringing his hand up along my waist and grabbing the hem of my camisole. He hesitates before going further and looks at me. "Is this okay?" I nod and he slips the silky fabric up over my head. He runs his fingers over the lace of my strapless bra. "I wondered about this. No straplines."

"Women are full of secrets." I assume he's fully aware of most of them. He's not a guy who's making his first trip around the bases.

"I'm not talking about mechanics. I wondered what you'd look like without it."

"Only one way to find out."

He reaches behind and unclasps the bra. Just like I thought, he didn't exactly need lessons. "You are stunning," he says. He surveys me for a moment before rubbing the back of his hands over my breast, gently circling and teasing. Then he lowers his mouth and I feel his tongue circle my nipple, and I'm swirling into ecstasy land. I want his hands on every part of me, but he's taking his time, which only increases every sensation.

Jack is all man, incredible looking, built like a marble masterpiece and crazy brilliant, all of which adds up to the biggest turn-on I've ever experienced. "I can't believe I worked so hard to dislike you," I tell him.

"It seems like a serious waste of energy."

"I see that now."

With his lips still grazing my breast, Jack's hand makes another pass up my thigh. This time he slips under the hem of my skirt and runs his hand up to where I can tell my panties are already damp in anticipation. My breath hitches when his fingers reach the apex of my thighs and he runs one finger under the elastic, hinting but not insisting.

At the rate he's moving, he'll have me naked and he'll still be fully clothed, so I need to remedy that situation. I reach for the hem of his shirt and pull it up over his head. "I like things to be equitable," I say.

"I think I could've guessed that about you."

Getting his shirt off forces him to move his hand away, which is disappointing, to be sure, but he doesn't seem like someone easily deterred from a mission.

With his shirt off, I lay both hands flat against his chest, which is a smooth wall of muscle and perfect skin. When I run a finger over his abs, I feel the muscles jump, and I take another slow tour from top to bottom.

He smiles and resumes his worship of my legs. "Are you a runner?"

"Nope. I ride a bike."

"Like, mountain biking?"

"Spinning." I'm amused at his ability to be a reporter and ask questions, even now. "Do you really want me to tell you about it right now?"

"Not even a little. I want to do this," he says, somehow deftly flipping me over so I'm lying on the couch and he's lifting the hem of my skirt higher and scooting himself down lower. Now his lips have taken the place of his hands, kissing a trail up one thigh. He pauses and kisses me squarely against my panties before going to the other leg and running the entire glorious gauntlet again. By the time he gets back to the top of my thighs, I'm halfway to orgasm and I can barely answer when he loops a finger under the elastic and begins to slide my panties down. "Is this okay?"

I nod, unable to explain how very, very okay it is. "You don't have to keep asking. I'm good with all of it."

There's no use pretending we might stop.

"Just making sure. I never want to assume."

"I'm giving you permission. Assume." My voice is breathy because that's what he does to me.

He slips my panties down my legs and I fling them across the room with my foot. Then he returns his attention to the sensitive skin at the top of my thighs, kissing there as he makes his way to the spot that's been moaning for attention since he grabbed me on the lawn hours earlier.

"I've been dying to taste you since you kissed me at the bar," he says, pausing and causing the heat to build within me even more. I can't even process that piece of information because he's so close to giving me what I want, and he's making my body ache for it.

I feel his breath hot between my thighs and then his tongue lightly stroking. His lips and his tongue work their magic, swirling and circling until I'm a barely coherent mess of trembling desire. I feel my hips rise as he sucks gently.

"Mmm, you're good at that," I say, twisting my fingers in his hair.

"You make me good at it." Then he does the whole series of moves again, each time bringing me higher and closer to orgasm. I'm grabbing the sides of his face and savoring the feel of his sandpaper skin against my hands, feeling the amazing contrast with the softness of his lips and the incredible stomach-clenching glory he's eliciting.

The man can't possibly have any idea what he's doing to me. My moans might be giving him a tiny idea and I hold on, feeling the build until I can't wait any longer. "Come on, baby," he whispers, his eyes on me as he continues to kill me with his tongue. And then I'm lost, surging to a place I didn't know existed, wrapped in blissful sensations; coming apart completely.

Oh.

My.

God.

I'm a pile of putty in his hands. Breathless and barely able to do anything except run my hands through his hair as he rises up to place a row of kisses up my belly, ending at my throat where he lingers. The warmth of his breath against my skin sends a new ripple of chills through my body. "How're you doing?" he asks.

"I... That was... I'm... just kiss me again."

He chuckles and his lips find mine. I'm carried away again at the sheer force of being with him. When I wrap my hands over his shoulders, I feel the unconscious twitch of his muscles at my touch and his kiss gets deeper, needier. He's lying on top of me and propping himself up on his forearms.

I reach down between us for his belt buckle and unclasp it, flipping the button at the top of his pants. I run my hand down inside his boxer briefs to his hard length and he lets out a low groan at my touch.

"Pants need to go," I say, helping push the pants down his legs until he's freed from bulky fabric constraints. I reach my hand down again and watch his face. His fiery blue eyes are consumed by wanting. I hear his breathing hitch as I continue to stroke.

"You ready for another orgasm?" he asks, a smile on his lips.

I don't want him to think I'm completely at his mercy. "*Ha.* Cocky. Confident you can do that?"

He licks the sensitive spot behind my ear and exhales a light breath, which lights me on fire again. Then I'm moaning, and he's kissing along my jaw and ending at my mouth, which may not be much with the words right now, but it knows what to do with his lips.

"I feel pretty good about my odds," he says. I nod and I work his boxer briefs down over his hips.

"I like a man with a plan." Oh, I am completely at his mercy.

He grabs his wallet from his pants and unwraps a condom.

The last thing to go is my skirt, which he skillfully unbuttons and has on the floor in seconds flat. Then I feel his fingers, first one, then two, getting me ready for what I can already tell will finish me off and delete my vocabulary entirely, except for two words: "Don't stop."

"C'mere," he says, though he's the one moving into me, slowly at first, teasing. Then, when I think I will lose my mind with anticipation, he sinks in, filling me. I can't begin to recall anything about work or why we're here, other than to do this. It's so, so good.

He moves gently, then more urgently, taking his time and building me back up. Which isn't hard. As soon as I feel him inside me, I'm done for.

Once again, I'm appreciative of his strong shoulders and tilt up to look at him. He doesn't break my gaze as he moves rhythmically.

"If you keep doing that, I'm gonna come," I say. I can barely get words out.

"I was kinda counting on that."

"I mean, if you keep moving... like that..." I feel my eyes roll back as sensation takes over.

He keeps moving. Like that. "Yes, don't resist it."

I can't resist it. My orgasm is spinning me from the inside out. His lips crash onto mine, his hips moving more insistently and taking us both closer to the edge. Until there's nothing to do but hold on for dear life as I lose my mind again. Right before he does the same.

"Fuck, Linden," he growls as his eyes flutter shut and I see the release in his jaw. I love the lack of tension in his face.

We move together, grinding, moaning, riding the last wave until the end. It's not until he stops moving and runs a hand down my back that I start returning to earth. He knows exactly what to do with his body to take mine to places it's never been and I'm trying hard to keep perspective. It's probably because we both know we only have the weekend, a finite amount of time, which seems to make every touch that much more intense.

He looks… like a completely different person. One who doesn't carry the weight of the Examiner on his back and the fear that we'll lose our position at the top of the journalism food chain. I don't realize I'm giggling at him until his face changes to a look of concern.

"I'm not sure laughing was the response I was after," he says.

"No, no. I just finally realized this is apparently what it takes for you to relax."

He presses his lips together and smiles, caught. And maybe a little bit amused at the observation. "Possibly true."

"I'm starting to figure you out."

"Does that mean you'll continue to help in that mission? While we're here this weekend?" he asks. And I'm cognizant of the limiting factor. It's just while we're here. Just for the weekend. When we go back to work, we go back to the normal, stressed, and driven people we are. Separately.

And that's a good thing because I can't let him in. No late nights that turn into oversleeping or fog brain that causes me to make a reporting mistake. It's just for the weekend.

"Well, there are an awful lot of couples here and we are supposed to be courteous guests who blend in. I'm all for verity."

"Wouldn't want to look like a couple of impostors."

"So then, yes. I think I can help."

He leans in and kisses me. It's a good thing we've agreed it's only for the weekend. Because otherwise, he could be very, very distracting.

JACK

I WAKE up to the soft churn of the ocean and bright light streaming in through the slatted shutters which I've neglected to close all the way. As I shuffle off sleep, I start to remember where I am and who I'm with. And how much I enjoyed our night.

Linden's arm is draped across my chest and I'm hesitant to move because I don't want to break the connection. But now that I'm awake, I need to do something. Even checking my phone requires me to scoot away, so I gently move her arm to the side and sit up. Now I can really see her, and in the golden morning light, she looks beautiful. I don't want to wake her, but I can't stop staring at her. The lips parted and pillowy, the fan of auburn hair splayed out on the pillow next to me, just like I imagined she would look when I drove Linden home and tucked her in and wished I could stay all night.

I can't believe it's only been a week since then, and I find it even harder to believe she's lying here next to me now. The pleasant recollection of last night will keep me going all day. That is, unless we replace those images with a few more this morning. I can't believe I'm this lucky. Or this stupid. This is not a good idea. For so many reasons. Not the least of which is the lingering issue I have to deal with when we get back: I may end up being her boss.

I initially put my hand up for the job, figuring it was worth being considered, even though I'm not sure it's what I want. For one thing, it would gut my reporting record. If I'm editing half the stories written by other reporters, I won't have as much time to write my own, which will mean I'll have to divvy up some of the companies and stories on my beat among the other reporters—for two years. There's no way to know if I'll ever get them back, especially if the other reporters make big strides in getting scoops. From a strict reporting standpoint, I'd be crazy to give up any of the territory on my beat. But there's prestige, and a huge salary bump in being an assistant chief. It could lead to Stuart's job or a post at the New York headquarters.

It's the natural next step for any reporter who wants longevity at the paper. And Stuart has made it clear I'm his first choice for the job. It should be a no-brainer for me.

But starting something up with a reporter who I may have working for me will cause all sorts of problems. And knowing that Linden already thought I was out to get her fired, having me in a position to do so isn't going to make her comfortable. Let alone, that the longer I wait to tell her, the more she'll think I have the worst of intentions.

Unfortunately, my intentions aren't clear, regardless of the potential job change. I've been watching Linden and noticing her at work since she got to the bureau, but she always made her disinterest in me it very clear. More like, total disdain. I never really understood why she had such a problem with me until last night. And now I'm a little mortified that she overheard my conversation with Jeremy and a little relieved to know her animosity had a logical source.

I'm still not sure she actually thinks better of me now,

though I have a feeling the multiple orgasms might have stacked the odds more in my favor.

I take another look at her. She's the kind of person I could fall for if I was looking for a relationship. Which I'm not. Especially if I end up taking the Assistant Chief position, while still trying to maintain a good part of my existing beat reporting. It's an almost impossible job, even for someone without daily beat stories. Stuart actually suggested I give up the beat entirely and focus on the editing and a few bigger picture, long-term stories. That's how Jeremy got his monster book deal, by pursuing longer-term assignments and letting the slow pace of reporting lead him to an even bigger, book-length story. I guess that could be interesting.

From beside me, I hear a quiet stirring as Linden starts to open her eyes. She can't possibly feel well-rested since we only slept a few hours, but that bright sun is merciless. I'd be shocked if anyone could sleep through that, let alone someone who's used to getting up at the same time every day.

When I turn my head to look at her, she has a sleepy smile on her face and half-opened eyes. "Hey." Her voice is raspy and cute.

"Sleep okay?"

"Like a rock. Is it late?" I expect her to reach for her phone which she left on the table next to the bed. But instead, she rolls the opposite way and reaches out toward me. She runs her fingers along my arm, forcing her eyes open a bit more. Their intense brown sparkles under heavy lids as she reluctantly wakes up.

"It's seven," I tell her.

She looks surprised. "How long have you been up?"

"About an hour."

"Why?" she asks, as if no sane person would get up at six without a reason. Maybe she's right.

I shrug. "I'm just used to it. And once I woke up, that was it."

"Really? So, on weekends… you get up at six?"

"Usually, yeah."

"And do what? Like, hit the gym and start reporting on something?" she asks, laughing a little at the thought.

"Pretty much. Yeah."

"Oh. I mean, of course. Me too. That's why I asked, to make sure you weren't some kind of a slacker." I know she's making fun of me, but I also know I'm not about to let this stunning naked woman talk to me about work right now. I pull her closer and wrap my arms around her back. She doesn't hesitate. Her body fills in every gap of space between us and I know she can feel how hard I already am for her. "Mmm, nothing slack about that," she says, reaching her hand down and running her fingers over my cock. I feel my nerves dance at her touch.

"Don't want you to think I'm all work."

"I'll never think of you quite the same way again."

Dipping down to lick the soft spot next to her ear, I run a trail of kisses down her neck and across her collarbone. I continue to one breast, running my hand over the other one while I give full attention to this one. I'm definitely a leg man, but that doesn't mean I'm not in heaven circling her nipple with my tongue. I want to enjoy every inch of her toned, beautiful body and I won't take my mouth off her breast until I elicit a moan. It only takes a minute. I whisper, "Of course, if you really want to, we can talk about reporting. Page one stories and scoops. Does that turn you on?"

She laughs. "Not particularly."

"Liar. I'm picturing you walking into the bureau in the morning, your hair kind of messy because you stayed up late reporting," I say, my voice low and gravelly in her ear. I take one of her hands in mine and brush my lips across her fingers, kissing each one before continuing my seductive tale.

"You see your name on the front page. Above the fold." I put one of her fingers in my mouth and suck lightly. Linden moans and threads the fingers of her other hand through my hair.

I run my hand down her ribcage to where her luscious hip curves. God, she's so sexy. There's no part of her I don't want to touch. As I move my hand lower, to the soft spot where her hip meets her thigh, she shifts, moving closer to me, which tells me she wants me to keep going. "You know the story is good, but you don't know how good until Stuart gets to the office—"

"No Stuart. Ruining the moment." She's breathless but insistent.

"Sorry. The other papers are screwed. They missed the biggest story of the year. You're the only one who has it. It might even be Pulitzer-worthy." I slip a finger inside her, feeling how wet she is.

"That's too much," she says, her breath jagged. "No Pulitzer, not yet." I love how even in my seductive fantasy, she wants to work harder to earn it. I slip in a second finger, getting into a rhythm that matches the way my tongue is now stroking hers. I don't want to rush this. We have hours before we need to be anywhere today, and I'm not interested in work right now. All I can think about is her.

Her hips rise up and flex against my hand, and I can tell by her ragged breath that she's getting close. "Come on, gorgeous," I'm watching her face. She's so feisty and capable all the time. I want to see her let her guard down for me and slide into her orgasm.

"Oh…" She doesn't complete the thought. Her eyes flutter and she grabs my face in her hands, locking her lips on mine. The intensity is matched only by the writhing of her body as she comes.

She slows down the kiss and sucks lightly on my tongue. I am helpless against the tide of her. She presses her lips to mine before running her tongue across my bottom lip and taking a tiny nip at it.

Now she leans in toward me, her voice sultry in my ear. "I really want this story. I may even want it more than an orgasm." Her breath is hot against my skin and her voice has me wrapped in knots. But I'll play her game.

"Your devotion to your job will get you far."

"I'm counting on it," she says, all breathy and adorable.

"But I see no reason why you can't have both," I say, flipping her on top of me. She doesn't resist, and her warm body relents and melds perfectly with mine.

"You're the one with the Pulitzer. I'll trust your judgment."

She can't talk anymore because I need her mouth on mine and really, what else is there to discuss? Her hips arch to meet me, rubbing against the head of my cock and making it almost impossible to hold off from what I really want to do, which is to get inside her. I tease her relentlessly, loving the way her hips are moving against me. Wanting, urging me closer. I kept a condom nearby, so we barely have to pause before I slide inside her. The second I do, I'm aware of how much I need to feel the clench of her muscles and the warmth that envelops me.

"Oh my god, it's too good," she says.

I don't want to talk or think. I just want to feel this woman, every spectacular inch of her, moving in perfect rhythm with me.

She's right. It's too good. I'm gonna be completely fucked on Monday morning when I have to go back to work and resume our normal lives. But what's the point of thinking about that now?

I just follow her next orgasm with my own, until we're both crashing into each other and I'm realizing that my feelings for her are going to follow me home after the weekend. There's no use kidding myself. I'm definitely fucked.

25

LINDEN

IT SHOULDN'T SURPRISE me that Ken and Judy have an entire itinerary planned for the weekend. Just as the dinner table seating was crafted to ensure that we mixed and mingled, today is set up for strategic interaction designed to ensure that we all come out of this weekend feeling like life-long besties.

Fortunately, lunch is a leisurely come-when-you-want buffet with minimal forced socializing. I need at least two cups of coffee before I can put on my game face and after an orgasmathon that resulted in very little sleep, I'm already not at my best.

In the harsh light of day, I'm annoyed at myself for doing the exact thing I swore I wouldn't do—get distracted by a guy. Granted, that guy was nothing short of masterful, and my eyes involuntarily close when I think about the things he did to my body last night. And again, this morning. But didn't I promise myself I wouldn't derail my career with distractions? And Jack is one hell of a distraction.

That's why it's probably a good thing that Judy has already divided us into two groups—supposedly randomly—for a morning sail on two of their boats which I can see bobbing on top of the water in the distance. Jack and I are not in the same group. "It's all about bonding with new people," Judy explains. "But of course the groups are merely a suggestion. There are no hard, fast rules," she says with a wink.

It's convenient that she's giving us that leeway, because I plan on maneuvering to make sure I'm on whichever boat Chad happens to be on, so I can begin working on him again. Jack definitely has the trickier job of trying to get Ken to admit what's going on at *Bachelor Bay*, even if it's off the record to start with. But if any reporter is capable of getting someone to talk, it's Jack. I've seen him in action many times and I always marveled at how he seems to tread the fine line between seeming like a really interested pal and a hard-edged authority no one wants to misinform.

After a very enjoyable morning that culminated in the giant rain shower, Jack left to do a background interview with Jim Culligan and I haven't seen him since. He did warn me to make sure to get to lunch by twelve-thirty. "To make sure you have your coffee. I know you've got your morning ritual and I, for one, don't want to be around a person who hasn't been pumped with the requisite amount of caffeine."

"I'm not that bad."

"Are you forgetting we work together? You're absolutely that bad."

"Fine. I'll make sure to get there by twelve-thirty."

"Boats leave at one."

"Got it. Don't worry. I won't be late."

Of course I'm running late.

It takes me a little while to decide what to wear, knowing we'll be on a boat and not knowing how the weather will be on the water. I opt for a pair of cutoff denim shorts with a loose blousy top over a white tank. I'm pretty sure the sailing isn't supposed to include swimming, but just in case, I have a red bikini on underneath and a bulky, warm Sherpa zip sweatshirt in case it's cooler on the water.

I've gone in the direction of very casual and I'm a bit alarmed when I see Hillary, the blonde woman who was sitting next to Jack at dinner flounce across the patio in a floor-length pool coverup with gold threads running through the gauzy fabric. She's wearing a giant straw hat and large Jackie O sunglasses and looks about as glamorous as I do homegirl.

Maybe I should go change. I grab a quick cup of coffee and decide to make a dash back to my suitcase in hopes that there's some miracle perfect outfit I've forgotten about when Ken comes down the stairs with Jack and starts pointing everyone toward the beachfront below. They're both wearing khaki pants and boat shoes and as I glance around, I notice that I'm the only one wearing shorts. Most of the women have on capri pants or some version of Hillary's caftan-like beachwear. If there was a memo, I wasn't on the distribution list.

Jack smiles at me and I see him take a not-so-surreptitious look at my bare legs. When he comes closer, he whispers, "Not that I'm complaining one second about those shorts, but you're gonna freeze."

"I was just coming to that conclusion. Do you think I have time to change?"

He looks down at the coffee I've barely sipped and the small plate of fruit I haven't eaten. "Lemme guess, you just got here five minutes ago?"

"I needed to wash my hair. After going eighteen rounds with you, it looked like a bird's nest."

He runs a hand through my hair, which is still damp underneath, though I've done my best to blow dry it and slap on a little makeup in the time I had. "It looks gorgeous. But you need to eat. And maybe find some long pants."

Jack goes over to Ken and pulls him aside for a moment, then comes back over to where I'm doing my best to slurp down too-hot coffee without burning my throat.

"You've got five minutes. Go change and I'll put your coffee in a to-go cup."

"Only five minutes? Is everyone on the planet a stickler for timeliness?"

"Everyone but you." He takes the coffee from me and I make a mad dash up the stairs and back to my room, where I find a serviceable pair of pale blue pants and substitute them for the denim shorts. I sprint back to where Jack now stands with my coffee in a paper cup with a lid. And he's holding a paper bag which he hands me.

"Thank you." I take a peek inside, spying a muffin that looks amazing. Like a giant hunk of blueberry cake with a billion carbs and sugar sprinkled on top. "Wow, that looks great. Tell me, Mr. Gym Workout, that you've ever had blueberry muffin-cake for breakfast."

"Today I had an egg white omelet."

"Of course you did."

"I wasn't late."

"Thank you for the muffin."

I take the coffee from him and we join the others, who are still making their way along the lower lawn to the path that leads to the beach.

Once we hit the sand, I see that four dinghies await, bobbing in the water at the edge of the surf. Judy is busy directing traffic, and I see that she's already indicated that Chad will be in one of the boats on the right, along with Ken. I glance at Jack and he nods. Looks like we'll be heading for the same sailboat, despite whatever Judy intended.

While people are situating themselves one-by-one into the dinghies, Jack pulls me to the side, away from the rest of the crowd. When we're a few paces away, I look at him, wondering what's on his mind. "What's up?" I ask.

He plays with a loose tendril of my hair and smiles. "I'm quite fond of this dating charade." He lowers his lips to mine and kisses me lightly, nibbling on my lip. It's a good daytime kiss, appropriate for a public place, but barely. "Mmm, that will tide me over. In case I'm too seasick to do it later," he says.

I'm momentarily alarmed. "You get seasick?"

"Nope." He puts his hands up. "Caught. I just wanted to kiss you, sailor." He leans in again. This time it's less polite and much less forgiving. I feel my insides twist as his tongue melts me into a trembling puddle of a sailor, who has to try hard to remember we're on a beach in front of other people, so I don't dissolve into moaning.

I'm not thinking about anything but the heat I still feel on my lips when I follow Jack to one of the small boats and take a seat next to him. If there was any question about being able to play the part of his plus-one, I have no doubt that we look like the real thing.

In minutes, I find myself motoring out to a beautiful fifty-foot sailboat that looks far larger than it did from the shore. The mast soars into the sky, its sail still furled. When I climb the ladder to get in, I see that all the controls are electronic. There will be no hustling around the boat for us passengers, pulling sheets, and cranking winches.

This boat has an upper deck that's all honey colored wood polished to a glossy sheen, with lounge chairs facing in both directions and set out along the sides of the sail. I can see the boat's captain and crew checking the dials and going over whatever plan they have for us.

As the wind whips around me, I'm grateful for the wardrobe change and the fuzzy sweatshirt I immediately wrap around myself. Ken is downstairs talking shop with the captain and coordinating with the other sailboat so we can sail a similar course without getting in each other's way.

I glance around at who else is on our deck and see Hillary and Buzz on adjacent lounge chairs and a few of the other people I met last night lingering on the deck below. I'm trying to see where Chad is sitting because I'll want to make my way over there sooner rather than later. I barely caught a glimpse of him when I was busy pouring my needed coffee, but he looked like he'd been dressed by his show's wardrobe department for a day on the high seas. He had on linen pants and a loose-fitting, striped linen shirt, tucked in and accented by a preppy canvas belt buckle with some sort of design. If I had to guess, I'd imagine there were tiny dolphins or starfish on it. And of course he wore a pale straw fedora.

His hat is what I use to try and spot him on our sailboat. That's when I notice that he's still in the dinghy, which is now taking him over to the other boat. The boat I would be on right now if I'd kept an eye on Chad and hadn't gotten lost in seaside PDA a few minutes before boarding. This missed opportunity is all my fault for letting my guard down and saying yes to my libido instead of my brain.

Jack comes up the stairs to where I'm looking over the railing wistfully. "You look like a kid whose balloon just flew away," he says.

I point, so he can see what I see. "Oh. Shit. That's your guy."

"Uh huh. How long are we gonna be out here on this ocean cruise?"

"Ken said three hours or so."

"That's three lost hours when I can't get any closer to my story."

"*Your* story?"

"Our story. Are you really gonna fight me on semantics?"

He puts an arm on my shoulder but I'm not in the mood to be placated. I can see my reporting opportunity sailing away before me and I'm not about to let him make me feel better about it by playing to my orgasmic side. I wriggle out from under it. "I want to get off this boat." I survey the distance between the deck and the water.

He laughs. "You plan on swimming to the other boat so you can interrogate him?"

"It's better than sitting here for three hours doing nothing. Why is this funny to you?"

He puts a hand on my shoulder, tentatively, probably unsure whether I'll snap at him again. "It's not funny," he says calmly. So I relent and look at him. I need his brainpower to help me decide what to do. He looks serious for a moment, but he can't hold back his smile. "I'm sorry, but it is a little funny."

I want to smack him. And the smile won't leave his face. I don't understand why he thinks this is so hysterical. "Aren't you the guy who puts the story before everything else? This should matter to you."

He makes an effort to look serious but I can tell it requires effort. "It does matter. It's just, we're on a goddamned boat. I mean, if ever there was a reason to give up on a source for a couple hours, this is probably it."

As if on cue, a gentle ocean breeze that doesn't feel at all freezing wafts over me with its salty smell and its damp comfort. I look out over the water. "It really is pretty."

"Exactly. Aren't you an ocean girl?"

"I am an ocean girl." And right now, taking in the view of endless blue from the upper deck of a million-dollar boat does have its appeal. "I'm just disappointed," I say, hating that I have to admit defeat for now.

"I know you are. But we have lots of time here. You can still get him to open up."

I look over again at where Chad is now climbing up the ladder to the other sailboat, which I now see has far fewer people than ours does. I guess a few too many people opted against following Judy's seating chart and we're overloaded. "Should I volunteer to go on the other boat so it's more balanced?"

He shakes his head and takes my hand. "You should spend three hours sitting on a lounge chair looking at the ocean and enjoying the day."

"Of all times for you to suddenly become relaxed, this is not ideal."

"Noted. Now let's find a spot for you to look at the ocean. Maybe even take a nap."

"I don't take naps." The only time I could is on a weekend but there's always way too much other stuff to do. I can't imagine Jack's a big napper either; I'm curious. "Do you?"

"On weekends sometimes. It's a nice thing. You should try it."

"Never. I'd rather exercise, read a book, or see friends. Or go to the farmer's market. Or take a walk. Plus, it messes up my sleep pattern the next night." He probably doesn't want to know all of that, but apparently, I can't stop oversharing.

"Come," he says, leading me to a pair of empty deck chairs draped with navy and white striped towels, very nautical chic. He gestures to one and I climb onto it, feeling the wind die down as I become horizontal. I don't even need my sweatshirt, so I toss it under the chair. I feel the sun hit my face and as much as I hate to admit it, it feels great. He's standing over me, waiting expectantly for my reaction. I'm tempted to continue being difficult, but that's only because I'm still frustrated that I missed the boat—literally—on the Chad situation. I shouldn't keep taking that out on him.

"It's amazing," I say and smooth out the towel on the chair next to me before he lowers himself into it.

"Oh yeah, that's good stuff." For a guy who I've never seen without a concerned furrow in his brow before this weekend, he's sure finding a way to unwind quickly. "See, glass half full. You can't grill Chad for details, but you get to spend three hours hanging with me."

His confidence amuses me. "What if I still don't really like you?" I ask.

"You like me."

He reaches across to my lounge chair and takes my hand in his, then he closes his eyes in the sun. How nice for him that he can gather background color for his profile by sleeping on a magnificent sailboat. And it truly is a thing of beauty. The mast soars into the perfect blue sky and the polished wood has clearly been maintained and kept pristine by a crew of elves who are nowhere to be seen. The white decks are spotless and broad on either side of the mast, leaving us all plenty of room to spread out and enjoy the peaceful outing.

The crew begins to raise the mainsail until it's bowed out slightly to expertly catch the wind as it starts to move us along at a nice, leisurely pace. Because we're already in deep water and there are no other boats around, we don't need to ride further out under power of the motor. We can set sail right away.

It takes a few minutes to unfurl the jib and set the sails at the proper tack, but then the boat starts to pick up the pace, tipping to the port side and sailing on a diagonal until the sails really catch. I lean back in my deck chair and look over at Jack, who still has his eyes closed.

The other boat is on a similar course but it's yards and yards away, keeping a safe distance so the crew can maneuver without the risk of the boats colliding. There's no point in trying to spot Chad and his fedora, and the acid in my stomach churns with the lost opportunity.

But I can see when a situation is beyond my control. Unless I really do want to jump ship and swim to the other boat, I might as well give up the fight and enjoy the time on the water.

I have to admit, it's not a bad place to spend a few hours. I curl onto my side so I'm facing him a little more, ball up my sweatshirt under my head and close my eyes. Life at sea feels pretty damned good.

26

JACK

AS MUCH AS I'd like to stay right next to Linden and sleep with her hand grasped in mine, this three-hour tour is an opportunity to sit with Ken and get my reporting done. Nothing better than a captive audience—if Ken doesn't like my questions, he'll have to swim to get away from me.

As it turns out, he's more than amiable. It's a welcome change from how he normally is when I interview him. Don't get me wrong; he's one of the most personable, genial people I've ever come in contact with. He's the perfect face for a media company that serves up big tentpole superhero movies and family entertainment. But it's a bit of a facade. It's his work personality and his media smile that most people see. He speaks at shareholder meetings and conferences with an even tone and a sweet expression. As far as he's concerned, that's all anyone needs to see.

Most powerful CEOs are careful about image, and Ken is no different. There's the smart, genial side that's fit for public consumption, and there's the more ruthless business side that he shares with adversaries and senior staff. He has ice in his veins when it comes to firing subordinates he doesn't think are running their subdivisions at peak performance. He expects a lot from his executives and he's merciless when it comes to his work ethic. When you work for him, you either perform or get fired.

He comes by his exacting standards honestly. He famously puts in sixteen-hour workdays and spends his commuting time making calls. Since he took control of Worldvision fifteen years ago, the company has gone from also-ran in the media business to the five-hundred-pound gorilla no one can beat. He's made millionaires of over a hundred people at the company.

I've been privy to his temper, often directed at me when I've printed something that paints one of the company's moves in an unflattering light, but he knows I'm just doing my job. He respects what I need to do to retain my reputation and he doesn't begrudge me the need to ask him the hard questions. He just doesn't always answer them in the explicit way I'd like. That's the job.

Ken is on the lower deck, standing at the front of the boat alone. It isn't wasted on me that he's wearing a navy sport coat, white pants, and a white baseball cap that makes him look every bit the seaman. He plays the part, whether he's being the gallant host or the stubborn head of a company or the glad-handing frontman in front of the cameras. When I coax him over to the bench so we can chat, I make a small notation about his outfit and his easy manner on the piece of scratch paper I'm using for notes. I also turn on my phone's recorder, but I find that scribbling on a scrap of paper that looks like nothing puts people at ease. Like I can't possibly write anything too damning from the notes I have on that thing.

"Here we go. I'm ready for your hatchet-job," Ken says, winking. People in his world do a lot of winking.

"I'm so glad we're on the same page about the story."

Ken laughs. If I didn't know him better, I'd think he was looking forward to talking to me and sharing all the details of his life he's kept out of the media thus far. It's a pretty big deal that he's let me come for the weekend and he's given me pretty much universal access to the people in his life and the run of his villa. But I do know Ken, well enough to wonder about his sudden change of heart when it comes to guarding his privacy.

"Thanks again for having both of us this weekend."

"Linden seems sweet. How long have you two been an item?"

Two days ago, I would have had no problem feeding him a line of bullshit about a date for the weekend, a casual relationship, something perfect for right now. Instead I feel a little bit protective of her. I don't want to make her seem like the usual string of women I date with no thought of a future. But that's crazy because we're not even dating. We had one night of incredible sex, end of story. I don't want more from her.

Sure, keep telling yourself that, and maybe you'll believe it.

"It's new," I tell Ken.

"Well, I can see she's really something. Don't do the stupid thing and let her get away from you. Trust me. I know people. I've made a fortune because I'm a good judge of people, and that one, she's a keeper."

"Is that on the record?" I'm trying to keep it light and change the subject back to him.

"Sure. Whatever you want." He looks out over the bow of the ship. The mist coming off the water showers his face before he turns away. "I sure do love it out here."

"Linden does too." What the hell am I doing? I'm not supposed to be squandering this time with Ken talking about Linden. "I mean, tell me about that. Did you always like boats? Did you grow up around them? Linden was raised in a landlocked area and that made her a little obsessed with boats and the ocean."

Seriously, stop looking for excuses to bring her up.

"I did, actually. My dad was a teacher, so he had summers

off. He used to take me out fishing every summer starting when I was eight. I didn't eat anything we caught, but I loved being in the boat. The one thing I knew, no matter what kind of job I'd end up having, was that I wanted to own a boat someday." He looks off into the distance again then glances around at the boat we're on. It's not really fair to call the yacht a mere boat, but I can see from his expression that he's happy with his choice.

"Did your dad ever come out on this one?"

"Couple times," he says. He tells me more about his dad, the relationship they had. I can tell his dad was influential in how he runs Worldvision, even though his job was nothing like it. Ken opens up easily about his family. He's not at all acting like the guarded man he normally is. I've definitely asked him questions about his upbringing in the past and he's shut me down.

I'm grateful he's open to me writing my profile and I'm not about to squander the opportunity. But I can't help wondering what's changed to make him suddenly willing to talk.

In fact, I'm still a little surprised Ken allowed for this profile at all. It makes me wonder if he's got an announcement brewing or some other reason why he wants to raise his personal profile. I've seen a lot of CEOs do that, almost like a bait and switch. They make a big splash by giving a reporter access to their personal lives and while everyone is busy reading about what they eat for breakfast and where they forage for antiques, some part of the company is dropping a news bomb and hoping the profile is enough of a distraction to compensate.

I'm fairly certain this is one of those times because there's really no other reason for Ken to decide to give me access suddenly after all these years. He wants the profile to run for a reason and before the weekend is over, I need to find out what that is.

~

AN HOUR LATER, I'm feeling pretty good about my profile. Ken has been a wide-open book about his family, his hobbies, even his philosophy on the correct ratio of work to leisure which allows for a long career.

Between the interview and the background, I can write the profile in my head after hanging around this weekend and seeing his off-the-job life in action. I know exactly how it will lay out.

But I'm a little uneasy. Something doesn't feel right and I can't put my finger on it. Maybe it's just a side of Ken I've never seen before. He's been so open, and I don't want to seem unappreciative.

On a gamble, I throw a different line of questioning at him. "Hey, so I met Chad last night. Good guy," I say, curious about how it is that they have a personal relationship.

"Yeah, he's a bundle of fun, isn't he?"

"Is this the first time he's been at the villa?"

"Oh, I believe he's been here once or twice before."

"Yeah? How'd you get to know him? Do you socialize with a lot of the people affiliated with shows Worldvision produces?"

"I wouldn't say a lot. But some."

"Could you give me some examples?"

It's tiny, but I see it: a slight look of unease passes over Ken's face before he harnesses his composure and forces his mouth into a smile. But it's a tell. He's uncomfortable. It wouldn't be obvious to a casual observer, but I've been interviewing this man for ten years. "Oh, you know, hosts of various shows. I'd be lying if I said I remembered all their names."

He knows people's names. It's part of his business acumen.

"Sounds like you have an affinity for Chad," I say.

"Well, he does host our most profitable show. I like to demonstrate my appreciation." He doesn't look at me. His gaze is fixed on the water.

I, however, am watching him when I ask my next question. "How's everything going on that show? After this many seasons, there's bound to be some drama behind the scenes. Tempers, bad behavior."

He shakes his head, but I'm certain I see another flinch discomfort. "Quite the opposite. After this many years, it's a well-oiled machine. No drama at all."

I decide to let the issue lie for now because I don't want to jeopardize the goodwill I've fostered so far, and I may have more questions for him this weekend. But I'm not letting go of this.

Maybe the reason Ken is so willing to talk about his childhood is to avoid talking about something else.

27

LINDEN

UNFORTUNATELY, I end up missing most of the scenery. Turns out the gentle rocking through the surf and the warm sun are a lethal combination when it comes to staying awake on a boat. I slept on my deck chair for over an hour before I'm nudged awake by Jack who runs a hand along my cheek.

I blink my eyes open and look at him, momentarily unsure where I am. Then I feel the breeze and smell the sea air and it comes back to me—I'm on a sailboat, and it's Jack who has his hand cupped under my jaw. "Hey," he says when I can finally focus on his face.

"How long was I asleep?"

He glances at his phone. "Almost two hours. We're on our way back."

"Seriously?"

"Yeah, for someone who swears to never take naps, you're looking like a liar."

"I guess all that's been missing is the sun and the boat."

"Or maybe me."

"Aw, that's sweet," I hear someone say and I turn to see Chase sitting on the end of Jack's lounge chair. Glancing around I see that most of the passengers of our particular boat have moved to the upper deck where I've apparently been sleeping in full view of a dozen onlookers. Some are focused on the ocean view, but there are enough on the chairs around us for me to know Jack's comment was heard by more people than just Chase.

Jack is smiling at me, being the cute half of our pretend couple. I reel my emotions in, the ones that sent my pulse racing when I felt his hand on my face. When we go back to work on Monday, we'll just be two regular colleagues who happened to end up in bed together one weekend. Because of the ocean views and the drinks. And the lust. I need to keep reminding myself of that. And I need to stay focused on the reason I'm here this weekend. It's not because I'm Jack's girlfriend.

"Thanks for waking me," I say, leaning in to kiss him. Like the better half of a pretend couple would do. "I'm gonna have a little look at what I've been missing." Then I haul myself off the lounge chair and walk over to the railing, feeling the salt air hit my skin. It really is beautiful out here on the water and I'm a little bummed I slept through so much of the trip. But the sleep did wonders. Shaking off the slightly dizzy feeling from sleeping in the sun, I think about how I haven't been at my reporting best today. It's fine, but it just puts a little more pressure on the rest of the day.

By the time the sailboat makes its final turn, I'm no longer in a place of calm. As the boat sails back toward the villa, I feel my heart start beating faster because I'm forming the beginnings of a plan. It will require me to be a little more aggressive in my approach to Chad, but I know what I need to do.

The villa is getting larger as we get closer. From this vantage point, I can really see how large the property is, spanning at least twice the space of the nearest coastal neighbor, who may be Oprah for all I know.

I look back at Jack, who's chatting with Ken. He has his

phone out, so I'm sure he's recording whatever Ken is telling him. I won't have the luxury of doing that with Chad, but I have a pretty good memory, and I'll make strategic trips to the bathroom, if necessary, to make notes on my phone.

We disembark the sailboat for the small dinghies and motor back to shore. I check the time and it's already a quarter to five, which means we're due for the obligatory sunset cocktails in just over an hour. I need to get the salt air and grime out of my hair before dinner. It's not looking like I'll have any chance to hit up Chad for a conversation until the cocktail hour.

But then it's go time. Which means serious questions, alcohol in his glass, and no holds barred to getting what I want. No more wasting time for me.

28

LINDEN

JACK THINKS it's a little strange that after how much I enjoyed his *casita* earlier that I'd want to shower and get dressed in my own.

"Please don't take it personally. Think of it this way. If we both had to use the same bathroom, it would take us twice as long to get ready."

"Actually, probably four times as long because there are activities I can think of that would go well with a shower."

"Mmm, that's awfully tempting… but I think it may have to wait." It takes a considerable amount of self-restraint to stand in front of him and say no to anything he's proposing, least of all a soapy sex-fest. He's wearing his navy sweatshirt tied around his shoulders—preppy overload—which means his rock-hard biceps are visible, stretching the limits of the fabric of his grey t-shirt. Maybe I could spend an hour in his room…

I take a deep breath and reaffirm my resolve. "I have to do my reporting."

I catch the look of disappointment on his face and feel bad that I'm so hell-bent on getting to Chad that I'm kind of pushing him away. "It's the reason we're here: to get Chad to talk. I'll be a whole lot more relaxed once I accomplish that." I pull him in and press my lips to his, kissing him long enough to give him a preview of what might come later if I'm successful in my mission.

"I do want you relaxed," he says. "And we don't really have that much time before we're due for cocktails, at least, not enough time for what I have in mind." He lets me go.

When I knock on Jack's door an hour later, he opens it like he's been waiting for me. At first, I'm flattered by his enthusiasm. But his eyes go wide and I'm struck by what I assume is the reason for his look. "Oh shit, am I late?"

"It's worth it." He smiles, taking in the red dress I'm wearing tonight, which is just as short as last night's but this one is all one piece and a little tighter in all the right places. It's my favorite dress and I've only worn it once to a wedding. I know, I don't go out that much. "Wow, that dress, that's… wow."

"Thank you. You look pretty good yourself." He does. His hair is wet and slicked back and he hasn't shaved since Friday morning, so his scruff looks even hotter now. His blue eyes sparkle as he meets my gaze.

"I'm sorry if you spent a lot of time on your lipstick, cuz I'm not letting you get out of here without messing it up."

He pulls me in, one hand on my back while he gently takes ownership of my lips. His kisses go from teasing to possessive as he licks, kisses and sucks every last bit of Crimson Fire off my lips. I am dizzy and limp when he stops. "I could kiss you for days," he whispers, igniting a sea of desire inside me.

"Maybe you should." I can't get over what he does to me. Part of it could be knowing that the weekend is all the time we have to do this. We both agreed to it, and the fleeting time makes every touch, every kiss that much better.

I'm leaning into him, partly to hold myself up, because kissing him makes me lightheaded and breathless. After a few more minutes it's clear that we either have to break the kiss or head into his *casita* and be very, very late for dinner. With a sigh, he backs away, his lips a little rosy from the residual lipstick. I reach up and try to wipe some of it away. As I rub my thumb across his lower lip, he watches me. I can't tell what he's thinking because he always has that steady stoic look on his face, but after I rub back and forth a couple times, he sucks the tip of my thumb.

He shakes his head. "I've gotta stop. This will just lead to more of that." He gestures inside. "And you have a story to report."

"You don't want to have a go at trying to get Chad to open up? You're pretty persuasive," I say, brushing one last kiss across his lips.

He shakes his head. "No. He likes you. And you're good with people. He's all yours."

DOWN ON THE LOWER LAWN, there's an appetizer spread fit for a wedding. Along with wine pairings and a waiter passing flutes of champagne. In the time we've been here, I've seen one or two waiters and bartenders setting up food and pouring drinks, but there's no way the few people I've seen account for the full staff of this place. Too much is being prepped, displayed, cleaned, and beautified.

"Who's making all this happen?" I ask Jack when we reach the lawn and take in the massive *charcuterie* platter, a shrimp cocktail ice sculpture, and a table-wide cheese platter that looks like it was airlifted from France.

"Yeah, it's pretty unbelievable." He looks around like he's noticing the display for the first time, as if he wasn't paying attention earlier. "They don't really talk about their staff. I know Judy likes them to be invisible."

"Yeah, I kind of have the sense that a team of fleet-footed fairies make midnight deliveries or something."

He laughs. "Maybe."

"It's good stuff for your story. I can see now why this weekend was so important to you. I hope I didn't get in the way of you getting what you needed."

Buzz and his girlfriend are at the bar and Ken's golf buddies and Judy's team of fitness instructors are seated at tables scattered in perfect symmetry on the lawn. There are still plenty of guests missing, so I'm not worried we're late.

More people are starting to filter onto the lawn. I see Jim Culligan and his daughter, Chase, who seems to wear a permanent frown. I've barely said two words to her and based on her attitude, I'm not sure I want to say more. "What's her deal?" I ask Jack.

"Her parents dragged her here because they're trying to set her up with Neve, and understandably, she's miserable."

"Neve, the little guy who teaches Pilates?"

"I guess. She's actually awesome when she's not around her parents. They've never really gotten along. She and Shane are super close though."

"Maybe we should hang with her, keep her parents from driving her too crazy," I offer.

Jack nods and picks up my hand. "I'm glad you're here."

We each grab a glass of champagne and a tiny plate. I fill mine with olives and Jack puts together a balanced array of prosciutto, sheep's milk cheese, and tiny pickles. He looks over at my plate. "Not much for variety?"

"I don't want to smell like salami and cheese. Fresh breath is key to good reporting."

I look around for the hundredth time. Still no Chad. I wonder what's up. He seems like a cocktail party kind of guy. Jack gestures to one of the small tables. But I hesitate to sit.

"What's up?" he asks.

"I'm just thinking, this is a table for four. If we sit here, there will only be two empty seats."

He nods, as though he's working hard to follow along. "Okay, four minus two is two, still with you. And?"

"I just mean, anyone who sits with us is great for you and your profile because you can work some little tidbit of information out of them, but I need to get stuff out of one specific person."

"Ah. You want to sit with Chad."

"I want to get the story I came for. I'll just glue myself to the guy if I have to until he spills his guts."

He gestures me to come closer, but I'm hesitant, as if it's some kind of trick. He waits, unwilling to tell me anything until I give up some ground. I take a step closer. He gestures to the seat. I take a look around, trying to see if Chad is somewhere and I'm missing an opportunity, but I don't spot him or his fedora. Maybe he's not wearing the hat. Maybe he's late, a possibility that endears him to me a little bit. I lean on the arm of the chair next to his and look at Jack expectantly.

"I know you want the story. Maybe too much. I think you need to dial it back a notch."

I can't decide if that's good advice or if he's trying to distract me with his smile and his clear blue eyes that are currently surveying me like he's plotting only one thing: how to get me back to his room before the appetizers are served. Which can't happen.

It's easy for him to be casual. He already got his sit-down with Ken. I can't be so relaxed.

"Why would I dial it back?"

"So you don't come at the guy like a crazed interrogator on a reporting mission and scare him out of talking to you at all. You can't just bulldoze your way into getting what you want. Good reporting is an art form. You have to build up to the hard questions with easy ones."

Seems like solid advice, but I'm not sure how to do that. "What are you suggesting?"

"Have an appetizer. You haven't eaten anything today."

"You gave me a muffin earlier."

"Which you didn't eat. I saw you put it in your sweatshirt pocket." I thought I'd been stealthy about that. I didn't realize he noticed.

"I'm trying to be semi-healthy."

"Which is awesome. Do that. Eat your olives."

"I don't want to," I say. I know I'm acting like a bratty child, but I'm frustrated that things aren't working out today. I pop one olive into my mouth to placate Jack and immediately regret my choice of snack food because each olive contains a pit I somehow have to dispose of gracefully. I spit this one into my hand. I'll just hold onto it until I figure out where to put it.

Jack leaves me at the table and walks back to the appetizer buffet, coming back with a plate like his own, laden with cheese triangles, flatbread, tiny pickles, and a few cherry tomatoes.

"Here. Eat this. And explain to me what's going on with you."

"I'm just antsy and I feel like I lost three hours of reporting time already today." I pick up a piece of cheese, place it on a rectangle of flatbread, and take a bite. It's delicious and I realize that part of my problem is that I'm hangry. Much as I hate to admit it, Jack is right. I need to eat.

"You have plenty of time. Trust me, if anyone can get him to talk, it's you. He likes you; I can tell." He puts his hand on my thigh, rubbing his thumb lightly over the skin that's very exposed because I chose this short dress. My leg jumps at his touch and I feel a warm glow under his fingers and despite myself, I feel my shoulders relax. He smiles. "By the way, so do I. I was regretting telling you to change out of those shorts all day, but this dress is something else."

"I can always put the shorts on underneath if you liked them so much."

"No, please don't," he says, nuzzling my neck and planting a few kisses along my throat. If there's any question about us being a couple, it would be clear to anyone looking at us that we get along. Maybe that's the point of all this public display of affection. Maybe Ken will give him a more personal story if he's seeing what he thinks is Jack's personal life. I never know with Jack if he's working an angle. I still don't completely trust him.

Why not? He's been nothing but sweet since we got here.

I can already feel the champagne going to my head and I don't want to go off on some rant that might be avoidable with a little something to soak up the alcohol. I eat another piece of flatbread and the rest of the cheese. I'm starting to feel a little better. Jack moves his hand down and caresses a spot behind my knee, which I didn't even know was sensitive until his fingers send a new shock wave of desire through me.

At the smallest touch from him, my insides light up and I feel myself wanting more. I'm caught between the urge to wrap my arms around his neck and be his weekend plus-one for a few more minutes—or hours—and the competing urge to hunt down my elusive reality show host.

"Maybe you're right," I say, thinking it won't hurt to have a quick little faux-girlfriend PDA, especially if Chad happens to walk by and get all hot and bothered by the display. I reach a hand out for him and shift off the arm of my chair and onto his lap.

"Ah, I'm so glad you've seen the value in my plan." He smiles and immediately puts a hand on my back, moving his fingers along my spine and twisting them in my hair. I feel a surge of pleasure every time he touches me, and I realize how easy it is to be with him. For now, at least, while we're here in this magical setting that doesn't seem like the real world.

I don't want to think about Monday morning when we'll

be back to our usual jobs. There's no point in thinking about that now.

Jack is no longer looking at me and he doesn't seem to have heard my response because his gaze has shifted to Jim, who's sauntering over with his wife. I can't tell if he wants them to join us or if he's dreading the intrusion in our space. I get my answer when Jack puts a hand up and waves them over. "Jim, Claudia, why don't you join us?"

Jim smiles but then I see Chase coming up behind her parents, scowling.

OVER THE COURSE of the cocktail hour, I'm very distracted, looking over my shoulder every few minutes to try and catch a glimpse of Chad. Every so often, Jack reaches over and guides my chin back to look at him, reminding me that there's a conversation taking place at the table and I'm being rude.

"Sorry," I mouth to him and try to focus again on the conversation Claudia is having with Jack about hooking up, much to the embarrassment of Chase, who's probably about my age and has therefore probably done her share of hooking up. Not that anyone wants to talk about that with her parents.

"I just don't understand," she keeps saying to Jack. "It doesn't make sense."

"Mom, you're being kinda dense. It's just normal dating," Chase says, looking around like maybe someone will come along and rescue her from the conversation. I realize that Jack and I are her best bet and I feel suddenly bad that I've been falling down on the job I offered to do.

"It's not dating, though. If it was dating, you'd be starting a courtship, building up to something little by little. Hooking up is just, sex," Claudia says. "Am I missing something? How is that ever going to lead to a relationship if you're giving the milk away?" Chase looks as if she'd like to be swallowed up by the resplendent lawn. For his part, Jim seems to have found salvation at the bottom of his bloody mary and hasn't looked up in twenty minutes.

"Mom, seriously, a courtship? This isn't the seventeenth century."

"Well, I just don't know what to think. Linden, can you explain it to me?"

I'm surprised she's dragging me into this, but if she wants my opinion, I decide I need to try for a save. "There aren't rules like maybe you're used to," I tell Claudia. "Our generation is more easy-going. We like to have fun without ascribing meaning to every action. It takes the pressure off." I hear my words and I wonder if Jack is hearing me describe our last twenty-four hours in the process. I don't look at him to find out.

"But surely sometimes the fun has to be leading to something more serious," Claudia says.

"Not necessarily. It's about where you are in your life. Sometimes fun is all you can handle with work and everything else. In that case, there's nothing wrong with a hookup." I feel like I'm justifying my orgasmathon, and I don't know if I'm doing a good job of explaining anything to Claudia, but Chase seems relieved that her mother's eyes are now boring into someone else.

"Casual sex. You might as well just call it like it is," Claudia says.

"And what's wrong with that, Mom? Seriously, you dragged me here for the weekend and it's the snooze of the century. If I find a decent looking human—over five feet tall— with a pulse and a cock, you better believe I'm hooking up. Just to keep from gouging out my own eyeballs to combat the boredom." With that, she pushes her chair back and dumps her plate on an unattended silver tray and stomps off toward the bar.

"That went well, as usual." Claudia straightens her shrimp fork next to her plate and looks at Jim. "You might've helped me out there."

He looks up from his drink for the first time like he's not sure where he is. "You seemed to have it handled."

"Oh, what do you know? She could end up alone at thirty," she says. Her words come out like a hysterical screech.

"No one's ending up alone," Jim says, patting her hand.

I look at Jack who has been silent all this time but looking plenty amused. He finally jumps in, putting his hand over hers and giving it a squeeze. The gesture seems far more effective than Jim's hand pat because she lets out a giant sigh and her face relaxes for the first time since the conversation began. "Claudia, you just have to understand that it's not that different from when you two probably first met. It's just less formal, less pressure until both people really decide they want a relationship."

He's not saying anything Chase or I didn't say a few minutes earlier but somehow the calm way he approaches it placates Claudia. She nods at him. "I just worry about her, you know?"

"Of course you do. She's your daughter. You want the best for her."

"That's all I want. I don't think she sees that."

"I think she knows." Jack nods at her until she starts nodding too. Finally, she picks up her fork, her appetite apparently returning and with it a more jovial mood. She elbows Jim and asks if he'd like another bloody mary and suggests he bring her one too.

I turn back to Jack, trying to figure out how he handles people as well as he does. I'm also struck with the fear that over this whole weekend, he's just handling me too, bending me to his will without me realizing it. But to what end? Just for sex? It's already clear that's beginning and end of our weekend escapades. We've both affirmed as much.

"You want another glass of champagne?" Jack asks.

"Maybe." I don't have time to think about what angle Jack may be working. I really need to turn my attention to Chad. Almost as if on cue, he walks past the terrace, headed in the direction of the pool. Jack watches me watching him. "Looks like I'm spending the dinner hour at the pool," I tell him.

"Okay," he says, looking a little disappointed.

"It's different for you. You've already proven yourself, so no one is looking at you with the same kind of scrutiny as I have on me right now. But I'm trying to claw myself out from under a series of screw-ups. Doing a good job on this is really important to me."

He nods. "I know it is. I get it. Don't worry."

"You'll be okay on your own for a bit?"

He shrugs, his hand still on my leg. Now he moves it a little higher, where my inner thigh jumps under his touch and I let out an uncontrollable gasp. I wish I was less transparent. I'm doing everything in my power to stay focused and all it takes is the smallest touch for a big part of my brain to want to abandon my plans and wrap my legs around him. "I'll manage. I think you'll feel better once you get what you want from Chad, so, do what you need to do."

He's right. So why am I not standing up and going off to get the information I'm after? Because his thumb is lightly brushing my thigh and weakening my resolve. I look down at his hand and his eyes suddenly go wide. He stops and pulls his hand away. "Oops. Sorry."

I know.

I am too.

29

LINDEN

I'M nervous as I walk over to the pool where I'm pretty sure Chad will be sitting alone. Everyone else is at the cocktail hour, which sounded mandatory, so I'm curious why he's chosen to bail.

I swear, this villa feels more like a luxury hotel than someone's house. The pool is surrounded by mature olive trees and it has its own bar and three cabanas with wide lounge chairs inside. As I expected, no one is there besides Chad.

He's sitting on a lounge chair facing the pool, a drink in one hand, his phone in the other.

After I grab a towel from a stained-wood bin, I set myself up on a lounge chair across the pool from where he is. He's a decent-looking guy, all told. From where I'm sitting, I can see the effects of gym workouts and ample sun time on his taut abs and toned arms. He's not my type at all, mainly because he seems a little shallow, and there's no bigger turn-off for me than an inability to keep up with a conversation. But physically, I can see how he's been able to make a living in front of the camera.

It doesn't take long before he sees me and waves. I shoot him a look of pleasant surprise like I didn't notice him initially. It's getting dark, but the lighting on the trees and around the pool would make it pretty hard not to notice him. "You out here alone?" he yells across the pool. It's okay. We're the only ones there.

"Yup, just me."

"Well, I don't wanna yell across a pool. You want to come to this side?"

I pick up my champagne and make my way over to a chaise on the other side of the small table where he's put his phone.

"There she is. The belle of the ball."

I laugh. "That sounds so charming and antiquated."

"I was only going for charming."

I smile, giving him my best flirtatious glance up from under my heavily mascaraed eyes. I'm pretty bad at flirting and I haven't had many occasions to improve my game.

"You good on drinks, baby? Sure you don't want something stronger?" I bristle at him calling me baby, but I'm forced to smile through it. I fight the memory of when Jack used the same word last night, right as he was coaxing another orgasm from me. In that context, I was fully on board. But Chad is in the junior leagues by comparison.

"Maybe in a bit. I'll stick with this for now."

I still can't get over how different Chad looks in person. I didn't realize how much makeup they must put on him before the cameras roll. He seems mellower than his on-air persona, and maybe even a little bit sad. "So. Not interested in the dinner?"

"Nah. I'm still a little queasy after the sail, believe it or not."

"Oh. Sorry to hear. That's no fun."

"It happens every time I go out there, and every time, I think it's gonna be different."

"Aren't you constantly on a boat for the show? How do you deal with that?"

He smiles. "Meds, seasick wristbands, ginger chews. I do it all. Wouldn't look good for me to be puking my guts out on TV."

"Some people might find it entertaining."

"I'm not interested in knowing those people. There are other shows for people like them." Now that we're away from the other guests, Chad is decidedly more normal. And likable. I might actually enjoy spending the next few hours—or however long he wants to hang out—talking to him. "Only I would end up on a boat show when I seriously hate boats."

"Couldn't you have at least skipped today's outing?"

He shakes his head. "That's a big no. Ken's my boss's boss. He says sail, I sail."

"I didn't realize he had that kind of influence."

"It's his company. He influences everything." It makes me wonder if Ken is aware that the show buried Jake's indiscretion with a crew member, if it ends up being true. I'll have to talk to Jack about that and I have a feeling he won't like the insinuation. One more instance of me trampling all over his coveted beat.

I want to ask more about the show, but I know better than to come out swinging, as Jack reminded me. I need to gain his trust, develop a rapport. I'm good with people, I remind myself. I can do this. It's just a regular conversation, with Chad at the center.

"It's nice that you got the weekend off."

"Yeah, we have a one-week break between seasons, then it's back on the boat." He makes a vomiting face. His liability is ratcheting up by the minute.

I can hear the sounds of conversation and laughter drifting over from where everyone's eating dinner or having drinks on the lawn. I feel a pang of regret at bailing on Jack, but he's right. I can do this myself and I need to do it. "Your schedule sounds brutal. How do you have time for a life?"

"What life?"

"Seriously? Is it all about the show?"

He wipes the back of his hand across his forehead like he's dabbing sweat, but it's not hot out here, despite ample heat lamps. "It's just… yeah, it's a lot."

"So… girlfriend?" I ask. I'm curious. Maybe he's not even straight. He plays it all close to the vest.

He flashes his thousand-watt smile, the one that melts the hearts of women around the country. He seems to return to reality show host mode when he gets uncomfortable. "I don't know, baby. You tell me." He winks.

He's nice enough looking and he seems like a decent guy. But somewhere along the way, no one seems to have told him that calling women he barely knows baby and winking like his charms are self-evident are mannerisms most women find cringe worthy. I'm pretty sure I can speak for all women when I say this. And it occurs to me that it may actually be the best way to gain his trust. Instead of trying to flirt and be someone I'm not, maybe I can gain points with him by being a straight shooter. It seems worth a try. Maybe we can be that kind of friends.

He looks at our empty glasses and holds up his own. "Time for another round?"

"Works for me," I say.

He gets up and takes my empty from me. "Thanks. And when you get back, I'm gonna tell you why you should cut it out with the 'baby' stuff and all the winking around women you're getting to know."

He laughs. "Okay, well I guess I had that coming. Deal. Please, impart your wisdom."

"Drinks first."

He holds them up as if to toast and carries them away for refills.

~

THE CONVERSATION with Chad has been a therapy session about his dating life for the past hour. In trying to let him lead the conversation and gain his confidence gradually—much the same way I did with Megan, by talking about anything but the story—we've fully shifted into how he can get his dating life in order. The guy seems genuinely distraught over his prospects.

But we've made some progress. He understands that laying on the bullshit doesn't work, and he's started to articulate what he actually wants in a girlfriend. "I want a confidante, a lover, someone to dream with, someone to experience life's tiny moments with," he says, plaintively.

After a few hours of conversation, I see that he's nothing like the smarmy host he plays on the show, which makes sense since most of what he says and does is scripted. He's an actor, and he's good at it.

The problem is that he's lost sight of where the reality show persona ends and he begins. Maybe that's what happens after that many seasons in front of the camera. The guy sitting with me is an honest, hard-working guy who just wants what most people want: to fall in love.

"I want to travel and laugh and take naps and eat ridiculous meals that don't represent all the food groups. Is that too much to hope for in a soulmate?" he asks.

"Not at all," I tell him. It shouldn't be. "I think it's hard with your job and all the time you spend traveling. But you'll find her. She's out there. Maybe when you're done on the show and have more time on land. It bodes well for your love life if you're not puking on your dates."

"Yeah. True. I think that day may arrive sooner than people expect."

"Why's that?"

He shrugs. "It's been eleven seasons. Maybe it's time to move on."

"I'm sure it's a hard decision. You don't want to say no to

a good thing, but if it's impacting your personal life and preventing you from taking on other career opportunities… only you know when the time is right," I say.

"Yeah. Sometimes it's good to try something new." He suddenly seems worn out, not from our conversation, but from the endless hours smiling in front of the camera. No wonder he'd rather sit by the pool than talk to people at dinner.

He puts a hand on mine. I can tell it's a genuine show of appreciation for listening. I tell myself I have to stop doubting my reporting abilities. It's about doing this—listening—and building a rapport with people. It's something that actually comes naturally to me. And Jack was right. My ambition was bigger than my ability when I first came to the paper. I didn't have all the skills I needed. But maybe I have them now.

I decide to dip a toe in the water and press him a little more about the show.

"Do you mind indulging a fan in a little more of the behind-the-scenes of the show?"

He takes a sip of his drink and doesn't answer right away. He looks out over the pool and points to the tiny reflections of the twinkle lights on the water. "Ken and Judy did this place right, down to every detail. Or their decorator did. Either way, it's amazing, isn't it?"

"Gorgeous." I wonder why he changed the subject, but I know better than to press.

He's quiet a moment, then he turns to face me. "You want to know about how the show works. What, specifically?"

"Oh, just the stuff we talked about the other night. How you draw the lines between what people are willing to do on camera and what should stay out of the public eye. There's always such drama." I almost feel like it's a conflict of interest for me to report this story since I love the show so much, but I won't let it be a problem.

"Yeah, that's what I thought you meant." He's quiet again.

His demeanor is different from last night when he seemed more forthcoming about the show. It's strange because I feel like we have a better rapport now, but he seems hesitant to talk. He looks me in the eye. "Are you a reporter? Like your boyfriend?"

"He's not my boyfriend." The answer comes so quickly I'm shocked at how insistent I sound.

"Okay. Could've fooled me. But let's put a pin in that. You didn't answer my question."

I can't lie. What would be the point? Even if Chad does end up telling me everything I want to know, if I want to print any of it in the paper, I need him to be on the record. Plus, right now I'm seeing a softer, more human side of him. I actually like him. "Yeah. I'm a reporter too."

He flashes his TV grin. "Thought so. You're just a little bit too interested in the background machinations for a regular fan."

"I'm sorry I didn't tell you."

He waves a hand. "Don't be. I work in reality TV. Assume I live in a world where people lie about much bigger things than that."

It sounds awful. I feel a little guilty for all the hours of joy I've gleaned from it. "How do you stand it?"

"It's entertainment, baby," he says, giving me the show biz smile with the perfect white teeth. "When I have to turn it on, I do. When I don't need to be on set, I'm hell and gone from there. And someday, when I meet a version of you who isn't in love with someone else, I'll be gone for good. "

"So now that you know I'm a reporter—for the Examiner —can I ask you about an allegation I heard?"

He nods. "Can't promise I'll answer, but maybe I can let you know if you're onto something and you can take it from there."

"Fair enough." I take out my phone and use it to type

notes. "If you say something's off the record, I won't attribute it to you, but anything on the record I can quote."

He nods his head. "What've you got for me?"

"I understand a member of the camera crew was laid off. Do you know why that would happen in the middle of the season?"

He smiles. "On the record? I have no knowledge of why her position was no longer needed, but usually those things happen for budgetary reasons."

"Okay, but I'm told she was involved with one of the contestants."

"Off the record, yes. She wasn't fired because that would imply she'd done something wrong, and admitting that would have had a domino effect."

He goes on to tell me that Megan and Jake's fling was not as hush-hush as she believed. Other contestants knew and were paid extra money to keep quiet about it. A lot of extra money. The kind of money that would show up as an expense on a balance sheet—one of those line items I'd memorized this week. Megan was laid off and paid a severance package and Jake, the audience favorite, was coddled so he can keep appearing on the show every week and keep it at the top of the ratings list.

Even though I can't quote him by name, Chad's given me a lot of what I need to write the story. I can quote "an unnamed source who works on Bachelor Bay." And maybe now that I know the details, I can convince other employees on the show to talk on the record. It's worth a shot.

He leans back and tucks his hands behind his head, elbows out to the sides like he doesn't have a care in the world. I kind of admire his ability to shift attitudes on a dime. "Tell you the truth, I'm sick to death of pretending this shit doesn't happen on our show. I feel bad for Megan because she lost her job over it, that's the worst part, but that decision came from above my paygrade."

I'm not sure I'm really hearing him correctly. Is he saying it was a corporate decision to get rid of Megan and let Jake stay? "How far above your paygrade? Like, the very top?" I ask, pointing in the direction of where his boss's boss, Ken Nichols, is still entertaining guests on the terrace.

He shrugs. "Something like that."

I reach over and wrap my arms around his neck. "Thank you. I can't even tell you how much this means to me. It's a big story."

"You just pay it forward, sister. Find me a nice single woman who looks a lot like you but maybe doesn't ask so many questions. And you send her my way."

I promise him I'll do my best.

30

JACK

I HAVEN'T SEEN Linden in hours. I'm pretty sure I know where she is—still at the pool with Chad. Neither one of them made an appearance at dinner and I have to assume that's a good sign. He must be talking. That, or they're in his room— or her room—having sex in exchange for a story.

Ew. I have to get that image out of my mind, pronto. I know Linden wouldn't do that.

I watch Chase, who's on her way back from the bar with a round of drinks for the two of us. I offered to get them, but she insisted she needed to stretch her legs. So, fine. I'm not gonna argue, especially after all the years when she'd visit Shane and me at school and she had the whole bunch of us running around bringing her drinks and anything else she wanted. Being Shane's little sister got her all kinds of special treatment. It didn't hurt that she was cute, but Shane made it clear that if any of his friends had even a fleeting idea about kissing her, he'd beat the crap out of all of us. I was probably the only one who took him at his word.

"He was out of gin so I had him make us margaritas. Does that work?" Chase asks, handing me a glass with salt around the rim and a couple clinking ice cubes inside.

"Good for me." Not good for me, since the combination of gin and tequila is likely to give me a massive headache in about an hour and I'm still hoping to be in good form when Linden finishes with Chad. We only have one more night here. I'll be disappointed if she doesn't come find me.

"Thank God the 'rents went to bed. They've been driving me fucking crazy all weekend," Chase says, taking a long slug from her drink.

"Why'd you come?"

"Didn't you hear? They were trying to matchmake me with a Pilates instructor. At first, I thought it was going to be a female because, honestly, I don't know any men who teach Pilates. So for a minute, I was a little bit psyched because I thought it meant my parents were leaning into me being gay."

"Since when are you gay?" I ask.

"I'm not. But I liked the idea of them thinking I was. I dunno. I just like to mess with them, I guess."

"They're really on you, huh?"

"Yes! It would make it a whole lot easier if Shane would get married and start pumping out grandchildren. Take the pressure off me."

"Maybe he will," I say. Although knowing Shane and his love for variety, it's doubtful he'll settle on one woman and have babies anytime soon.

She takes the lime from her drink and bites into it, then cringes, likely from the sour taste.

"No, I just have to face it. I'm my parents' bitch until they decide otherwise."

"Well, here's a thought. Maybe don't do everything they ask you to do," I say. She has to learn to say no to her parents. If she doesn't, she'll have bigger problems than a string of hookups. And there's nothing wrong with hookups. That has me thinking about Linden again and wishing she'd reappear.

Chase finishes her drink and pops one of the ice cubes into

her mouth, talking through it. "I love my parents. They're a pain in the ass, but I don't want them to worry about me and my unstable relationships."

"They don't seem that worried. I think it was just a conversation."

"Maybe. Yeah, you're right. I'm here. It's gorgeous. I can't let my mom get to me." I'm feeling whiplashed by the about-face, but I'm glad she's not spitting venom for the moment. I need to extricate myself. It would be more fun to hang in the room. "So, catch me up. How'd you find the love of your life? Probably not at a weekend key party with your parents' friends."

Is she talking about Linden? "Oh, we're colleagues. She works at the paper with me. Not the love of my life, trust me."

"Oh, come on. I saw you two together. It's so obvious that you have it bad for her."

"I'm not sure what you saw, but—"

"OMG, it's the way you look at her. It's everything. It's exactly what my stupid mom is hoping I'll find, and the crazy thing is, for the first time, watching you two, I actually thought I might want it myself."

I'm not sure what to do with all that. "Oh."

"Uh huh. So, you love her. Have you told her?"

"What? No. I don't love her. This whole thing between us, it's not a thing. It's a weekend thing." I don't think I've ever been more inarticulate.

She laughs. "Oh, okay. You just keep telling yourself that. But one of these days, you're gonna realize I'm a genius."

I really don't know what to do with all that. She's rambling and probably drunk, and I should put zero credence in what she's saying. But I am feeling a little bored and lost tonight without Linden hanging with me, which is crazy. I've done reporting junkets hundreds, maybe thousands of times. I just put on my reporting hat and go. Like a robot. None of those ever made me feel the aching emptiness I feel right now.

None of them included her.

Stop it. Stop letting Chase get in your head. It's all good. Just get through the weekend.

I don't have to suggest that maybe Chase should slow down on the drinks because she's now put her head down on the table. I worry for a minute that she's passed out and wonder if I should carry her back to her *casita*. Then she looks up at me and winks. "It's all good. And you've always been a sweetheart. I hope I find a guy like you someday." Now she's standing. Wobbling, but standing.

I walk her back to her room and make sure she gets in the door. Then I take one last look in the direction of the pool, wondering if Linden is still out there with Chad. I don't see any sign of her. I walk into my dark *casita* and head to the balcony so I can listen to the ocean.

31

———

LINDEN

WHEN I POUND on Jack's door, I don't mean to sound like a drunk sorority girl begging to be let in after curfew, but that's what comes to mind. I'm still out there pounding, and I think it's already been a minute or two. Why isn't Jack opening the door? It's not that late. At least, I don't think so.

I pull out my phone to check the time just as the door swings open. Jack is standing there in the same button-down shirt he was wearing earlier, with its sleeves rolled up over his forearms like he does at work. His tie is gone, and he's untucked his shirt. He looks just as hot and sexy as he did when we left for cocktails on the lawn, hours ago. Actually, he looks better. The second I see him; it hits me how much I missed him.

"Hey!" I'm super amped.

"Hey. You okay?"

I feel better than okay. I don't have time to ponder why he asked me that. I could have eyeliner all over my face right now, but I don't care. I'm too excited. "Oh my God, Jack. I got it. He told me everything!" I still can't believe it's true. I still can't really fathom how big a story this is, but I know I've got something good.

"Wait, what? Chad? He corroborated Megan's allegation?" His eyes light up. I know that look. I've seen it in the office so many times when Jack has some big news he's about to break in the paper. I love that look.

I'm nodding like a bobblehead doll on crack. Then I'm launching myself at Jack because the only thing better than getting this story is the feel of his mouth on mine. I'm hell-bent on getting to his lips. He doesn't make any attempt to slow me down, which is good because I'm not in the mood for anything slow.

He leads me back out to the patio, where I barely notice the mashed up pillows where he was sitting. We land on the wide chaise and I'm slightly conscious of the ocean roaring in the background as Jack pulls me on top of him. "I want to hear all about it, but it'll have to wait," he says, pulling my dress up over my head. "You look gorgeous in this, but so much better out of it."

I'm sitting up, unbuttoning his shirt, his pants. This is a race to get rid of any fabric that separates us. "I want to feel your skin." Mission accomplished in seconds and he pulls me back down so I can feel the skin-to-skin contact of his chest against mine. I wrap his face in my hands and kiss him with an urgency fueled by the thrill of landing the story and the knowledge that our colleagues-with-benefits weekend is almost over. I don't want to stop, and I don't want to think about the limited time we have.

He's trying to slow down my frantic pace, moving me over him so my breasts are above his face, and he takes full advantage of gravity, closing his mouth over one of them while his fingers reach lower. I'm a ball of pre-orgasmic energy, ready to explode.

He stops, rolling me to the side and runs a hand over my cheek. He's looking into my eyes and even though I'm desperate, ragged, I try to regain my focus and meet his gaze. "I don't want a quick fuck," he says. "I want to take you right to the edge and let you feel every delicious bit of every orgasm I can pull out of you. Then I want to do it again."

I don't have words to match his so I just nod, easily convinced to take whatever journey he has in mind. I brush my lips against his, concentrating on the contours of his lower lips, feeling the stubble from his chin against my hand. He's right. There's no rush. It feels good to kiss him like this, changing the angle and going again. His lips part, and he pulls me in deeper with his tongue and pushes his hands into my hair.

"C'mere," he says, guiding me to the end of the chaise and hopping down to the ground in front of me. The gleam in his eyes betrays his plan of attack. He starts with one foot, caressing it and running his hand up my calf to my knee. Planting a row of kisses as he goes. Then on to the other leg.

"Praise the spinning bike," he says. "You have the most stunning legs." He smiles, his hands still running up and down my lower legs. His hands move higher, and his lips are tracing a path up my inner thigh. When he gets to the rim of my panties, he slides a finger underneath, sending a ripple of pleasure across the skin.

"Okay if I take these off?"

"Good god. Yes."

Before he does, he plants a few more kisses, moving over the fabric right in the center. I can feel his hot breath and the lightest kiss before he hooks one finger under the elastic and slips them down my legs.

He looks up at me and smiles. I'm certain what he sees is a wild-eyed, half-sane woman, building to the orgasm of her life. I can't even speak, and when he hits me with his tongue, I'm halfway to heaven.

I don't want to know why he's so good at this. In my half-conscious brain, I chalk it up to impeccable reporting and a strong work ethic. He circles languidly with his tongue, adding friction with his thumb as he licks and caresses down the center. It sends me so close to the edge that I'm holding onto his shoulders for dear life. One more stroke and I'm... yeah, it's crazy good.

"You are so... everything." I don't even know what I'm saying, but I know I mean it.

I'm not sure if he's watching me because I can't keep my eyes open as I fall apart for what feels like four minutes.

When I finally have the wherewithal to scoot back on the chaise and try to get my eyes to focus, I notice that he's still in his boxer briefs. And looking to burst right through the fabric.

"You're still wearing clothes," I say. "That's a party foul."

"Easily remedied."

I help him roll them down his legs and he kicks them to the floor. He reaches into his pants pocket for a foil packet and rips into it. "Are you still on a mission to take things slow?" I ask, as I wrap my hand around his erection and begin stroking it.

"Shit, not if you do that."

I cock an eyebrow and continue what I'm doing, watching his face as he gets more riled up. Then he slips the condom on and moves so we're perfectly lined up.

When he slips inside, it feels so good I'm already screaming his name.

"All day, all I could think about was being inside you," he says.

He moves and I circle my hips and he groans. I move and he thrusts, and I think I'm going to black out, but I stay with him. And it's amazing and we're both right there, riding out the orgasm together.

"*Mmm...* I want to do this forever," I say, the words out of my mouth before I can edit them. I don't want to freak him out. I know forever isn't an option, so I try to cover. "I just mean I'm not ready for this weekend to end."

His kiss tells me he's not freaked out. "We have loads of time left. I don't plan on sleeping."

He's good for his word.

32

———

LINDEN

THE MORNING IS lazy like the sun that's just starting to peek through the haze of clouds by noon. I've barely spent any time in my *casita*, but I head over there to pack up my suitcase before we say goodbye to Ken, Judy, and the other guests.

Jack's been gone for an hour, determined to get in one last sit-down with Ken before we drive back to LA. I finish the remains of the latte I brought back with me from breakfast, which was a six-yard spread of pastries, fruit, egg sandwiches, and a barista making custom drinks. It will be hard to trade this place for the real world. For many reasons.

Hugo knocks on my door and grabs my two bags from the entryway. On our drive in the golf cart, I ask a few more questions and learn he has two kids and an alpaca farm at his house about sixty minutes from here. He and his kids shear them every summer and sell the wool to a knitting store in Santa Barbara. I'll never get tired of meeting different people and learning how their lives are different from my own.

I'm lucky to have the job I do. It gives me the excuse to ask people questions for a living. Right now, I'm eager to get back to LA and lay out the bones of the story.

Jack is already waiting by his car when we pull up. He

and Ken exchange a somewhat terse goodbye that seems out of character for them. Jack avoids my eyes when I try to intuit what's going on. Ken is gregarious and Judy is his gracious partner in crime, both pulling me in for a hug and telling me how glad they are that I got to spend the weekend with them.

"This is our special place and we love sharing it with our friends," Judy says. Jack leans in and kisses her cheek before we hop into the car. I'm a little wistful about leaving, only because it was *our* special place this weekend, and driving away means we're leaving it all behind. I know it's expected and necessary, but I'm still a little sad. Having two hours on the road with Jack will give the return to reality a slightly softer landing.

Jack is quiet for the first fifteen minutes we're on the road, but after we hit the part of the coast highway that's right next to the ocean, I can't let him stew in his mood any longer.

"You have to admit, this is beautiful," I say, staring at the hard line that separates the blue sky from the deeper azure of the ocean.

"I can't look. I'm driving."

"You can look. Just for a sec."

He gives the ocean a micro-glance. "Yes. It's pretty."

I let him drive in silence for another minute, but then I start to get annoyed that he's not telling me what's bugging him. "Dude, what is up?"

A tiny smile creeps into the corner of his mouth. "Did you really just call me *dude*?"

"I did. You're being very dude-like, driving all angry and silent. What's going on?"

Even from the side, I can see his face relax a little. He reaches out and puts a hand on my leg. I put my hand on top of his. I already feel a little better since he's starting to thaw.

He shakes his head. "I just didn't end things well with

Ken. We had a pretty… unpleasant conversation right before we left."

"Is he not letting you do the profile now?"

"That's not how it works. He doesn't dictate what I write. You never let an interview subject tell you what you can or can't write. And you never give them approval before you print."

"Okay, journalism sensei. I get it. You can save the lecture."

"Sorry. Bad habit."

"What's up with Ken?"

He's silent again and I'm not sure he heard my question. Then he responds, "I asked him about *Bachelor Bay*. I kind of had a sense he was trying to distract me by agreeing to do the profile, and yesterday, I started thinking maybe he was doing it to hide the problems on the show."

Chad implied as much, but I'm not about to tell Jack what's likely to be true at a major company on his beat. "Okay…"

"This morning, I flat-out asked him. Let's just say he was not happy."

"Not happy that you found out?"

"Not happy I 'dared bring it up after he'd welcomed me into his home,' not happy I would 'believe that crap about *Bachelor Bay*…' He went on for quite a while with his outrage."

All kinds of thoughts are going through my head. I want to know if I'm getting kicked off the story, now that the CEO might be involved. I want to know what else Ken said. I want all the details of his outrage. But there's time to hash that stuff out. For now, I'm a little worried about why Jack seems so aggravated.

"So, what now?"

"He gave me a standard denial when I asked about what

Chad told you. When the story runs, we'll have to say he knew nothing about it."

"Well, that's okay, I guess. We still have the story."

"Yeah. I just hate printing something I know isn't true.

"You're sure he's lying?"

"I know him pretty well. He's lying."

THE REST of the drive home is still on the quiet side. I think neither one of us wants to think about how we're leaving the protected bubble of our Montecito getaway and going back to the grind. Reentry's gonna suck.

I'm pretty excited about the story though. I have to stay focused on that, not the pit in my stomach that makes me feel like I'm going to die.

When we get back to the office, where I left my car on Friday, Jack helps me unload my suitcases and packs them into my trunk.

"So… you free tonight?" he asks.

I'm not expecting that. We're back in LA. The weekend is over; so are we. "You mean, like… more Montecito fun, only here?"

"I was thinking. Sure."

I was hoping he wasn't thinking. Because now I'm thinking. And neither one of us should be thinking about it.

I shake my head. "This can't go any farther than the weekend," I tell him.

"Because you didn't have a good time? Or because you still think I'm a dick?"

"No. Option number three. Because of my job. And your job."

"Our jobs have nothing to do with what I'm imagining doing to you in the privacy of your apartment. Trust me, it doesn't involve a computer or a lot of words or a deadline. Definitely no deadline."

"Okay, maybe it doesn't matter for you. You've already won your Pulitzer and all that. But I still have a long way to go and I don't want to get there by sleeping with every reporter in town."

He laughs. "Ah, I see. Well, have you slept with a lot already? Because if you're even sleeping with most of the reporters in town, I hardly see it being a problem to toss in one more." He really doesn't get why this is a problem. Of course he doesn't. Men rarely suffer the same consequences as women for bedding their colleagues.

"You're hilarious."

He waits. I have more to get off my chest, but I don't want to blurt something out that I'll regret. Finally, he takes a stab at the conversation. "You said we can't do this. I'd like to give you my argument in favor of why we can."

Despite my overall wariness of the guy, he's been growing on me since the night he drove me home from the bar. He's still arrogant as hell and I still need to avoid having my career tanked by my libido.

But he's freaking charming standing here right now, ready with all his verbal ammunition in hopes of convincing me why abandoning all wisdom is a good idea. I'm entertained enough to hear him out. "Okay, shoot."

"Well, I think it goes without saying that I find you insanely sexy and attractive, stiletto heels notwithstanding."

"Good opening, but I'm still going with my original argument: I can't derail my career with dating. It will seem fun and fine, but I'll be the one to suffer for it."

"Why?"

"Because I always do. It starts out as one night when I stay up later than I should and I feel sluggish the next day at work. Then it happens again and I'm careless on my fact-checking and I have to print a retraction. Then I screw up even worse because I can't stop thinking about the incredible sex long enough to do my job correctly and bam, I miss a story, some other paper gets the scoop and I'm out on my love-struck ass."

Jack looks at me like I've just gone 'round the bend. "I was just asking about one dinner." He picks up my hand and runs a finger over my palm, then along my wrist. It's hard to believe that feels so good. No matter where he touches me. Which makes me even more resolute. Trying to spend time with him outside of work would be too big a distraction for me.

"I'm not willing to sabotage my career for a guy."

"A guy? You say that like I'm some sort of generic organism with a Y chromosome."

"I don't mean it like that," I say. I need to articulate this better so I'm clear about my boundaries without insulting him. "I can see how much I already like you and it feels like a slippery slope. I've never been able to manage both."

"Both what?"

"A job and a relationship."

"Again, I was just thinking dinner."

"But what about after dinner? You wouldn't want to come back to my apartment? If I wanted you to spend the night, you would, right?"

"Um, in a heartbeat."

"Exactly. And the sabotaging of my career begins."

"But I'm not trying to sabotage your career. If anything, I'm constantly impressed by your instincts. And your big gorgeous brain. I want you to have every measure of success that you deserve in your career. But at this particular moment, our work is done I just want more of you."

I still can't look at him because now I know if I do, I won't be able to keep my hands to myself. Or my mouth or any other part of me. I focus on the ocean and try to explain. "I'm just… bad at this. At doing two things at the same time. If I even kiss you again, I might as well say goodbye to my job at the paper because I'll lose my focus. And I can't. This job is too important to me."

I can tell he's looking at me and I'm doing all I can to avoid his gaze. Then he reaches a hand to my cheek and grazes the skin with his finger. Without intending to, I lean into it. His fingers burn against my skin and I don't want to lose the connection. I turn slightly to look at him. "Hey. I get it," he says. "I don't want you to lose your focus."

As I try to inhale, I find the air catching as my heart beats in a ragged tempo. I can't believe what he does to me. "I think it's too late. You're very distracting."

"I'd say I'm sorry, but I have to be honest, I like distracting you."

"I know. I like it too. But I don't trust myself. Maybe when I've been at the paper longer and I feel like I'm on better footing…"

He nods because he's a smart guy and he hears what I'm telling him, which is that I've made a decision. He may be relentless when he's reporting a story, but this is different. He kisses the back of my hand and doesn't let go of it.

"I get it. And I support whatever you need to do."

"Thank you." I stand on my toes to kiss him on the cheek. It pains me not to move a couple inches to the side. Or take him home with me. But I have to stick to what I know is right for me.

So I get in my car and drive away.

33

———

LINDEN

I'M at the office by eight, partly because I know it's my job, and partly because I'm looking forward to seeing Jack. I know I shouldn't be. It's not like anything from our weekend together will continue now that we're back. But he's a better guy than I thought he was, so maybe I can like seeing him at work in a friendly kind of way.

Sure, let's see how fun that is.

It's not like I have a choice. We agreed to throw caution to the wind for the weekend and it was good. So good. Maybe more than good.

But we're back now. We both have demanding jobs and we both love what we do. Dating doesn't enter into the equation.

"Hey." I hear Jack's voice before I get through my first cup of coffee. "This is early for you." I look at the time and see it's only a quarter to eight.

Yeah, I was early. Eager?

"Turning over a new leaf." The truth is, I couldn't even go to spinning this morning and have my usual conversation with Cassie about *Bachelor Bay*. I couldn't think of anything but getting to the office. I hate to think it's because I'm eager to see Jack. Leaving him in the parking garage yesterday gave me the worst feeling I've ever had.

He unloads his laptop and notes and starts rolling through voicemails. He's using his headset and I don't hear them all on speakerphone. Strange. It's the first time he's done it. Did I tell him it annoyed me when he did that?

I peek over the partition. "You're using your headset?"

He punches the button on his phone to pause the messages. "Yeah, I don't want to annoy you with my messages."

"Didn't mind annoying me before."

"Maybe I was trying to get you to notice me."

I have no response to that. If he was playing his voicemails loudly for my benefit, does that mean…?

Forget it. It doesn't matter. Do your job.

We both get to work typing up our notes from the weekend and starting to outline our stories. Even though I ultimately got the story out of Chad, Jack started working his sources and has some leads on people involved with the show and the company's legal team who might be willing to speak on the record.

I used all the binders of data I read to add background reporting into company financials that round out the story and show why *Bachelor Bay* is such a cash cow for the company.

For an hour, we type in silence, as other reporters filter in. We're both waiting for Stuart. Like kids coming back from a treasure hunt, we want to show him what we found.

TO SAY Stuart is happy about our story is an understatement. He's like Michael Flatley, Lord of the Dance, skipping through the newsroom without his feet touching the ground. I've never seen him this giddy about anything, especially once

Jack tells him he suspects Ken Nichols had full knowledge of the payouts to other contestants and the bogus layoff.

Stuart is ecstatic about the story. "No one else has this. And it's big. If Nichols knew and looked the other way, heads are going to roll."

"He's still not copping to it, and his inner circle is protecting him, saying he didn't know," Jack says. "But my gut says he knew. He may have even suggested it as a way to save the show. Doesn't matter though. Right now he's giving me squat."

"His canned denial might be the best we get if we want to run the story sooner rather than later."

"Exactly. If we want to go after Ken, I'll need time to work sources at the company."

"Okay, let me know what you decide. Either way, great work, you two."

We head back to our desks. Neither of us says anything while we walk but we're both glowing with quiet satisfaction for what we've pulled off. It's a good story. There's still a lot of work to be done before they're ready for publication but we have the broad strokes of what we need.

I sit at my desk, deciding where to begin, and an inter-office text pops into my in-box.

Jack: *Kudos. You worked hard for this. Well done*
Me: *Thanks*
Jack: *I think it calls for a little celebratory dinner. Whaddya you say?*
Me: *With you?*
Jack: *Um, yeah*
Me: *But we're back in the real world. We don't eat dinner together*
Jack: *We could*
Me: *Doesn't that violate the terms of colleagues with benefits? And my No Dating terms?*

Jack: *Maybe, but I want to have dinner with you*
Me:

It's quiet in the cubicle next door and I'm sure Jack's waiting for my response. My fingers hover over the keyboard, as I decide what to type. I don't know what to say. I want to have dinner with him too. But... that's where things get complicated and I've been doing my best to avoid complicated since I took this job.

I stand up and look at him over the partition between our cubicles. He's still staring at his computer screen waiting for my response until I let him know I'm there. "Hey."

He turns, his serious computer face brightening with a smile when he sees me. "Hey. So..."

"I thought we said..."

"I know," he says.

"So..."

He shrugs.

For two people who make their living writing words, neither one of us seems to have any.

"Okay," I say.

"Yeah?"

"One celebratory dinner," I confirm.

"Just one."

"When?"

"Tonight?" he asks.

I nod and sit back down at my desk. I can't wipe the dopey grin off my face, even though I know it's just one dinner. The idea of it makes me happy. Because this guy, he makes me happy.

Damn it.

34

———

LINDEN

JACK PICKS me up at my apartment at eight. Even though we could have gone straight from work, I told him I wanted to go home and change. Mainly because I was wearing jeans at work and I wanted to put on a dress. Jack seems to like me in them. This one is black and a little form-fitting.

When I open the door, I think Jack looks a little nervous. His face softens and he hands me a giant bunch of lavender mixed with white roses. And a jar of olives—pitted.

"Aw, it's like a mini Montecito. Thank you."

He nods and checks out the dress, which I can tell he likes. "I didn't think it was possible for you to look more spectac-ular than you did all weekend, but oh my God." His hand runs over the curve of my hip and around my back, pulling me in. I wrap an arm around his neck and shiver as his hands make their way higher up my back. "You're gorgeous. And I'm not talking about your big intellectual brain."

He makes me smile. And feel all kinds of other feelings in other parts of my body. I'm wearing eye makeup because I know he likes the way it brings out my eyes, but I decided to forego the lipstick in favor of a swipe of gloss. He reaches out and runs his thumb across my bottom lip. "I thought I'd save you the trouble of kissing off the lipstick."

He pushes both hands into my hair and pulls my face to his. "Lovely thought. I want those lips. I want you."

Kissing him is the best thing I've ever felt in my life. Well, it's one of the best things and it leads to the rest of the best things. It turns out he timed his arrival well, so we have time for all those other things before we need to be anyplace.

And he brought me olives.

Jack insists I pick the restaurant, so I opt for an Italian place that's casual, but it has good wine and small tables in a romantic setting. I've only been there once before, when my mom was in town, but I remembered how good the food was.

Our date is so sweet. It feels different than the weekend. There, I felt like a guest in someone else's fantasy life. The sailboat, the perfect catered food, one romantic setting after another. Who wouldn't give in to that? I left Montecito believing that Jack and I wouldn't really translate well into the real world. We'd been working together for six months prior and had never really thought much of each other. I assumed we'd go back to a version of that, which would make it much easier to forget about the weekend.

But tonight, I have a whole different sense of us. Being with Jack—talking to him, holding his hand under the table—feels more tender and genuine than what I experienced over the weekend.

When he runs his fingers over my knee and rests them on my thigh, it's so much sexier because it feels real. We're back in the regular world where we live and it's just as good. Actually, better.

Which is a little bit scary. Because this is me and I tend to lose my shit at work when I'm involved with a guy.

But maybe… maybe I can do things differently this time.

Fortunately, I don't have a lot of time to overthink things during dinner. We just talk. And laugh. And eat.

"Is your family still in Fresno?" he asks.

"Yup. My half-sisters are in college there and my mom and stepdad will never leave. I think they're scared to live anywhere else."

"Do you see them often?"

I feel guilty when he asks because I haven't been back to Fresno in months, even though it's only a few hours to drive. "Work always gets in the way and I don't love it there."

"Yeah, I hear you. My family's out in Boston and I haven't been back to visit in over a year. My mom is not happy with me." It's funny to think of him being in trouble with his mom. He's so in-control all the time.

"You're a pretty likable guy. I doubt any mom could stay mad at you."

He suddenly lights up, his smile wide. "I'm likable? Does that mean you're finally over thinking I'm a dick?"

I take a sip of wine and look him over like I'm still considering. Then I relent. "I think I got past that impression when you said you had my back."

He picks up one of the garlic knots the restaurant is known for and breaks it in half, handing me a piece. Like we've already done this dozens of times and he knows I want a piece. It's delicious but I cringe. "Garlic breath! There goes my end-of-date kiss."

"Then I'll just have to kiss you now." He leans in. His lips are soft, and they taste like wine and garlic, but I don't care. I also wouldn't care if we skipped dinner and spent the rest of our date on my couch, but I'm trying to stay on good first-date behavior and not jump him. It's hard.

"Okay, so you're from Boston. I don't hear it in your voice."

"Years ago, when I thought I was going into broadcasting, I had a voice coach who beat it out of me."

"Ah, so all those threats to go on-air weren't out of nowhere. Why'd you choose print?"

"I like longer stories. The depth. Plus, I'm not into wearing makeup every day." He runs a hand over my cheek and tucks a strand of hair behind my ear.

Our entrees arrive and for a while we focus on the food, but we both like to ask questions, so the quiet doesn't last long. By the time we've shared a panna cotta, I've learned about his parents, his childhood summer vacations on Cape Cod, and all the jobs he had before he finished college.

It just might be the perfect date. Jack is sweet and open and for the whole time we're together he looks relaxed. I take that as a good sign.

When we pull up to my duplex, he leans in and kisses me over the armrest, which is awkward and reminds me of many uncomfortable teenage nights out with awkward, acne-faced guys. I don't mention that part to Jack.

"I'd ask if I could spend the night, but I'm gonna act like a gentleman who's on a first date. I'd never spend the night on a first date."

"Never?"

"Well, generally not if I was plotting to have a second date."

"You're such a player."

"Not really. Definitely not with you."

He walks me to the door, and we kiss on my doorstep for a very long time. That seems perfectly acceptable for our celebratory date. It also makes me wish we didn't have to stop at one.

When we pull back, I keep my arms around his neck. "So... since you're being such a gentleman, does that mean you're plotting for a second date?" I ask, feeling my resolve wavering. I'm mad at myself. This is how it begins...

He looks surprised, then inordinately pleased. "I don't think it's appropriate for me to reveal details of my plotting."

He leans his head toward me so our foreheads are touching. "But… no. I heard what you said and I don't want to be the reason you stop short of knocking it out of the park."

I feel my eyes start to sting with the welling of tears. No one has ever listened to me and actually heard me in the way he has. I guess that's why he's so good at his job. I don't want to cry all over him. I just want to kiss him. "Thank you," I say. It comes out a whisper.

"However…" he says. There's more? "I believe in you and that means I see things that maybe you can't. And what I see is a person who is extremely capable, someone who can handle all the challenges this job throws your way, as well as the challenges presented by someone who desperately wants there to be a second date."

"Jack…"

"I believe in you. You can do two things at once. You don't have to derail work with kissing. I'm not going to pressure you. Just… something to think about."

He uses his sleeve to wipe the tears out of my eyes. Then he traces my jaw with his finger and follows it with a row of kisses. I feel his lips cover mine and I block out everything else.

I want this. I want him.

35

JACK

I SHOULD HAVE TALKED to Linden before dinner. Or during dinner. Or before we made out in her doorway for an hour and came just shy of tearing each other's clothes off.

Any time before now would have been great.

What I shouldn't have done was pretend the conversation with Stuart was going to go away without me giving him a firm answer or figuring my life out.

At any rate, I should have realized that by not telling Linden, everything would blow up into a shitstorm eventually.

Or immediately.

Last night confirmed everything I didn't want to believe when I told myself we could have a little fun for a weekend and leave it behind. Who am I kidding? Why would I leave behind the best thing that's ever happened to me? It makes no sense. No one would believe a story that ended like that, even one written by a prize-winning reporter. They'd just think I got my facts wrong and maybe not trust me to report the truth going forward.

I come back from a vending machine run with a Hansen's

apple-peach smoothie for me and an organic protein and grain bar for Linden. I know she hasn't eaten lunch again.

I find Stuart leaning over the wall of Linden's cubicle, finishing up a conversation. I can't hear any of it, but from Stuart's expression, I can tell something's up. As he passes me, he pats me on the shoulder like a sports coach readying his player for an ass-kicking by an opposing team with a perfect record.

Linden has her back to me, but her shoulders are hunched and she's not writing anything. I can't tell what's bothering her, but I have a feeling I know. "Brought you one of those bars you like," I say, showing her my paltry offering, which I have a feeling is no match for whatever is about to go down.

She turns and I catch her grim expression and the moisture in her eyes. This isn't good…

"Were you ever gonna tell me? Or was I just supposed to come in one day and see you at Jeremy's desk?"

I can't imagine why Stuart mentioned the promotion to Linden, but that's not the issue right now. I need to do damage control. Fast.

"I haven't decided whether I'm taking the post."

She looks even more insulted now. "Oh, please. You're the most ambitious person I've ever met. Of course you're taking it."

"It's not about ambition. I'm not sure it's the right move."

She throws up her hands. "Fine. So you're thinking about it. Why not tell me? We had the whole weekend."

Most of our colleagues have their Bluetooth earbuds in but I still try to keep my voice low in case any of them can hear our conversation. Linden doesn't seem to have as much concern for volume. I motion for her to follow me to the back room where the vending machine is. She shakes her head but stands up, her shoulders still hunched.

I walk out the back door of the office and hope she's following me. When I turn, she launches in again. "Seriously,

Jack, what's the deal? First, you make a case for a second date —and a very good case, by the way. And now I'm probably gonna lose my job for sleeping with the boss."

"You're not going to—"

"You can't promise me that!" She's really pissed. And she's right. Not only can I not promise her that, I know the company forbids any relationships between a superior and a lower level employee. We both could lose our jobs. "Jesus, Jack. I told you why I was reluctant to get involved in a relationship and this is why. It always blows up in my face."

"Will you please give me a chance to tell you my side of things?"

She shakes her head. "What's the point? I wouldn't trust that you were telling the truth."

It's the worst possible thing she could say to me, especially since I worked pretty hard to gain her trust. I can't believe I've screwed that up so royally by not telling her about the deputy chief position. "So, what? Is it too late for me to fix this?"

"There's nothing to fix. I can't date a superior. And I want to be a reporter more than I want to be your girlfriend. I know that makes me sound like an asshole, but I'm sorry. I've always been honest about this. I'm really sorry."

I can see the internal fight as she says those words. Her eyes well up with tears but she's balling her fists, every bit the fiery redhead I think I'm falling in love with.

Screw that. I'm already in love with her. It's probably been a given since the day she walked into the newsroom, but I'm acutely aware of it now. I love her.

And she's walking away.

36

LINDEN

KAYLA MEETS me at my apartment when I get home, a bottle of sauvignon blanc in one hand and twin bags of pretzels and pink and white frosted cookies in the other. "I brought snacks. And wine."

"You're like the cavalry, but with carbs."

I already have a couple glasses ready and the bottle is a screw top, so we get right down to getting our cocktail on. This is a situation that may end up requiring more than one bottle.

"Your text sounded dire."

"I might have just screwed myself."

"Fuck that, I wanna hear about what went down when you were screwing the hot guy from the bar."

"Jack. I may be too depressed to relive the weekend. It will only make me feel worse."

I log into my computer and look up the company handbook. It takes me a while because it's buried on the corporate website and it's clear no one has spent much time making this thing easy to read. "This is the worst-written web interface I've ever seen," Kayla says, trying to read over my shoulder.

"Ironic for a company that owns newspapers, right?"

I finally find what I'm looking for, and the result doesn't raise my spirits at all. Kayla reads, "Company policy prohibits dating relationships between two employees who are separated by two or more levels in the chain of command. Under no circumstances will a manger and reporting staff member engage in a romantic relationship or pursue a situation that results in the perception of detrimental or preferential treatment for the employee... blah, blah, blah."

"You're the lawyer. Is there any way I'm misunderstanding what this means?"

She's already refilling my wine glass as she shakes her head. "It's very clearly spelled out. If you're dating him and he's your boss, they can fire you."

"That's so unfair. They can't fire him?"

"They can fire both of you, but from what you've told me, he has job security, especially if they're offering him this big promotion. You're gonna be left holding the bag."

"I always am."

"I mean, you can fight it and you definitely should. He should absolutely be fired if they're calling you out. We have a whole employment law division at work. I can get one of the top guys to take it on."

But I already know I'd never do that. "I don't want to be known as the reporter who got her boss fired and got herself fired for sleeping with him."

"It's your call." She breaks open the bag of pretzels and grabs a handful. They're the tiny twists, my favorite kind, but I don't have the appetite for them. I already know the answer to her question. I knew it before I kissed his face off at the bar.

"I just can't date him. It is what it is."

Kayla looks horrified. The romantic in her is dying a slow and painful death because I'm not fighting harder for love. I slug down half the wine in my glass like it's water. It burns my throat, but the pain feels satisfying.

Love? Who said anything about love? I didn't even like the guy until a week ago.

I'm so full of shit. I already know I feel more for him than I've ever felt for anyone. I'm falling hard for him, but so what? It's not worth getting fired over.

"I've said it before. I can't have a great relationship and a great job at the same time. This time I'm choosing the job."

"You're so full of shit. You've never had a great relationship *or* a great job before now. Why are you so convinced you can't have both?"

I feel defensive, thinking back on some of my relationships. There was Seth, the artist who painted late into the night and called me even later. He was a night owl and the source of too many faux sick days. There was James, an accountant who talked in his sleep. He was adorable but I never got any shuteye when I stayed at his house and that's a big reason why I was always so tired and unfocused at work. Yeah, maybe they weren't great relationships. They definitely never made me feel things I experienced in multiples with Jack.

So what? This is about the current situation.

"I can't date him if I want to keep my job."

She shrugs because she knows me well enough to understand that if I've made up my mind, the issue is closed. "If that makes you happy…"

"My job makes me happy. The rest makes me miserable."

Kayla refills my wine glass again. I was right. We're going to need a second bottle.

37

LINDEN

ONE THING I've learned in my time at the Examiner is that committed reporters don't take a lot of personal days or vacation days. It's almost like a badge of honor to leave most of the two weeks of annual vacation days on the table at the end of the year. It means you're a diehard, serious reporter.

I want to be like that. For eighteen months I've been like that.

Today, though, I'm staying in bed. I called in and said I needed a personal day, and Stuart was only too happy to accommodate me since I spent my whole weekend working and he's happy with the result.

I just need a day to wallow, then I'll get right back to work and put this whole Jack thing behind me. I'm a very focused person. One day is all I need to get my head turned around the right way and get back to it.

There's a chance I won't see as much of Jack anyway, which will make it easier. I assume he'll move over and take Jeremy's desk, and there's actually a path I can take through the cubicles that will get me to my desk without having to lay eyes on him at all. I'm actually looking forward to the day

Jeremy goes on leave and Jack takes over, simply for that reason.

In the meantime, I'm taking one day to feel sad. I pulled out my rattiest grey sweatpants, the ones with holes in both knees, and an orange hoodie that says, "It's all good," on the front, even though today is far from good.

I've made a giant pot of coffee because I'm not in the mood to go anywhere, even for the promise of a latte. The couch is my home for the day.

Surprisingly, after a fitful night of sleep last night, punctuated by tears and too much time reading some of Jack's older stories, I'm exhausted. Settling in on the couch with my laptop, I page through more of Jack's stories, apparently to torture myself. He's a damned good writer. Reading his stuff confirms that I'm doing the right thing, choosing my job over a boyfriend I can't trust.

Somehow through the caffeine and the occasional explosions of tears, I manage to zonk out on the couch. I have no idea how long I've been asleep when I start to become conscious of a knocking sound. Like someone's hammering.

No, someone's knocking at my door. Annoying. I wonder if people often come to my door during the day when I'm at work.

I consider not answering, because I'm not expecting a delivery, and solicitors annoy me. But the knocking continues and it's preventing me from falling back asleep, so I stagger over to yank open the door and glare at whoever's out there.

I'm not expecting it to be Jack. He's holding a jar of Nutella and a bunch of celery. It would be sweet, but I don't want him here, so it's just annoying. I shake my head at him. "No. I don't want to do this."

"What? Talk to me?"

"No, let you in so you can be cute with your snack."

"I'm not trying to be cute. But I do want to talk."

He's so frustrating. I'm taking the day off to get away

from him and clear my head. I don't need this. "Why? We talked. Just… let it go, Jack."

He looks deflated. "Is that really what you want?"

I want to say yes. It would be the easiest way out of the conversation, and I could go back to wallowing on the couch and moving on. It's important that I move on. Then my mouth starts in before my brain has a chance to control it. "No."

Dammit!

"Neither do I."

"It doesn't matter. You can't have what you want. You're about to be my boss and I don't want to get fired."

"That's not the only scenario. There are other ways this could all shake out," he says.

"I don't see how," I tell him. He looks pained but he obviously doesn't have an answer. He hasn't thought this through like I have, and I don't blame him for that. Like me, he's focused on doing the best thing for his career. "Look, I get it. It's a great opportunity. I can't fault you for wanting to take it."

I suppose I could look for another reporting job. After working at the Examiner I'd have an easier time getting hired. But I love this job. This is where I want to work.

Why should I have to make the sacrifice so the man can have the job he wants? It just doesn't seem fair.

So I'm led to the conclusion I drew before any of this even started with Jack. I can't have both, a great job and a great relationship. And at this point in my career, I need to choose the job.

I can't bear to even articulate it again to Jack. He knows how I feel. What's the point of explaining it over and over again?

"I want to go after Ken Nichols. I can't get my conversation with him out of my head. I knew he was up to something when he was willing to let me come to the villa for the profile.

That's so unlike him. I think he was trying to distract me from the bigger story."

"How'd he know you'd find the bigger story?"

Jack nods, a satisfied smile on his face. "Because too many people know about it. He got nervous and tried to placate me with a puff piece. But I want the real story."

"What's that mean?"

"We keep digging, find people high up at Worldvision to corroborate that he knew. Then when we publish, it's a much bigger story."

He keeps saying we. There's no we. I'm going to hand the whole story over to him just to avoid dealing with him at work. "What if it causes fallout with some of your sources?"

"It won't. If anything, they'll be scared to fuck with me. Fourth estate," he says. I see the elation on his face at the power of the press. It's what's always been so attractive about him. "It's why I went into journalism. To get to the truth that underhanded people don't want us to see. It's why I'm not taking Jeremy's job," he says.

I'm not sure I'm hearing him right. "Hold on. What?"

He gestures to the couch behind me, but I'm wary. I've still got my arms out like I'm holding up the doorframe. "Can I please come in and explain?"

Fine. He's not going to stop badgering me until I let him talk, so I move out of the way and let him bring his celery snack to the couch. I follow him in that direction, but I don't sit down.

I'm more comfortable standing six feet away from him, glaring with my arms crossed. "What in the hell are you talking about? You're taking the job."

He shakes his head. "I never wanted to be an editor," he says.

"What do you mean?"

"I mean, that's not why I went into the field of journalism.

I don't want to spend most of every day rewriting other people's stories."

"But you're good at it."

"So?"

"And it's the best opportunity you'll ever have at a newspaper to make good money."

"I make good money now."

"You'd make more."

"Maybe that's not the most important thing in the world."

"So, what is?"

"Doing what I love. And that means reporting. Every day, shoe leather reporting," he says. I nod. I get what he's saying. I love it too. "And it means you. With me. I can't see any path forward that doesn't include you. I just... love you."

I'm so caught off guard by those words that now I'm wary. I wait. Maybe he didn't mean to say what he did, so I allow some time for him to backpedal. But he doesn't.

"You... you do?"

"I adore you. I can't stop thinking about you. And it breaks my heart to think that I screwed up a beautiful beginning with you by not telling you about the job. I was pretty sure I wasn't going to take it. And after the weekend with you, it sealed the deal.

But I'm sorry. I should have told you. And I promise I'll never be an idiot again."

"We're all idiots sometimes," I say. "I just..." I close my eyes because I can't look at his face. "We've both had problems trying to do both, the work and relationship thing."

He gets up, carries the celery to the kitchen, and turns on the faucet. The guy likes to multitask.

"The problem I had wasn't that I couldn't balance work and my fiancée. It was that I didn't want to. I think I worked as hard as I did back then to avoid spending more time with her."

He dries the celery and putters around opening drawers,

looking for a knife. I point to the one where I keep them. "Thanks," he says.

"So, what are you saying? You use your job to avoid people?"

"People I don't like? Absolutely. It's a pretty handy excuse." He cuts the celery into smaller pieces and grabs a plate from my cabinet. He only had to open two to find it. He puts the celery sticks in a circle around the now-open jar of Nutella and walks back to my couch. I follow him.

"Okay, but I still have my own issues. I've tried to mix work and relationships and my work always goes into the toilet," I say. Each time I hear myself say the words, I feel more like it's a lame reason, though. I'm more disciplined than I used to be. Maybe I'm making excuses too.

Jack dips a celery stick and hands it to me. "Those guys who kept you up all night, so you were too tired to do your job, they were only thinking about themselves. That's where I'm different. I only want what's good for you," he says.

"I know, but maybe I don't trust myself."

"Do you think you can trust me?"

"I want to." I take a moment and think about why I've had trouble trusting him, and in each instance, I've been wrong in my assumption about him. He's proven himself trustworthy. Now it's my turn to stop jumping to hasty conclusions and assuming the worst. "Actually, I take that back. I do trust you. I do."

"I hope so. I'm not going to do anything that will interfere with you becoming as big a star at the paper as you want to be. We can have a nine p.m. curfew if you want."

"That seems excessive."

"I'm just saying, I'll follow your lead. If the only thing that's keeping you from spending every night with me is your fear about screwing up your job, you've got nothing to worry about."

I like everything he's telling me. If he's a regular reporter like me, there's no issue with us dating. And the job I love will be even more magical when I get to see him every day at the bureau. Where he should be right now... "Hold up, why aren't you at work?"

"Because I was out shopping for celery. I even put it in the interoffice memo."

He did? I pull out my phone and look at the interoffice message system. I see, *Jack OUT: buying celery for woman I can't live without. See y'all in the ayem.*

"You ended a sentence with a preposition," I say. I know that's not the point. But maybe it is.

"That's how much I want to be with you. More than grammatically possible."

I process all this information. "You're not going back to the office today?"

He shakes his head. "Not unless you kick me out. And even then, I'll probably just go drown my sorrows in a bucket of Nutella alone."

I take a step closer to him. Then another. Then I put my arms around him and feel what I've been missing for the past twenty-four hours. "I'm not gonna kick you out. Ever."

"I want you, every day, every night, until a reasonable bedtime hour, with me."

He's so freaking cute.

"I want that too," I say, feeling my heart beating fast in my chest because I think that means I get to kiss him again. He doesn't disappoint. Ever.

EPILOGUE

Jack

Initially, people at Worldvision are reluctant to talk on the record. Of course they are. No one wants to be the first one to put their name in print, saying something bad about the guy who can get anyone fired for far less.

But over the course of a couple weeks, I start wearing people down. Maybe they're just tired of hearing from me. Or maybe they recognize that if they don't talk now and get ahead of the problem, they're going to look complicit later.

In either case, people start admitting that saving Bachelor Bay from scandal was Ken's first priority. He wanted to make sure the show stayed on the air with its stellar ratings intact.

One of his deputies dreamed up the idea of paying off everybody who knew about Jake and Megan to keep them from talking. Or complaining, in the case of the other contestants who were almost guaranteed not to win prize money if Jake stayed on the show.

It turns out Worldvision paid each contestant the same

hundreds of thousands of dollars given to the winner. That means that instead of having a budget of four million dollars an episode, the show doubled its budget.

Ken was instrumental in what came next.

He decided to wrap all the extra show expenditures into a line item on the company's tax return earmarked as legal expenses. That's where Linden's encyclopedia knowledge of the company's financials came in handy (I've apologized to her many times for making her read through all those binders, but she says she's grateful. This is one of many reasons why I love her).

She recognized the irregularity which turned a minor reality show scandal into a major financial story. The financial wizards at the company, in trying to save their own hides, quickly implicated Ken.

I was eager to call him for comment because I wanted to give him space to explain himself. After stonewalling initially and claiming he knew nothing of the irregularity, he finally talked to me on the record. He didn't say a lot, but he said his piece.

He'll be in all kinds of hot water with shareholders when the story runs in the morning. The story will probably result in him stepping down from his position. I'd feel bad for him, except that he had a choice to be a better person and he chose company profit over doing what's right.

People like him are the reason I became a journalist in the first place.

The last thing Ken Nichols said to me was, "I invited you into my home." He leveled the words at me like an accusation. He said it as though hosting me—or Chad or anyone else—ought to have been enough to buy our silence.

It was the wrong assumption to make about a journalist. We're rarely silent.

OUR STORY IS RUNNING on Page One of tomorrow's paper. Linden and I share a byline. We're finishing up the last round of nitpicky changes from the slot editor before the story goes off to get typeset for the morning edition.

I offer one final time to take my name off the story because I feel like Linden did the lion's share of the work, but she won't hear of it. "I like the idea of our names together on one story. I'm going to frame a copy, and when I look at it, it will always remind me of our weekend," she says.

I can only agree. "It was a great weekend."

I grab her shoulder bag from her cubicle while she waits for the editor to sign off on our final draft. When she gets the okay, she gets up and grabs my hand. Exhausted and exhilarated, we're the last ones to leave the bureau for the night. We walk toward the elevators.

I'm surprised Linden's so calm considering we're about to break a huge story in the morning.

As soon as the elevator doors close, Linden lets out a screaming whoop and jumps on me like a koala, her legs wrapped around me and hands holding my face. "We did it!" She kisses me in about a dozen places and nuzzles into my neck.

"We did. It's a good story. You should feel proud," I tell her.

She's shaking her head. "No. I mean yes, I do feel proud, of course, about the story. But we've been working non-stop on this for more than a month and we've spent every night together. And I haven't slacked at my job at all and you haven't tried to use work as an excuse to stop kissing me."

"Ah, I see. I'm proud of that too. But you should know, I'm never going to stop wanting to kiss you so your fears are unfounded."

The elevator reaches the parking garage and she's still clinging to me, so I carry her out and set her on the hood of my car so I can prove my point. Her lips are soft she responds immediately with fierce intensity. I get lost in her like I do every time.

When she pulls back, her voice is quiet but sincere. "I believe in us. I just wanted you to know that."

"I believe I us too."

"I'm going to find a nice frame for our bylines."

Some people frame photos of themselves on beach vacations or at dressy events where they look their best.

My girlfriend is going to frame our names on the same Page One story together. I kind of like the simplicity of it.

Her name is first. I made sure of it.

THE END

SIGN UP for Stacy's fabulous newsletter for exclusive bonus content, giveaways and more!

PREORDER STACY TRAVIS'S next book, The Summer of Him. Read on for a sneak peek!

ABOUT THE AUTHOR

Stacy Travis is an author of contemporary romance novels and romantic suspense fiction.

Stacy lives in Los Angeles with her husband, two sons and a poorly-trained rescue dog who hoards socks.

She loves to hear from readers so please connect with her on social media and join Stacy's Social Club for giveaways, information about upcoming books and excuses to drink rosé. SIGN UP here!

stacytravis.com

BONUS CHAPTER

COMING JUNE 19TH...

THE SUMMER OF HIM

If our breakup was as inevitable, so was our initial hookup. I'd planned it, because I was a planner, and Johnny went along with it because he'd do anything if it seemed new and fun. He wanted one thing from life—a party. Well, he also wanted sex, but he took that as a given. He made a pretty decent effort to find a party on a daily basis, looking for a cliff to dive from or a door to sneak through if it seemed like something interesting lay on the other side. Johnny made everyone around him have a better time, no matter where he went. He woke up in the morning in a good mood, ready to have a great day. He insisted on having fun, and he never did anything if it felt like work.

Johnny P. Royce did have a job. He worked as a bartender at Moby's, a tiny craft-beer bar and fancy burger place a dozen blocks from my apartment. Moby's was my go-to spot when friends came to Santa Monica and wanted a place to hang out. It didn't take long before I noticed Johnny, who always looked like he'd just come in from playing beach volleyball—suntanned with streaks of blond in his sandy-brown hair and sunglasses on top of his head, even at night. He was always laughing and smiling as if he would be there, loving his job, even if the place were empty. It turned out he liked it even more without customers, because he'd turn the bar into his own private watering hole.

He was always in motion, swinging out from behind the bar to wipe down three tables, scooping up empty pint glasses and dumping them in a grey kitchen bin, and wiping his hands on a long white apron without letting a single customer wait more than a couple of minutes at the bar. He'd fill a glass, holding the tap open with the same hand so he could use the other to wipe off the bar or pop a napkin down for a newly arrived customer. Moby's had a steady flow of people, and Johnny kept up. It made me think he had to be smart if he was able to stay on top of everything without letting a task go unfulfilled.

Later, I found out that his multitasking skill had more to do with a god he revered above all else—beer—than with anything else. He made it his personal mission to ensure that customers went the least amount of time possible without having their glasses filled. It was his own kind of religion, born of the need to have a drink in his hand as soon as his shift ended for the night or as soon as the clock struck five on his nights off.

"He's cute. You should ask him out," my friend Maggie said after I'd dragged her to Moby's for the third time just because I liked his vibe and because he always implored us to come back when we left, like it was personally important to him. That might have been a well-honed act to keep customers flowing through the door, but I bought into it and kept returning to see him.

Maggie humored me, probably out of a continued sense of gratitude because I'd introduced her to her boyfriend two years earlier. Back then, she'd just colored her strawberry blonde hair with hot-pink streaks and pierced her ears for the fourth time, so she wouldn't look the part of a "lawyer at a stodgy firm," as she termed it. Her new look had made me think of Ben, my department head at the public relations firm where I worked. He played in a band a couple of nights a week, so I'd dragged Maggie with me one night to watch. They'd started dating the next day. They would probably get married someday. She definitely owed me one.

"Ask. Him. Out," Maggie said again. I realized I'd been staring at Johnny for the past five minutes.

"I could," I said, not sure if I was ready. I wanted to be reasonably certain he'd say yes before I went down that road.

"You should. And I'm gonna hold you to it. If you don't want to do it tonight, fine. Just come back by yourself. Feel it out. If he's into it, you'll know."

"Don't women who go into bars alone just look like they want a cheap hookup? Doesn't it seem desperate?"

"You need to rethink that," Maggie said. "It's empowering to go places alone. If you were in a foreign city by yourself, you'd do it, because the alternative would be staying inside your hotel, and that would be lame."

I wanted to believe that I would go out by myself in a foreign city, but I couldn't say for sure. "You're right. I could just pretend I'm on vacation. I'll go to Moby's alone and have a beer, all good and casual. I'll just bring a book."

"Okay, that might seem lame."

"Fine. I'll do it without the book. Sometime. When I'm ready," I said, still not entirely convinced I'd ever be ready.

"Just be safe. *Empowered* doesn't mean dumb. Don't leave your drink unattended, and if you're going out solo, call me so I know you got there and back safely."

"Yes, Mom," I said.

After a few more months of stalking Moby's with friends, I ventured in by myself. Johnny recognized me and greeted me with his usual wide smile and a hug that made me feel like I'd stepped into my best friend's living room. He led me to a seat at the bar and leaned in to hear my order over the noise in the place. And after an hour of sitting across from Johnny while he worked, I had tuned out everyone else in the room. There might have been ten people in the bar or fifty. It didn't matter. All I saw was Johnny. It felt like we were on our first date, even though the place was packed and he was working the room.

Until that night, I'd barely talked to him other than to order a drink with my friends. This felt different. Maybe I felt more open to talking to him because I had no one else to talk to, or maybe he felt more of an obligation to entertain me because I was alone, but he kept coming back to me and picking up where we'd left off. Our conversation was a series of aborted attempts at finishing a get-to-know-you Q and A.

"So where are you from?" I asked.

"San Diego originally, but we moved around," he said before spinning off to plunk a coaster down in front of a pair of twenty-five-year-olds with long eyelashes and perfect teeth.

Each time he left, I wasn't sure he was coming back unless it was time to offer me a refill. But whenever the rush died down and he had a moment to breathe, he'd head back my way as if I was an old friend who didn't mind waiting. I didn't. I felt like I had special status, like a touchstone he enjoyed returning to with new questions and bits of insider information.

"Those two come in every Thursday," he said, gesturing with his eyes to the women with the eyelashes. "They always start out together, but after a couple drinks, one inevitably leaves with some guy and the other skulks away. I sometimes make a bet with myself about which one will be left hanging."

"And what are the odds tonight?" I asked, noticing that they weren't as gorgeous as I'd imagined them to be when they'd first walked in and commanded Johnny's bright smile. Jealousy had blinded me. All I'd seen had been their short skirts and his undivided attention as he laughed and winked at something one of them said.

"I'm thinking Jill. The one in the big earrings," he said. Jill was surveying the patrons in the bar with a disappointed scowl like she'd already failed in her mission to find someone worthy. "But that means you get Holly. You wanna bet?"

I didn't even need to look at Holly to know I wanted in on Johnny's game. I wanted a link to him, a reason for him to come back over to me throughout the night, even though I thought I'd taken a sucker's bet. But it turned out that Jill found someone first, so I won.

"That means you get a round on the house," Johnny said, already pouring me a second pint of Sierra Nevada Pale Ale.

I'd only finished half of the first one and knew I'd never make it through a second, but it was the gesture that counted. He winked at me and toasted my pint glass with his bottle of water, which made me feel like we shared a secret. I had no interest in leaving the bar that night until I saw where that wink would lead.

"I grew up surfing," Johnny told me in between customers. "You have a board?"

"Ha. No. I'm barely capable of boogie boarding. I think I'd fall off a surfboard, get conked on the head, and never be heard from again."

"Nah, not with me, you wouldn't."

"You inviting me surfing?"

"Maybe. You saying you'd go if I did?" he asked, leaning in closer. I wondered if anyone else in the place noticed that his face was about two inches from mine, definitely too close for someone who hadn't known my name a couple of hours earlier. I didn't care. I didn't dare look away from him.

"I'm saying I would." In that moment, I believed it.

The truth was, I'd always been pretty terrified of the

ocean. In a pool, I had a reasonable chance of emerging without drowning, since there were no waves and the maximum depth was about ten feet. The ocean was a different story. I'd grown up in California, but after getting beaten up by the waves as a kid, I'd stayed on the beach, just dipping my feet in up to the ankles or wading in up to my knees when it got really hot. And there I was, after only a couple of hours, telling this cute guy with flashing sea-green eyes that I'd get up on a surfboard with him. I was clearly under his spell.

"If you stay after closing, you'll see where the real fun starts," he said, winking. He went off to fetch a new tray of clean glasses from the back. I kind of marveled at how he kept the whole place running by himself. Granted, there were only about twenty seats, but sometimes the bar would be crammed with a couple dozen customers all wanting to order at the same time, and no one ever seemed perturbed. Johnny would come over with his big smile, tossing his hair out of his eyes and offering free tastes of different beers while people made up their minds.

"Did you decide?" he yelled over to me in the middle of pouring a pint of Guinness. "You gonna help me close up?"

"Still thinking about it," I said. But of course I stayed. I had no idea what *closing up* meant, but I was in for whatever it turned out to be.

The minute the last Moby's patron left, Johnny locked the front door and cranked up a Led Zeppelin playlist. He smiled at me, poured me a small glass of cider from the tap, and toasted it with a tall glass of his own nut-brown ale. Then he went to work clearing away all the glasses from the bar in a sweeping motion that landed them all in a grey bin without breaking a single one.

What happened next was a combination of cleaning up with the two barbacks and a wild party starting at two in the morning. It seemed like Johnny's goal was to taste every one of the bar's thirty-six brews. He wouldn't let me help with the cleanup effort. "You're a guest. Just hang and keep me company."

He insisted I stay perched on my barstool. Then he went to work, polishing the metal taps with a rag until they shone, replacing empty kegs with full ones, stacking clean glasses behind the bar, and mopping down the countertops and floors. He did all of it without it seeming like work, his smile never fading. He worked with pride in his job and a love for Moby's that I'd never seen in a person who didn't own the place.

He'd come over from time to time and ask, "You still good?"

I'd nod. The longer I sat, the more it felt inevitable that we'd hook up. That was what I wanted, but sitting in anticipation made me nervous.

"You're adorable," he mumbled, his face close to mine. My hands were folded in front of me on the bar. He lifted one of them to his lips and kissed it. Then he came around to the other side and sat on the stool next to mine. I glanced around and didn't see the barbacks. The music had segued to a quieter run of classic-rock songs.

"I'm glad you came in tonight." He stood close to me, his chin resting on his hand, staring right into my eyes.

"I am too." I felt my stomach drop a little when he talked to me. I hadn't realized how attracted I was to him until he was so close and I knew we were heading toward a hookup. At that point, I knew I wanted him.

"I've had my eye on you, you know."

"You mean tonight?" I asked.

"Nah, you've been in here before. I noticed. I'm just telling you so you know. I noticed that you're adorable." He seemed to like that word.

I felt my cheeks flush with embarrassment. I didn't take compliments well, but I'd learned over the years not to say something self-deprecating like, "Oh, you must have me confused with someone else." So I just said, "Thank you. You're not too bad to look at yourself."

He gave a boyish grin that showed all his teeth. He knew he was cute. And even though I'd seen him flash that smile at people all night long, I felt a shiver when he directed it at me. I took in his face, focusing in particular on his lips, which looked soft as he rubbed them together and smiled at me again as if to say we both knew where this was headed.

When Johnny moved closer to kiss me, I felt a rush of blood to my head and a beautiful ache in my chest, like my heart had swelled and I'd forgotten how to breathe. I could feel his smile when his lips met mine, assuring me that this was right. He was nodding as if everything made sense. I leaned in because I realized that it did.

He had no need for a subtle ramp-up. He kissed me that night like it was just part of our conversation. He never left his barstool. He kept his elbow on the bar and rested his chin in his hand, asking a few more questions and looking into my eyes like he really cared about the answers. I told him whatever he wanted to know. I knew I wanted to stay there, open to whatever came next.

He'd taken me so much by surprise that it sent my heart throbbing inside my chest so hard I was sure he could hear it. His lips were soft, lightly grazing mine then lingering a second more before he backed up a few inches and looked me in the eye.

"That was nice," he said, smiling and nodding.

"It was," I managed to say. I wanted him to kiss me again, but he twirled around and poured himself another half glass of amber ale. Not that he needed it. He was already swaying back and forth with a dreamy expression on his face.

I didn't move from that barstool for the next half hour while he mopped down the tables and helped the barbacks carry trash outside and mobilize a bucket and mop to clean the floors. He hadn't given me any indication whether he wanted me to stay or go. I didn't know if that last kiss had been the culmination of our time together. In watching him, I felt like I'd been granted a window into a kind of carefree being I'd never met before. Nothing seemed to stress him out —not that night, not ever.

I knew it was partly the alcohol that had fueled our hookup. I didn't care. I didn't care for seven more months, either, as late nights of kissing for hours and falling into sex turned to lazy mornings on weekends when I would lie in bed under a ceiling fan, my head on Johnny's bare chest, talking about what we'd do that day.

It was always a version of the same thing. "Kenny's having a party" or "Maxi said the surf's amazing" or "Jeb's having people over." His friends were bartenders or surfers or bartenders who surfed. After a few months of persuading, he even managed to get me on a surfboard. He guided me patiently and held onto the board until the waves came up and under me. "Okay, stand up now. Just hop into a squat, and when you're balanced, rise up and ride the wave." It took a half dozen attempts and more than a little water up my nose each time I fell, but I did get up on that board. I was having more fun than I'd had in ages, and it felt like the wave would keep on building.

That just showed how little I understood about relationships. Or surfing.

PREORDER now!